WENDY JAMES

WHERE HAVE YOU BEEN?

fi

*To my sisters
Blood
& Soul*

In the old nursery rhyme, when the cat went to see the queen, he caught a little mouse under her chair; that was long long ago and the queen was different from our queen, but the mouse was the same. Mice have always been the same.

Rumer Godden, *THE MOUSEWIFE*

PROLOGUE

November 1975

A suburban bedroom. Two girls. Sisters. One, a little girl, eight or so, sits on the bed. It's only early evening, six o'clock, still light, but she's all ready for bed: cotton pyjamas, Jiffies, teeth cleaned, her pale hair damp from the bath. The other, much older, seventeen, eighteen, practically a woman, sits at her dressing table applying make-up. She traces a heavy blue line around her eyes, darkens her lashes, reddens her lips, her cheeks, brushes a silvery streak across her eyelids. The little girl gazes at her sister's reflection, sits very still, very upright, doesn't make a sound; she barely breathes, so intent is she on the performance before her.

The older girl stands, takes a backward step or two, turns this way and that, trying to get a full view in the mirror. The dress she wears is long, the fabric a swirling combination of purple colours—lilac, violet, mauve, indigo. It is a glorious dress, with underskirts and bows, puffs and flounces. It shimmers and glints in the light. The young woman looks glorious: tall, slender, golden. Resplendent. The little girl gives a deep, a heartfelt, sigh.

'You look so beautiful, Karen,' she whispers, 'like a princess. Like a fairytale princess. Like Cinderella.'

Her sister smiles at her own reflection. 'I like that, Sukey,' she says, softly, 'Cinderella—that's me.' She turns to her sister, twirls slowly, her arms outstretched, 'And now I'm off to the ball.'

I

Susan

This is the moment when everything changes.

There have been other significant moments; a multitude of them if Susan cares to look back, and some (one in particular) even more significant than this.

She should have been prepared, of course; should have been awake to the possibilities contained within such an occasion—for drama, for revelation. For farce. *The Reading of the Will.* It isn't that the terms themselves are difficult to understand; she's understood what he's said well enough, but Susan asks him to tell her again, to explain. She needs time to recover. To compose herself. Right now she feels as if—no, she doesn't quite know how she feels.

'It's really quite straightforward, Mrs Middleton,' the solicitor speaks slowly, patiently, as if to a child. 'The house can be put on the market immediately, but any disbursements from the estate are to remain in trust until the executors are satisfied that everything possible has been done to locate your sister. If we do manage to find her, she receives half of your mother's estate; if we don't—which is by far the most likely outcome—you'll receive the lot.' His voice is low, sonorous, plainly his intention is to soothe, to smooth things over, iron out all the unsightly bumps and creases.

'But when did she make this will?' His bedside manner isn't having the desired effect: Susan's voice is pitched strangely, she can hear it—too high and too loud, and she's speaking too fast.

'I don't understand it. My mother hadn't been well—not for a long time. She'd been in a home for ten years. She had Alzheimer's. She couldn't even remember who I was. She couldn't feed herself. How could she possibly have managed to write a will? Surely it's not—it just can't be—valid. This is crazy. This whole thing's crazy.' She can feel her heartbeat now—and like her voice it's too loud, and much too fast.

The solicitor appears unruffled. 'It's certainly valid, Mrs Middleton. She wrote the will years ago.' He shuffles through the papers in front of him. 'In May, 1980. I'm surprised your father didn't tell you, he was an executor.'

She shakes her head, as much to clear it as to indicate the negative.

'Even if we do find Karen, your inheritance will still be quite substantial.' He leans towards her, lowers his voice. 'Your mother's house has been valued at more than eight hundred thousand dollars. And in this market—who knows.'

'It's not the money.'

The man says nothing, smiles a polite professional smile.

'No really, Mr Hamilton,' for some reason, she wants this man to believe her, to understand. Because it's *not* the money. 'I mean it—the money's not an issue. I don't care about the money.'

'Then what is the problem, Mrs Middleton?'

'I just don't understand,' Susan's voice has dropped to a whisper, and the man has to lean close to hear her, a little closer than is proper. 'Hasn't anyone told you that she's dead?' Susan is unravelling, she can feel it. She clutches his arm. 'Didn't anyone tell you that Karen's dead? How can we give her half of the estate when she's dead?'

The solicitor looks pained. 'Dead? Well that's never been—'

She interrupts: 'Karen disappeared more than twenty years ago. She was abducted, raped, murdered. God knows what. Anyway, she's dead. Gone. This can't be serious—it's insane! My mother wasn't of sound mind. I can contest it, can't I? Can't I?'

Mr Hamilton takes her hand, which has been waving about

dangerously. His hand—large, cool, comforting—covers hers briefly. 'Mrs Middleton. Susan. May I call you that?' He doesn't wait for an answer. 'Susan, this seems to have come as a terrible shock to you, and it may be that your sister is, as you say, dead. But the police files on your sister's disappearance have never been closed, a body has never been found, and most important-ly, as far as the terms of your mother's will goes, your mother herself never gave up hope.'

'But it's ...'

He covers her hand again, as if that will silence her. 'Listen to me for a moment. The will is completely watertight. There's no question that your mother was of sound mind when she made it, and that the conditions are completely legal and reasonable. You can leave the whole business to me—since your father's death I'm the only remaining executor. Anyway, I'll advertise and then conduct interviews in the unlikely event that there is any response. Even if she is alive, Susan—and yes, I know you believe it's highly improbable—but even if she's out there some-where, it's very unlikely she'd make contact now, after all these years. What's more likely is that our notices will attract a number of—er—false respondents. I've seen it before: any hint of a lost heir brings out all sorts of opportunists. Mainly cranks, but oc-casionally some very clever performers. Professional impostors.

'Of course it's standard procedure these days to have a DNA test, but as you're only half-siblings and we won't have a sample from your ... er ... shared parent, the test won't be conclusive. At best it will only advise that the possibility can't be excluded. Most unsatisfactory.' He sighs, then pauses, waiting for her to comment, but she has nothing to say. Instead she looks steadily down at the desk, at their two hands. She studies the dark hairs on his fingers, the ornate silver ring on his middle finger, the clean, neatly-cut fingernails. Her own: trapped; barely visible. He follows her gaze, releases her fingers without comment. Continues.

'If, and again this is highly unlikely, if a respondent *can* prove her identity; if a set of—shall we call them qualifying provisions—are met—well, then I think your involvement will become necessary. Will become essential, in fact ...'

'But—'

Mr Hamilton interrupts, 'At this point you would have to conduct any further interviews to determine true identity. The final decision will be yours.'

She wriggles her fingers and he moves his hand away. She breathes deeply for a moment, then looks up, meets his eyes.

'After all,' he says, and his voice is carefully devoid of emphasis. 'You're the only one left who knows her, aren't you?'

It's true that Susan's the only one left.

But know her?

The girl, Karen, is eighteen. It is the night of her sixth form formal—a big night, much anticipated. At ten to seven she is ready. She wears the gown that her mother has made for the occasion, her hair is curled, make-up carefully applied. *As pretty as a picture*, her mother says. The mother takes several photographs: Karen beside a mirror, in the lounge room, several in the garden, one with her young half-sister standing beside her.

She is walking to the dance. The school—where both dinner and dance are to be held—is only a few blocks away, and Karen has arranged to meet a friend—a girlfriend—en route. She says goodbye; the mother and sister wave to her from the front verandah. The phone rings and the mother hurries inside to answer it. It is her husband, the father of the young child, Karen's stepfather, calling from the north coast, where he has travelled for a business meeting. He has rung from his motel room to wish Karen luck, to wish her a fine time out tonight, to tell her that he's thinking of her, but has rung too late. By the time the mother rushes out to call her daughter back, Karen has already turned the corner, is out of sight.

Her daughter has been out late at night before this, but the mother waits up anyway. As mothers do. She watches television. *Ten o'clock. Eleven. Midnight.* She gets into bed. Tries to sleep. *One. Two.* Gives up and goes back to the lounge room. Tries to read a book. *Three.* The mother is mildly anxious—as mothers are wont to be—but what to do? Who to ring? It is the end of year formal after all. There was talk of a party after the dance, and Karen has been given money—more than enough—to catch a taxi home. She will be with her friends, good responsible kids, the mother thinks, they will look out for one another, keep one another safe. And they're not kids really, are they? At eighteen. Still—it's a dangerous world out there.

The young child wakes up, wanders out sleepily. 'Is it morning yet?'

'No. Get back to bed.'

Four. The mother drifts off on the lounge.

Eight o'clock.

The child is shaking her. 'Mum! Wake up. Mum, where's Karen? Karen's not here!' The mother checks the bedroom. It's empty, the bed still made. She panics. Dials 000 and disconnects immediately. Takes several deep breaths. Thinks. Finds her phone book. Dials another number, local. Speaks to a woman, another mother. Yes, her daughter is home, was back surprisingly early, just past midnight, is still asleep.

'Wake her? Is it really necessary? ... Karen's not home? Oh dear. Hold on ...'

A voice thick with sleep. 'Karen? She didn't turn up. I waited by the bus shelter for half an hour, but she didn't arrive. She didn't come to the formal at all. I thought maybe ...'

The mother disconnects. Her fingers are deft, knowing, they dial 000 again, while the rest of her body shuts down, freezes over.

'We'll approach it this way.' Mr Hamilton has assumed the proper distance from his client. 'I'll get the house organised: put it on the market, notify the tenants. I'll place the notice in the personals. On the off-chance that she, that someone, turns up, I'll have the appropriate DNA test kit sent to you. It's quite a straightforward procedure, I believe. You take a cheek swab and send it back to the lab.' He is brisk and businesslike. Susan is trying hard to look together, alert. She has an urge to take notes but hasn't the means. Instead, she nods every now and then.

'In the meantime I'd like you to put together something about your sister. On tape, or paper, whatever's easiest. Whatever you can remember. Again, just in case. I've got the basic facts and they'll probably be enough—date of birth, last known address, that sort of thing—but I'd like some additional detail, personal detail, from you. What she liked, what she *was like*. Whatever you can remember about her. I know it's been a long time, you were only a child, but I'd like to—to get a feel for her. That way,' he says, 'we can weed out any ... obviously false claimants—without going to the expense of testing them.'

'But she isn't ... she can't ...' Susan cannot finish the sentence.

'And in all probability she won't. But she might. You have to prepare yourself, Susan. She just might.'

She.

Susan drives home.

It's a little bit early, but she pours herself a whisky. Drinks it straight.

She unloads the dishwasher, brings in the washing, scrubs the bathroom.

She remembers, just in time, to pick up Stella and Mitchell from school.

She is vague and distracted, but the children are busy with their games, and don't notice, don't care.

Just.

Susan hangs out another load, takes phone calls, organises her next month's shifts. She prepares dinner, feeds the kids, runs their bath.

She pours another drink; a double this time. Adds a dash of water, ice.

She kisses Ed warmly, lingeringly, when he gets home from work. Asks him how his day's been. Tells him that the meeting with the solicitor went well. That everything's under control.

Might.

Susan can't face telling anyone, knows that to talk about it will somehow make it more real, will make it seem possible. So she puts off telling Ed until she's downed the required number of whiskies. She waits until she's blunted her edges, so to speak.

'Do you really have to talk to her? She's only a child, she won't be able to tell you anything.' Susan is sitting on the dining room floor, pretending to dress her Sindy doll. There are police everywhere—or so it seems to the child. Their big blue bodies crowd the small rooms. They're manning phones, taking photographs, talking to her mother who sits hunched over the table, smoking cigarette after cigarette.

'Any information would be valuable to us at this point Mrs Carter. We have to talk to your daughter—you never know what a child hears or sees. Karen might have confided in her.'

'She wouldn't tell her anything. *I know.*'

'Mrs Carter. Please.'

'Oh, if you really think it will help.' Her mother shrugs. 'Susy. Susy darling, will you come over here and talk to the police lady. She just wants to ask you few questions. About Karen.'

The policewoman squats down beside the child and smiles. At this level she seems very tall to Susan, taller than her father, and her dark hair is cut short like a man's. But even in the dim light, and through the fug of cigarettes, Susan can tell that she has a kind smile. She holds out her hand. 'Come on sweetheart.'

Susan puts down her doll and reaches out. The woman pulls her up gently. 'How about we go and sit over on the lounge, Susy. You might be more comfortable there.'

The child sits right in the middle of the big lounge. Her feet dangle, don't touch the ground, and she bangs her heels against the bottom of the chair. The policewoman sits close beside her. Her skirt rides up a little when she crosses her legs, flesh coloured stockings wrinkling a little around her knees.

'It's a little bit scary, isn't it—all these policemen? I know I'd think it was pretty scary if I were you, but don't worry, sweetheart, everything'll be okay.' She takes the child's hand again. The policewoman has short bitten-down nails—but her hands are soft and warm. 'Your big sister's probably just gone to a friend's place without telling anyone. Maybe it's a friend your mother doesn't know.'

Susan says nothing, looks down. Drums her heels nervously.

'Perhaps Karen has a friend that you know, Susy? Maybe she's got a new friend, someone she hasn't had time to introduce to your mum? Maybe it's a boy?'

The child says nothing. Gazes at the thick black belt the police woman wears around her waist, and the wooden handle—the gun—pressing in tightly under her ribs.

'It's okay sweetheart. You can say. Karen won't get into any trouble. We just need to make sure she's safe. Susy?'

'She doesn't have a boyfriend,' the child speaks at last.

'No?'

'She's never going to get married. She told me that. She doesn't even like boys.'

'Oh?'

'Me and Karen are going to get a big house far away from Mum and Dad and we're going to get a little puppy. Karen said I could.'

'That sounds like fun. Doesn't Karen like living here, then?' Her voice is very deep, and she's speaking so quietly that it's almost a growl. 'Does she fight with Mummy and Daddy?'

'My dad's not her daddy, you know. We've got the same mum, but her dad's dead.'

'Yes. Your Mum explained that, Susy. Does Karen fight with your dad?'

'Daddy's away a lot. He's a traveller. That's why he's not here now.'

'He'll be home soon, Susy. We called him this morning. He's on his way. Do Karen and your mum fight, sweetheart?'

'Karen said that when we got the puppy, it would be mine mostly. At *least* three-quarters mine. She said I could name it. But I'm still thinking what. I really like Scruffy, but I haven't decided yet.'

Ed

Ed stretches before he runs. Breathes in through his nose. Feels the air fill his lungs, pushes it down, down, down, all the way to his belly. Holds for ten. Then breathes out through the mouth. Slowly, slowly. *Aaaaahhhh.*

He takes it gently this morning, starts off walking, then eases into a jog halfway down the beach. He's feeling a little, not unwell, but low in energy, out of sorts. Susan's news of the night before has put him into something of a spin. He is simultaneously aggrieved (he'd made plans, who wouldn't?—pay off the mortgage, buy a new car, an investment property, take an overseas holiday), anxious and amazed. He had wanted to really *talk* to Susan about it last night—to gauge her response, find out what she expects, how she feels, what she thinks he should be doing, how he should be feeling—but after the initial (and, it must be said, rather blunt) revelation, Susan took herself off to bed, half-pissed, and by the time Ed followed her she was deeply and unrouseably (he tried nudging, tickling, groping, whispering in her ear) asleep. And the mornings—with the mad rush to get ready for work and school—lack both time and opportunity for that sort of discussion. He doesn't (how can he with so little information?), doesn't know what to think, what to make of it.

Ed has read somewhere that many successful people—those who are successful in a spiritual and emotional as well as material sense—conduct what might be termed a 'stocktake of the self' in times of stress or uncertainty. They look at themselves objectively, dispassionately identify what they feel to be their most significant attributes, their belief systems, their weaknesses and strengths. This supposedly grounds them somehow, allows them to face most situations with a positive and creative attitude, encourages them to move forward in a positive manner—to evolve emotionally. He has read that it is helpful to keep typed inventories of these attributes, which can then be pinned above desks and beds, stored in glove boxes and briefcases, as a type of ready reference, affirmations that can be re-assimilated in moments of self-doubt. Though Ed has never actually taken the time to type out such a list (he can't quite bring himself to expose himself—face himself—so literally, so permanently) he has frequently engaged in a slightly less rigorous mental stocktake. He undertakes just such an examination now, as he jogs, in the hope that this, in combination with aerobic exercise, will help clear his mind.

Ed (he finds that use of the third person gives him access to a starker objectivity) *is a partner in a family business, Middleton and Sons, a kitchen design and manufacturing company. His brother Derek runs the factory (established by their father thirty years ago) while Ed handles designs, sales and marketing. Ed loves the business passionately, is committed to providing what their advertising claims they provide: An Executive Quality Product, Teamed with Superior Family-Oriented Design Concept and Comprehensive Project Management. After more than a decade of slog, a not insignificant level of uncertainty, of risk, the anticipated return is in sight. The business plan is running smoothly—better than smoothly—and goals have been achieved far in excess of expectations. Since their father's recent retirement Ed and Derek have finally established a committed and congenial team. Ed has achieved a satisfactory—if not perfect—work/life balance: usually restricting himself to working no more than a hundred-hour fortnight. Ed runs two prestige cars, has a not-outrageous mortgage, a comfortable home, an efficient secretary, and a more than substantial pay-packet.*

His substantial pay-packet means that he is able to provide for his family single-handedly, without having to rely—as so many of his friends and colleagues do—on a second income. His wife Susan, a nurse, works only one part-time day a week. The decision to postpone her career has been her own, but there's no doubt it pleases Ed that she has chosen to stay home, pleases him that his children, unlike the children of so many of his colleagues and friends, have the security and stability that only hands-on, full-time parental care can provide.

He is finding it difficult to get the correct order, the right emphasis. He is describing the external detail, not the essential Ed. And it is the essential Ed that he needs. It may be that the jolting rhythm of his jogging is interfering with the process. He slows right down, moves over to the soft sand, walks. Starts again. Begins with the basics.

Ed loves his wife. He loves his kids. He loves his work. He loves the ocean.

He is respected by his employees and his colleagues. He has many friends. He would class a number of his employees as friends.

He is, in general, a responsible man. He would even say a moral man. (Though his morality does not extend to being judgemental— he has no problems with abortion, recreational drug-taking or soft-porn, for instance.) As far as he is aware he has never committed an illegal act, has never even been issued with a speeding fine. He never speeds. This is not because he is afraid of being caught, or not only, but because he believes in law and order. A civil society.

He also believes in market forces—though in the face of each new financial crisis he is wondering whether he needs to rethink some of his assumptions.

'No Man is an Island.' If Ed had to sum up his guiding philosophy, his take on life, that line would more or less encapsulate all that he feels most deeply. It goes without saying that, unlike the originator of this quote—some old white guy, no doubt—he'd include women. In fact, he'd put women first: No Woman or Man is an Island.

It is Ed's belief that in this one simple phrase the principles of the marketplace and any and all humanitarian concerns have been happily synthesised.

Ed likes to read. He's never been that strong on novels (though he read and quite enjoyed Hemingway and Conrad in high school), can never quite get the point, but is very keen on biographies (sporting figures, business people, rock stars—never politicians) and instructional books. Marketing manuals and guides to self-improvement. Not that there's really anything terribly wrong with him—nothing that really needs improving. He has no deep-seated hang-ups, no serious problems with his parents, his self-esteem, his sexual, emotional or work relationships. He's just keen to fulfil his potential.

In the last state election he voted for an independent. In the last federal election he voted for the Labor party. Naturally.

His name is Edward, but he prefers Ed.

He believes in spending quality time with his children. But is committed, too, to the ideal of quantity.

He believes that the family is the mainstay of the community. He believes that men and women are different but equal.

He is heterosexual and monogamous but this is not an issue, not a judgement of other choices, other preferences.

He is what other people describe as a good bloke.

He never misses his shout.

He is even tempered; easygoing.

He is a happy man.

He looks at his watch. It is seven o'clock and he has three more lengths of the beach to go. He hasn't even started on his negative points yet, but already his head is clear, he feels energised, his sense of purpose has returned. He knows who he is. He starts jogging again. Concentrates on his legs, his breathing. His head is clear but he can't think now. He has to run.

Susan

This is her first-ever visit to Linda Carmichael's house. Linda is not a particular buddy, is not even in Susan's class, but Linda's sister, Judy, was one of Karen's friends, and so Mrs Carmichael has offered to have Susan for the afternoon, is eager to help. Since Karen's disappearance six months ago Susan has spent afternoons and weekends with various friends, has spent very little time at home. Her mother seems to have barely moved since that night, sits hunched and smoking all day, waiting for the phone to ring, the key to turn in the front door. Susan's father, who has been given a temporary job in head office—just until things at home are resolved—explains that her mother isn't well, that she'll be better soon, but Susan's not too worried anyway. She likes visiting.

Linda lives too far from the school to walk home, so Mrs Carmichael collects the girls in her car, a big maroon station wagon. Susan follows Linda's lead and clambers over the back seat into the spacious luggage compartment, though she knows that her father, who is tediously strict about seatbelts, would disapprove.

'You're really my best friend, y'know,' Linda confides as her mother starts the car. At lunchtime Linda had told Susan to get lost, had said in her loudest voice that she hated Susan and didn't know why her stupid mother had invited her over anyway.

Still, Susan responds instantly, eagerly: 'You're my best friend too, Linda.' Linda is simultaneously the most feared and most admired girl in third grade: she is the junior girls sports captain, she has been to Luna Park three times, she has seen *Jaws* and *The Towering Inferno*, and she has (she boasts) ten new Barbies with an entire suitcase full of extra clothes—as well as the latest Ken doll. Susan has one black-haired Sindy. Her single outfit, which is only the one she came in, is coming dangerously apart at the seams. 'You're my bestest bestest friend.'

Linda shares a bedroom with her younger sister, Tracy, who has been banished to the backyard for the afternoon. Susan is surprised that other than the additional bed this bedroom is not so very different to her own. She had expected something else, something richer, more exotic. But it's only the usual: white painted furniture, faded chenille bedspreads, baby-print curtains, a battered desk and bookcase. There's a big shag pile mat in the centre of the lino floor and the two girls sit cross-legged, with a glass of milk and buttered pikelets, and prepare to play some serious Barbie games.

Linda scrabbles around in her wardrobe and finally produces a battered brown cardboard suitcase. It's a small port; designed for preschoolers. Linda unclips it and tips the contents all over the carpet. A plastic boot lands on Susan's pikelet. Linda laughs. Susan counts the dolls. There are only six Barbies, not ten, and they are all much older than Susan's Sindy. There is no Ken: instead, one of the dolls has hacked-off hair and a drawn-on moustache. The clothes are sad looking, too, homemade and old-fashioned.

'These were Judy's,' Linda tells her. 'My big sister. She's too old to play with them now.' Not one of the shoes makes a pair.

The girls play intensely for an hour or so, stage high-pitched Barbie battles and the occasional passionate love scene, though Susan never really accepts the moustachioed Barbie as Ken. Then: 'I'll show you something,' Linda whispers. She takes Susan's hand and they tiptoe in their stockinged feet along the hallway, stop halfway up in front of a closed door. Linda turns the doorknob slowly, pushes the door open carefully, quietly. She steps inside and pulls Susan after her, closes the door. They lean against it, half giggling, half panting. 'This is Judy's room,' she says. 'I'm not really allowed to go in here, but I thought you'd like to see it.'

Judy's room satisfies all Susan's expectations. It's a small room, and mysteriously dark—like a secret cavern. Instead of a proper bed, a few mattresses are piled up lengthways along one wall to make a lounge. The walls are covered in posters, not the usual bright images of ABBA and the Bay City Rollers, or the cute, furry animals that Susan is familiar with from her own sister's room, but strange signs and symbols, and some black and white shots of grimy looking men with guitars, women in leather. There is a desk against one wall—it is an old desk, made of some dark timber and has a roll-down top.

Judy keeps it locked, and wears the key on a chain round her neck,' Linda whispers, wide-eyed. 'I've never ever seen inside it. Or maybe once when I was a baby, but I can't actually remember that.'

Books are stacked in piles everywhere, and there's a guitar in one corner. The room smells strange, not the familiar comforting Pine O Cleen and Omo smell of the rest of the house, but sweet and slightly musty.

Linda sits on the lounge bed, pats the space beside her. 'Come on. I'll show you something.' She tugs at the fabric covering the seat, pulls a section of it loose. Holds it up close to their faces. The material is coarsely woven, scratchy looking, a jumble of colours and patterns. 'Look at this with your eyes half closed,' she says. 'Make it go all blurry.' Susan screws up her eyes and the jumbles miraculously resolve into silvery elephants, shimmering tigers.

'Wow.' Now she is impressed. 'And look,' says Linda, clutching a small satiny cushion. 'Look at this.' The cushions have mirrors no bigger than a fingernail sewn into tiny pockets. 'They're real mirrors,' Linda says. 'Real glass.'

'Wow.' Susan is stuck for words.

'Judy wants to lock the door even when she isn't here,' says Linda, 'only Mum won't let her. She's allowed to lock it when her friends come, but. Except when it's David, her boyfriend—and then they have to stay in the lounge room *at all times*, Mum says.' She opens her eyes wide. 'That's so they can't do it.'

Susan doesn't ask what *it* is, doesn't want to reveal her ignorance, instead searches for something to compare. 'I'm not allowed in my sister's room either,' she says finally. 'My sister's missing and the police can't let us in because it's ...' she pauses, relishing the big, important sounding word, 'evidence.' This is no longer true, but that doesn't matter, it has the desired effect.

'My mum says I'm not s'posed to talk about it.' Linda is suddenly far less certain.

'It's okay. I don't mind. I'm used to it now.' Susan smiles graciously.

'My sister says your sister's probably been murdered, that she's probably been *adducted* and cut up into hundreds of pieces with a big knife.'

Susan swallows. 'She might've been *adducted* and murdered, but I think she'll be home soon. Next week probably.' She shrugs. 'Anyway, that's what the police say.'

'You're lucky, actually. Big sisters are a pain. I wish Judy would disappear.' Linda says this carelessly, her interest rapidly waning. 'Now, let's play ABBA.' She jumps off the seat noisily, then remembers where she is. Tiptoes to the door. The two girls creep back down the hallway. 'You can be the blonde one,' Linda offers. Susan accepts without comment: she is growing used to such generosity.

Her parents separate in late 1976, not long after the new divorce laws are enacted, just after Susan turns nine. Karen has been missing for more than a year.

Her father tries hard to explain. 'It's not just because of what happened to Karen. It's nobody's fault. Things have been going wrong for a long time now. Your mother and I haven't really been good friends for a while, Susy. It would have happened eventually. And it's for the best, sweetheart. We'll all be happier, believe me. Even your mother. One day you'll understand. It's all for the best.'

Her dad moves into a flat in Manly, and Susan goes with him. She isn't given a choice: her mother can't cope with her, can't cope with anything, spends most of her days in a grief-fuelled drunken oblivion. The flat is big, new, and up ten storeys. There's a buzzer—an intercom—at the front entrance, and she has to learn to use the elevator—the stairs say EMERGENCY EXIT ONLY, and anyway it would take forever to climb all ten flights. There is no backyard, but there's a view of the harbour as well as the beach from the wraparound balcony. Susan is disappointed to discover that wall-to-wall carpeting doesn't actually mean carpet all the way up to the ceiling, but is thrilled with her mirrored built-in wardrobe, and the double bunk bed with its detachable wooden ladder.

Her mum stays in the house in Harbord.

'You're not selling it, James. That's all I have left. And what if she comes back? How will she find us?'

'She's not coming back, Helen.' Wearily. 'I wish you'd get it out of your mind. She's dead. Or better off. She's not coming back.'

For the first few months Susan spends a night or two each week, as well as every second weekend, with her mother, while her father's away working. But visits to her mother become increasingly difficult, distressing for everyone, and it isn't long before her father is forced to organise an alternative. A babysitter. Gillian. Gillian is youngish—younger than Susan's parents anyway. She teaches art at the local tech, but it's only casual work, and she needs the extra money. She has wavy red hair that's almost down to her bum and the most enormous boobs that Susan has ever seen. She wears no make-up and, when she whirls here and there in her colourful Indian skirts, fine orange hairs glint along her shins.

On the nights that Susan's father is away, Gillian sleeps in a fold-out bed in the lounge room, though Susan offers her the top bunk.

While nobody actually tells her, it isn't long before Susan realises that Gillian is keeping her father company on the weekends when she's away visiting her mother (small signs—the particular way Gillian stacks the crockery; folds the dishcloth; her underwear, still damp, left draped over the shower-curtain rod). After a while, when her father's away, the fold-out bed stays folded up, and Gillian moves out of the lounge and into his bed. And in a few more months she's sleeping there even when he's at home.

A Friday night—her mother's access weekend. Susan is alone at the small dining table—it's a card table really; her father claimed their old table, and her mother has yet to replace it—eating the meal that she has prepared herself. Cheese on toast and tinned tomato soup. Her mother sits slumped in front of the muted television with a tumbler of wine and her cigarettes. She does not eat with her daughter. Susan thinks perhaps she does not eat at all.

'You know that we might never find out what's happened to your sister?' Her mother speaks quietly, her eyes not moving from the silent screen.

'Yes.' Susan knows the questions, knows the answers, doesn't really have to listen. It's always the same conversation.

'You know that she might be dead.'

'Yes, Mum.'

A long pause, then: 'You know that this has destroyed me.'

Susan makes no response; what response can she make?

'I was a good mother, Susan. I was young and it was hard for me, but I was always a good mother to her.'

'Yes.'

'They can't take that away from me. Even if she's alive somewhere, even if she never comes home, they can never tell me I was a bad mother. I was hard, sometimes, but you can't always let your children have their own way, can you? You can't let them make their own decisions. Sometimes they're wrong, your kids. Wrong. Sometimes you have to be hard. But it's never for yourself. You do it all for them. Look at you. You take notice of me don't you? You listen to what I say, don't you Susy? You take notice. You're a good girl.'

She pauses, lights another cigarette, her hands tremble. Susan breaks the toast into small pieces, drops them one by one into the soup.

'I'm a good mother to you, Susy. Say I am. A good mother?' She still hasn't turned her head towards her daughter.

Susan follows the script. 'You're a good mother,' she speaks with difficulty, her mouth crammed with sodden toast. 'A great mother. The best.'

It has been more than five years since her father's death, but Susan still finds it hard to believe that he's gone. He was only in his early sixties; fit and healthy—a non-smoker, a jogger. He'd suffered a massive heart attack while walking along the beach—had literally dropped dead. Gillian (who was ten years younger and with all sorts of opportunities still ahead of her) had almost immediately moved back to Adelaide, where she'd grown up. By then they'd been living together nearly fifteen years, and though Gillian had always been good to Susan, and had taken on the role of stepmother and then step-grandmother with good cheer and considerable enthusiasm, without the connection of Susan's father they'd lost contact. There's been the odd phone call, the occasional letter, photographs, an exchange of presents at Christmas, but somehow they've never made plans to visit, to meet up. Still, it's Gillian that Susan contacts now, the morning after the reading of the will. She wants to tell her about Karen: to see what she thinks; to find out what she knows.

Gillian is, as always, pleased to hear from her. Susan explains, gives a lengthy and somewhat confused account. But Gillian seems undisturbed, unsurprised by the terms of her mother's will—it seems she has known all along.

'Why did Dad let her do it?' Susan asks, 'What was the point? It's ridiculous. A complete waste of time and money. Karen's dead. I can understand there was no way Mum would believe it, but why did Dad let her write the will that way? He had power of ...'

Gillian cuts into the shrillness of Susan's misdirected indignation. 'Hey Suse, it's not my fault. There's no point yelling at me.' Her voice is as it always was in times of conflict—impossibly calm, generously soothing.

Susan apologises.

'It's okay. I understand, but listen for a minute, Susan. I'm sorry I have to be the one to tell you this—I told your father that it wasn't fair, that you should have been told. But he—he didn't want it hanging over your head for the rest of your life. On top of the thing with your mother. He wanted to keep things ... clear for you. To give you some certainty.'

'Dad told me she was dead. I remember that. He told me she was dead.'

'It seemed the easiest way, the best way. And he ... well I guess at that stage he probably thought she was dead too.'

Susan's throat is dry and words are difficult. 'At that stage? What d'you mean? Did something happen after she left? What do you mean? What happened?'

'Jesus,' Susan hears Gillian's sharp intake of breath. 'This is bloody hard over the phone.'

'What's hard, Gillian?' Susan doesn't want to ask and doesn't want to hear the answer. It would be so much easier to just hang up.

'There was some proof that Karen may have been alive, Suse. Some family friend, in Melbourne, I think, swore she'd seen her, and told your mother. Your mother hired someone, didn't tell James.'

'And?'

'There was nothing definite. Some people who knew someone who met someone who just might have been Karen. But this was years after she left. Most people change such a lot at that age. No one was certain.'

'When was this? How long after she disappeared?'

'Oh, it was years ago—just before your mother ... before she got really ill, maybe ten years after Karen disappeared. She hired this person, this private detective and of course she couldn't pay. The bill and the reports ended up coming to us.'

'But why would she have been alive? Didn't the police ...?'

'The police file was never closed, Suse. You know that. There was no body, no evidence. Nothing conclusive either way.'

'And the reports, you say there was no positive sighting ...?'

'No absolute positives. Look, Suse,' Gillian sounds a little impatient, as if she wants to end this conversation, or move it elsewhere. 'I've still got those reports. I'll put them in the post in the next few days if you like. Now, tell me, how're those children of yours?'

It is not until Susan is twelve, has just started high school, that she stops believing that Karen is out there somewhere, that she will come back for her one day.

'She's dead, isn't she?' Susan asks, out of the blue, one Saturday morning. 'Karen's dead.'

Her father looks up, startled, from his weekend newspapers. 'We can't ever know, sweetheart,' he says slowly, 'not for certain—when there's ... no body. But it's probably best that we start thinking that way. No matter what your mother says.' Susan can tell that her dad is unsure about what to say, knows from experience that he is out of his depth, that such conversations make him uncomfortable, uneasy. But she needs some answers, some certainty, and she still has a naive faith in her father's assurances.

'She would have come back if she was alive, wouldn't she? She wouldn't have stayed away all these years, would she, Dad?' Susan doesn't understand her father's agonised look at Gillian, and her stepmother's slight shake of the head in response.

'She would have come back if she could,' he says finally, and with what seems to be complete conviction. 'I'm sure of it.'

Susan stops wondering about Karen. She stops dreaming about her.

Stops remembering her.

In the end it takes her almost an entire day, countless drafts and redrafts, but finally she has a file on the computer labelled KAREN, containing a single document. She makes it as official looking as possible: headings in bold, double spaced, title in capitals, centred:

KAREN MICHELLE BROWN

Date of birth: 12/6/57

Last known address: 24 Koolaroo Ave, Harbord, NSW

Appearance: Dark blonde hair, blue eyes, fair skin, some freckles. Medium build. Height when last measured: 161 cm. Please see enclosed photograph.

Family details:

Mother: Helen Mary Carter. Nee McGregor. Born Adelaide: 1936. Died 1996. Married Paul Brown in Melbourne in 1956. Married James Carter in Manly 1963.

Father: Paul Brown. Navy Midshipman? Born? Died 1959.

Sister: Susan Louise Middleton. Nee Carter. Born 1967. Married Edward Middleton 1987.

Extended family:

Maternal—Helen Carter's parents both died before she married and she had no siblings. Some elderly aunts in Adelaide, but they're long gone.

Paternal—none known.

James Carter—born 1929, died 1991. Family all English. Parents visited sometime in the early seventies. One sister, lives in the United Kingdom.

History:

Karen Michelle Brown was born in Melbourne in 1957. Her father died in a shipping accident soon after. Her mother trained as a nurse but worked in Myer when Karen was a baby. Met James Carter, a salesman, in 1962. Moved to Sydney soon after to marry him. Karen and Helen moved into Carter's Harbord residence.

Karen attended Harbord Primary School, then Manly Girls High. Worked Saturdays and school holidays at the local newsagent. She was offered—and accepted—a cashier's job at the ANZ Bank, Brookvale, a few days before her disappearance. Disappeared the night of her high school formal, 10/11/75.

School history:

Unknown. All reports and awards and other documents destroyed by mother.

Friends:
Best friend: Julie Walker. Julie moved to Brisbane with her family just before Karen disappeared. Other close female friends: Judy Carmichael, Amanda Hastings, Joanne Simpson.
No known boyfriends. Though rumour of her being seen with a man in a red car a few days before her disappearance.

Hobbies and interests: Netball. Swimming.

Personal qualities: According to others: quiet, well-mannered, hard working.

When she reads over what she's written, Susan is disturbed by the brevity, the starkness of the information. She could have been writing about anyone. A stranger, not a sister. She prints out the page and slips it into an envelope. She has the photograph ready—a school portrait, taken the year of Karen's disappearance. She seems so very young; an ordinary teenage girl—gleaming hair, bright eyes, a wide untroubled smile—waiting for life to begin. She slides it in, seals the envelope.

Later, she goes back to the computer, reopens the file. Scrolls to the bottom of the page, adds another category, another subheading: 'What I remember about my sister'. She types slowly, a single sentence:

> *'I remember that I thought my sister was wonderful, but I don't—I can't—remember why.'*

She realises that it's not all that unusual, has spoken to others who've admitted that similarly, they have very few memories of their young lives, of actually being themselves before they were four, five, six, whatever. But Susan's amnesia seems to be more substantial. Sometimes it feels as if she slept until she was eight. That she didn't really come to consciousness until Karen's disappearance and that her very existence is only a bizarre consequence of her sister's absence: her first conscious memory, her first real memory, she's certain, is of waving her sister goodbye on that particular night, of watching Karen's elegant figure receding in the distance, and then disappearing altogether as she turned the corner at the end of the street. After that night, after Karen left, Susan's memories are sharp, clear, focused; they come thick and fast and more or less chronologically. But before that it's almost a blank. Oh, there are a few random recollections—brief and unrelated, almost like snapshots, or dreams. And she can never be sure that they truly are memories, that they aren't constructions, reconstructions based on stories told to her by her parents, or made up collage-like from family photographs.

And it isn't just her sister. No matter how hard she tries, Susan can't really recall the woman who was her mother *before* Karen's disappearance. Her only enduring memory of her mother is of the woman she became—a woman to be feared and then, as her anger and grief became madness, to be guiltily avoided. Oh, the texture of certain fabrics, a whiff of hairspray, lipstick, a particular tune on the radio, all these can pull her back—but it's to a feeling, an indefinable sense of her mother as she was once—loving, humorous, interested—rather than a concrete memory or even an image. And with it comes always an associated sensation of loss and grief, of her mother, *that* mother, being lost.

Susan's memory of her father before that time is hazy, too. It's difficult to connect the smiling youthful man who, according to the photographs anyway, was physically demonstrative (in so many snaps he stands close, arm slung round shoulders; he hugs—unconsciously, easily) with the irritable and emotionally contained man she knew. In photographs there's an unselfconscious, irrepressible energy about him. He looks like he might be good fun. And that's the sense she has of him from that time: recalls, she's certain, being thrown up in the air; or tickled, tortured in that affectionate fatherly way. But after Karen's disappearance—though he was only in his late thirties—he became someone else. Someone unbearably burdened, not someone fun.

And Karen—the big sister who, they assured her, she worshipped—Karen has for years existed only in two dimensions, six by four, framed, and under glass. Karen she barely remembers at all. She has a handful of memories in which her sister features, but these are incoherent, without context. All meaningless. If not for the photographs, the few stories provided by her father, family friends, it would be easy to assume that she'd never even known her.

She wonders endlessly about those final months before her sister's disappearance. Did something happen, something she's repressed or denied or perhaps dissociated from? (Oh, she knows the jargon—she's read the books, done her homework, spoken to experts. Ed would be impressed.) Or is there something—some moment, some event that she just can't remember because she was too young?

It eats away at her, this blank. She scours her memory, but there's nothing there: no gleaming moment of truth just waiting to be to discovered beneath the burnt-on layers of the past. There's nothing—an absence.

Ed has cut the notice carefully from all of the papers. The nine copies are pinned neatly to the cork board in the office, waiting to be filed. Susan prises out the drawing pin and takes the top clipping.

> Would Karen Michelle Brown
> (formerly of Harbord NSW)
> or any person having information regarding her
> past or present whereabouts
> please contact Howard Hamilton at
> Shepard Hamilton Sloane Solicitors.
> Suite 6, 4 Peel Street, Chatswood.

She thinks about their names. Susan. Karen. Their lack of meaning, of connection. If their names held some particular association for her parents, Susan was never told—as far as she knows they were named for no one, for no particular reason. Their names have no history, no past. They are names typical of their era: Karen was fashionable and so was Michelle. At school Susan was always Susan C. to differentiate her from the three other Susans in her class. Susan's middle name is Louise—the bridesmaid of names, a perfect middle name, containing the required number of syllables, nothing more than a convenient filler. At home she was usually Sukey. Or Susy, Suse, Sue. She was only ever Susan when she was in some trouble or other. *If you don't stop doing that right this minute, Susan Louise Carter ...* It was impossible to shorten Karen's name. She was always just Karen.

Waiting, she is in a state not unlike those first days of pregnancy, when it seems that everywhere you look there are women lumbering with their eight-month bellies, or pushing new babies in prams. Everywhere Susan looks she see sisters. At the school gate a tiny kindergarten kid—her dress too long, shoes extra shiny—grips her sixth grade sister's hand tightly; another shouts something, gives her younger sister a sneaky shove with her bag before running off with friends. A pair of elderly women—their identical bright blue eyes the giveaway—walk slowly along the beach, trousers rolled up to their knees, shoes swinging loosely in their hands. Queuing at the supermarket Susan eavesdrops unabashedly as the young women ahead of her talk heatedly and unselfconsciously about their mother: 'I can't believe sometimes, that she's actually our mother. She's so irresponsible,' says one. 'She's just lonely,' her more generous sibling replies. 'She needs the attention.' Even stopping at traffic lights she imagines sisterly similarities in the faces of drivers and passengers, between female pedestrians crossing together at the lights.

For the first time ever Susan is envious. Is filled with a real sense—an adult sense—of what she's missed out on. Of what she's lost. She has female friends, good female friends—her best friend Anna, her sister-in-law, girls she went through college with, colleagues at work—but with none of them does she have that uncomplicated ease, that familiarity that she sees between these women. She notices the casual way they touch one another—the brisk removal of lint from shoulders, of lipstick from teeth, the hair brushed away from faces, sunscreen smoothed onto skin. She envies them their easy impatience, too, the scornful shrug of the shoulders, roll of the eyes, the knowledge of each other's shortcomings, fears, failures. She envies most of all their shared history, their shared past.

The week before she is due to start her college nursing course, Susan visits her mother. She visits only every month or so now—and then for just a few hours at a time. She goes for lunch usually, or sometimes brings Chinese takeaway for an early dinner. It has been years since she has stayed overnight—and anyway there is no longer anywhere for her to stay. Her mother has closed off most of the house, and lives entirely in the kitchen and lounge room, where she has set up her bed on the couch. She gave up working years ago, and Susan guesses that her father supports her, or at least supplements her government entitlements, though he never mentions it. She knows he or Gillian calls in every week to bring groceries and to check that she's okay, that she's bathing, eating regularly, but they never mention this either. Nobody ever suggests that Susan should do more—she is young and busy—and the time that she spends with her mother is painful enough.

Today her mother has set the table for a formal afternoon tea; the good silver teapot—a wedding present from an English aunt—has been brought out of storage, and the dainty china cups have matching saucers and tiny silver teaspoons. She has covered the table with a lacy cloth that doesn't quite hide the smeared and crummy surface beneath. Neat stacks of Scotch Finger biscuits grace a scalloped Wedgwood cake plate.

'Karen won't be long,' her mother says as she fills the cups. 'She called me from London last night and said she'd be here in time for afternoon tea. She said we should start without her, not to let it all get cold, not to let it spoil, waiting.'

The tea is stone cold, and the surface looks slightly greasy. Susan pretends to take a sip. 'Mmm,' she murmurs. 'Delicious. Just what I need. Thanks Mum.'

Her mother blows on the surface of her tea. She breaks a biscuit in two, dunks one half, and pops it into her mouth. Swallows the finger in a single noisy gulp. She's no longer the thin, haggard, underfed woman of Susan's childhood, but is unhealthily plump—a result of years of inactivity, overeating and medication.

'Did I tell you I start college next week, Mum?' Susan says brightly. 'Nursing's a three year course at college now, it's not taught in the hospitals anymore. Not like when you did it.' Susan keeps going, though her mother isn't even looking her way, is humming tunelessly to herself through another mouthful of soggy biscuit. 'I'll get a diploma in applied science at the end of it. And then I start work as a sister.'

Her mother nods and mutters. 'A sister. A sister.' Susan has her attention now. 'Your sister Karen is a very fine doctor,' she announces with a proud smile. 'All her patients tell me she's a fine doctor. One of the best.' She slurps her tea, lifts a corner of the tablecloth and delicately wipes her mouth. 'You should be proud, too. It's no small thing, having a doctor in the family. Your sister; you should be proud.'

She presents Susan with a cardboard carton as she leaves. 'I'm having a bit of a spring clean, dear,' she says, 'and I thought I'd give you a few of your old things, things you might not want me to throw out.' As far as Susan can recall, she's left nothing here, but she takes the carton anyway. 'I thought I might take a short holiday when I've finished here,' her mother says as Susan kisses her goodbye. 'I thought I might take a train down to Melbourne to stay with Karen for a few days. It'll be lovely to see Karen and the kids,' she adds, a little teary now. 'I'm lucky to have such lovely grand-kids,' she tells Susan earnestly. 'So many things to be grateful for.'

Susan opens the box when she gets home. They're not her things after all, but Karen's. A couple of netball trophies—best and fairest, 1973; most consistent player, 1975—and a random se-lection of her books: *Carrie, Jaws, Go Ask Alice*, some hardbacked Agatha Christies and a few old Nancy Drews. There's a battered address book and several dressing table trinkets: a Victorian pin-cushion and a pair of china kissing angels; a maroon-and-white Manly football beanie; a *Certificate of Merit* in Biology for the year 1974. Susan is surprised that her mother's kept anything belong-ing to Karen. Soon after the separation, all her sister's belongings were consigned to the incinerator, and everything that couldn't be burnt was sent to the tip. Nothing was donated, it was as if her mother wanted all evidence of Karen's existence destroyed. She must have hidden this collection of things away from herself. But this is a strange assortment, there's nothing here that's character-istic, nothing telling—they're meaningless bits and pieces.

At the bottom of the carton are several slim manila folders—all with *Karen* scrawled darkly across the top. Inside is a copy of some official document—a police report. In the second folder are newspaper clippings detailing Karen's disappearance and the subsequent search. They range from front-page articles in the *Manly Daily* with six by six blowups of Karen's last school photograph; to a single paragraph in the *Sun. Police give up hunt for missing teenager. Girl feared dead.*

Susan dumps everything back into the carton, tapes it up and shoves it as far back in the wardrobe as she can. She is starting college in a week. She has her own life to get on with.

She has chosen nursing because she has enough marks and because, as her father has pointed out, nursing is a sensible job for a girl. 'It's not as if you've got any burning ambition, Sukey,' he says, 'or any particular talent. Nursing's respectable and flexible and the pay's reasonable, though I can't understand why you have to go to college. Waste of time if you ask me. I

don't understand all this bullshit about careers for girls, anyway,' he adds somewhat irritably. 'You'll all just end up getting
married and having kids like your mothers.' Susan's father has
become unashamedly reactionary as he's aged, and she is often appalled by his curmudgeonly declarations, can't imagine
what Gillian sees in him, but has never braved asking, perhaps
fearing that underneath the flamboyant clothes and eccentric
opinions Gillian would secretly like to shave her legs and don
flesh-coloured pantyhose.

Anyway, Susan takes no offence, makes no objections because, as she sees it, her father's probably right. It's true—she
has no burning ambition, no particular talent. Judging by her
final exam results, she's reasonably, but not outstandingly,
bright. She has no flair for art or music or textiles or sport. She
abandoned the acting fantasy in her junior years of high school.
She has no desire to be a lawyer or a doctor, or to study arts or
engineering. But she doesn't want to be a check-out chick or
spend her life waitressing, either. So, ultimately, if rather un-
imaginatively, it's a choice between teaching and nursing, and
considering that her mediocre marks will barely secure her a
place in primary education in a rural college, nursing's really
the only option. She can't claim that she has a burning desire
to make people well, to heal or to nurture, but then, at her age,
who does? Like many girls her age, Susan's only significant desire is the usual one. And, were anyone to ask, she'd have to
admit that the prospect of meeting a nice young doctor (isn't
that every young nurse's dream?) is appealing.

He is not a doctor, but a business studies student at the CAE.
He's not quite a man either, but the same age as Susan: nineteen—just a boy, really. She is eating an early lunch—a pay-by-
weight meat and salad sandwich—between lectures; is sitting
contentedly alone at one of the courtyard tables at the college
cafe, when another student, male, asks if she'd mind sharing.
She says no, go ahead, but can't help wondering, after a quick

look around, why he wants to share when there are so many empty tables. The boy takes the seat across from Susan, heaves his backpack onto the vacant chair. Her initial impression is that he's reasonably good-looking—maybe his hair's a bit shorter than what's currently fashionable and he is, perhaps, a bit too boy-scouty, it's possible that he's a Christian or a young Liberal on a mission—so she keeps her eyes cast down, chews her food slowly, selfconsciously, trying hard not to gulp or dribble.

'You're from the beaches aren't you?' His voice is deep, his vowels neutral.

'What beaches?' Susan knows she sounds impatient, that her tone could even be taken as scornful, dismissive. It's just nerves.

He perseveres. 'The northern beaches. I'm sure I've seen you swimming at Freshie. I'm from Harbord.' He's smiling warmly, encouragingly. Susan wonders when it was that he saw her there—she hasn't been in the surf for months. She wonders what swimmers she was wearing.

'Actually, yeah, I do. I am. Well, sort of.' Susan tries to appear less wary. 'I live in Manly, but my Mum's at Harbord. I don't know if that counts.'

'Oh, yeah—Manly counts alright. Good surf.' He nods approvingly, smiles. 'Mackellar Girls?'

'Yep. You were at Manly?'

'Uh huh. Don't know how we've never met.'

He has great teeth, and the faintest of dimples in his right cheek. 'So. What're you studying?'

'Nursing.'

'Nursing? Then how come you're here? At college? I thought nurses trained in hospitals.' His eyes, wide set, heavily lashed, are an impossibly bright blue. They *twinkle*. She wonders how it is that she's never noticed him before.

'They've changed the system.' Her reply is too abrupt.

'Oh.' He seems suddenly at a loss, looks away, his shoulders slumped.

Susan contemplates packing up and going—her chemistry

lecture begins in five minutes—but she can't leave the conversation there. She tries hard to combat her nerves, to inject some casual warmth into her voice, 'So, what're you studying?'

He brightens at her enquiry. 'Business. Marketing options mainly.'

'That sounds interesting.'

'Oh, it's fantastic. I'm learning some unbelievable stuff. Huge. Life-changing. Did you know that just through the introduction of peer reviews, a company can increase employee productivity by up to eighty per cent? Just imagine it, eighty per cent!'

Susan has no idea what he's talking about, but she doesn't care. All the other boys she's met at college have been cool, restrained, have been trying hard to be cynical, to seem grownup. This boy is different. He's so unselfconsciously enthusiastic, so convinced of the wisdom of what he's learning.

'You should come to the three o'clock lecture, I'm sure no one would mind. He's an unreal guy, the lecturer—totally inspiring. He'll make it all much clearer than I can. Why don't you come?' He looks doubtful. 'I mean—that is—if you're interested.'

She's interested.

'By the way,' he says, holding out his hand, 'I'm Ed. Ed Middleton.'

Although there's the odd occasion when parents are absent and surreptitious overnight stays are possible, it's almost impossible for Ed and Susan to spend long periods of time together.

It even proves difficult to meet outside college during the week—Ed's mother, though not overtly hostile, doesn't approve of Susan. 'Ed's studying, I'm afraid,' she'll say over the phone, 'I don't think I should disturb him.' Or, 'He's helping his dad at the factory today, dear, and you can't call him there. I'll let him know you called ... er ... Sally, is it? Perhaps he can get back to you tomorrow ...?'

Ed, though anxious himself, and conspicuously nervous whenever they're both in his mother's company, tries to reassure her. 'I think it's just that you're so quiet around her, Sue, so reserved. I think quiet people make her uncomfortable.' He makes suggestions: 'Perhaps if you'd open up a little; try to be more friendly. Maybe *you* could start conversations; talk about the weather, the tennis …? I think she just doesn't know what to make of you.'

But Susan suspects that it is the little she does know of her that offends the respectable Mrs Middleton: her parents' divorce ('Such a sad thing, divorce,' she sniffs. 'We're lucky, in our family, we've all managed to keep together. Seven siblings between us, Mr Middleton and I have. And there's not been a single divorce. Not one!'); her mother's 'illness' ('Oh dear, a psychological problem is it? Fortunately we've never had to cope with that sort of thing in our family. It's just not in our make-up, I suppose.'); her father's live-in girlfriend ('Gillian's your stepmother, is she, dear? They're not actually married? Oh, I see.'); even the fact that Susan lives in a unit ('Oh, I do think that must be hard. All those neighbours. And no garden. No sunshine. It can't be healthy.'). It is possible too that, being local, she remembers Karen's disappearance, though Susan has never mentioned it to her. Or to Ed. Instead, she has told Ed that her older sister died of meningitis when she was a child. This is the tale she tells any new friends or acquaintances. It's an easier story to tell, somehow, and the more frequently she's called upon to tell it, the more real it feels.

While he doesn't disapprove of Ed in particular, Susan's father has made it clear (despite both Gillian's and his daughter's remonstrations) that he will not welcome frequent visits by young men. 'They take up so much space,' he huffs. 'Their big feet. Their pimples. Their callow arrogance.' He sucks in his cheeks, 'And they *eat* so much.' Ed's visits, as awkward and uncomfortable as Sue's visits to the Middleton home, are restricted to Friday nights, between the hours of six and ten pm.

Though neither of them are especially keen on the outdoors, out of desperation Ed and Susan take up camping. They go away together every few weekends when Ed can get away from work, stop at different beaches and camping grounds along the Central Coast, sleep in the back of Ed's newly resprayed EH Holden wagon, his pride and joy.

Susan tells her father that they are staying at a friend's holiday house at The Entrance. It is his imagined response to them sleeping in the back of the car, rather than to the outrageous fact of their sleeping *together*, that keeps Susan from telling him the truth—and though she knows he has reservations about Ed's driving ability and the age and reliability of his vehicle, he makes no real objections to their weekends away. Susan's not sure what Ed tells his parents, but assumes, noting his barely suppressed panic whenever they are held up on the congested freeway on Sunday nights and the frequent calls he makes from garage payphones along the way, that he, too, is lying.

'Why don't we move in together?' Susan has woken up cramped and cold in the back of the wagon. Ed is lying on his side, facing away from her, his knees pulled up almost to his chest in order to fit. They have been going out for more than six months, and with no perceptible diminution of interest, but Susan can no longer pretend to herself that the extreme inconvenience, the humiliating privation of their weekends together—the mosquitos, the lack of decent food, the vaguely sordid coupling on the hard floor of the wagon-tray (or occasionally, for variety, on the back seat), the interminable walks to the smelly amenity block for a pee—represents in any way the apotheosis of romantic love. Moving in together seems a reasonable way to avoid these weekends of deception and discomfort. 'Ed?' she nudges him gently when no answer's forthcoming, 'why not move in together?'

'We can't.' His voice is low, slightly muffled. 'How could we afford it?'

'Oh, Ed. Don't be so stupid. It's easy.' Most of Susan's school friends have moved out of home by now, so she knows how it's done. 'We'll both get some sort of student allowance. I can get more part-time work. You've still got your work at your dad's factory—it's not like he'll care. We'll be able to rent a little flat somewhere. We can get other people in if it gets too dear. I've only got another year of study, anyway. Come on, Ed—it'd be fantastic.'

'It'd be too hard. We couldn't. Not live together.'

'Oh Ed.' He doesn't say what is bothering him, but Susan knows without being told that it is his mother. She wouldn't approve. ('Living In Sin? No one in the Middleton family has ever ...')

'But we could get married.' He turns towards her now, grinning widely, wildly. 'Let's get married, Susy.'

'Married?' Susan is not yet twenty. Twenty-year-olds live together; share dingy flats with other cohabiting students. Marriage is something you do when you grow up. Marriage is something else entirely. 'Married?'

Ed shuffles about in the cabin until he is kneeling, one leg tucked awkwardly behind him. He takes Susan's hand, takes both hands, clasps them between his two, 'Will you do me the honour,' he says, raising her hands to his lips. 'Susan my love, my darling, my life,' he brushes the backs of her hands gently with his lips, then turns them over, kisses her wrists, 'will you do me the honour of becoming my wife? Go on. Say you will.'

And he looks so sweetly ridiculous, bare naked, his rangy body all hunched over in that small space, his face as crumpled and tender with sleep as a baby's.

How can she refuse?

'You're not what Ed needs,' his mother hisses the words, though she smiles politely for the camera. 'You're not the right kind of girl for my son,' she elaborates, making sure the message sinks in. 'And you'll never last.'

'Could you ladies stand a little closer,' the photographer calls. 'So your shoulders are just touching. Great. Now, how about a smile from the bride. This isn't your funeral, honey. That's better. Perfect. Perfect.'

It takes Susan a moment to recover from the flash and dazzle, and by then it's too late for any response—she's standing with her arm around Ed's waist, smiling triumphantly for the camera.

The solicitor's secretary phones. It is late afternoon, a month after the notice was first placed. 'Mr Hamilton's very busy, Mrs Middleton,' she says briskly, 'or he'd have rung you himself. He wants me to tee up an appointment with you. If you could come in as soon as possible?'

'There's been a response, hasn't there?' Susan tries hard to keep her voice level, detached.

'I really don't know anything about it, Mrs Middleton. How about ten tomorrow?'

She sounds so breezy, so offhand, so indifferent.

Doesn't she know what this means?

'I asked her what her mother's full name was, her mother's maiden name, her—your mother's date of birth. Her own full name, date of birth, place of birth, former residences. And,' here he sorts through papers, aligns them briskly on his desk, 'she knew all the answers. She hesitated a little when I asked her your mother's birthday, but the date she finally gave was quite correct.'

Susan is sitting in Howard Hamilton's office. It is only ten in the morning and the room is air-conditioned, but even so she is hot; the heat prickles her scalp, her legs stick moistly to the leather seat, she is conscious of the gradually spreading damp patches beneath her arms. It has been a struggle to get here, to get the children off to school on time, to drive through manic peak-hour traffic and find a park. She's had to hurry, in uncomfortably high heels, along the busy Chatswood streets. She's had no time to catch her breath while waiting. She arrived just on the hour, was ushered in still panting from the rush and is sitting now, trying to make sense, react sensibly.

'And the DNA?'

'Well, as I warned you, the test is not conclusive, but it seems it can't rule out the possibility that this woman is your sister. In my opinion, it's not likely that she'd have agreed to undergo a test at all if there was really any question.'

'What about looks? Does she *look* like Karen?'

'Well, from the little I had to go on, I would say that the woman I met yesterday is physically consistent with your sister. She's fair-haired, fair-skinned, blue-eyed. Regular features. She's thinner. Older. But that's only to be expected.'

'So do you think it's her? Do you think you've got enough to go on? If the DNA's inconclusive? And these facts? Surely anyone could know these ... these things.'

'Birth dates, Susan? Addresses? There's hardly been time for her to launch a full-scale investigation. The notices only went in a month ago. And anyway, how else *could* she know—who would she ask?'

'But you say she's got no documents, no identification. No proof.'

'Susan. Your sister ran away from home twenty years ago. It's not unusual for people who don't want to be discovered to get rid of anything that might connect them to their old lives. It's not—and it certainly wasn't back then—before photo IDs and hundred point identification checks—as hard as you might think to become another person.'

'I suppose not.'

'I think that at this point, Susan, we should be taking this woman's claim very seriously.'

'Oh?' Her resistance is as confounding to Susan as it is to the solicitor. She wants it to be Karen, wants it desperately, but somehow (what if it turns out to be a joke? a hoax?) she just can't grasp it, is finding it impossible to give in—to trust that what he is saying is true. That it could possibly be the truth.

'But it's not really a matter of what I think, is it?' he says. 'Because from here on in it's in your hands, not mine.' Mr Hamilton splays out his fingers as if to illustrate the point. 'It has to be your call, Susan.' He leans back in his chair, waits.

She capitulates. 'Okay.' Reluctantly. 'What's next then? What do we do?'

'What do *you* do?'

'What should I do, then? Should I meet her? Should I meet her now? Or should I wait?' She tries hard to tamp down the panic, the terror.

'Look, I have to say, given the facts, I'm confident that this woman is your sister. So, what are you waiting for? You must be desperate to see her again. Why not meet up with her now? That is, if she's willing to make contact. What I'd suggest is that you organise a meeting somewhere. For lunch, or for afternoon tea. Meet somewhere neutral. A cafe, a restaurant, a park. But not at home. Not this first meeting, anyway.'

'What about my husband? I guess this affects him too. Should I take Ed?'

'Oh.' Mr Hamilton looks a little put out by her question. 'Ed?' He rubs his hand over his jaw, considering. Hamilton is a short man, barely taller than Susan, but strong looking, wiry. His eyes are heavy-lidded, deep-set, his lips full, firm, his cheeks, despite his relative youth—he's not much past forty, Susan would guess—already heavily etched. His pale skin has a greenish tinge. Thick dark hair coats his wrists, the backs of his hands and fingers, curls above his collar. Already, even though it's still morning (surely a lawyer would shave before work?), there is a slight raspiness, the beginnings of a dark shadow under his chin. She wonders if, despite his name, he might be Mediterranean. Greek, Spanish. He has the characteristic dourness, anyway.

'No,' he says finally. 'No, I don't think that'd be a good idea. Meet her alone.' He smiles then, and somehow it's an unlikely smile in that sculpted facial landscape, loose and slightly snaggle-toothed. He looks younger, less predictable. Less lawyerly. 'I know it's harder to do these things by yourself, but really,' he says, scraping his hand across his chin again, 'you're the only one who'll know for sure. Aren't you?'

On the way home Susan drives slowly past her mother's old house, turns at the end of the street and drives back, parks on the other side of the road. She sits and watches, though there's nothing to see.

The house has been rented out for ten years, the money used to pay for her mother's hospitalisation. In all those ten years Susan hasn't been inside once. Until his death, her father had managed everything to do with the property, and for the past five years it's all—from the signing of leases to the organising of repairs—been left in the hands of real estate agents and solicitors.

It is a red brick and tile house in a street of other, almost identical, red brick and tile homes; its only claim to singularity being an extraordinarily large block of land—almost twice the size of most of the neighbouring homes. The acme of late fifties respectability. Solid, suburban, dull. Built for ease of maintenance rather than beauty or comfort. Secure against the corrosive ocean breeze, against the summer sun, against the whims of exterior paint fashions. Nothing about it has changed (what is there to change? How could you change it?). The walls are orangey red, the roof a darker shade. Oh, maybe the charcoal paint on the porch railings and window frames is a recent alteration (wasn't it a sickly pastel green once?). The guttering—the same charcoal colour—could be new, Susan supposes. And the front garden—though it barely warrants the term garden: a couple of frangipani trees, some ragged hibiscus, the innocuous dusty leaves of the deadly oleander—maybe the plants have grown a little, but they haven't been added to or cultivated in any way. The lawn is overgrown, full of weeds, and a jaunty *For Sale* sign is nailed up beside the mailbox.

Susan sits in the car outside the house for an hour, watching, waiting. She is trying to discover something—anything—that will give her some kind of clue to the life she once lived here, the life she once shared with both her parents, with Karen. There are half memories; she can see herself jumping down the front steps, swinging on the small square iron gate, collecting the deliciously fragrant frangipani flowers, balancing carefully along the low brick fence. The way the sun falls across the porch leaving one half in shade gives her an odd sort of pang. Inexplicable. Inexpressible. She winds down the car window and breathes in the familiar breeze as if the substance of her childhood might be contained within its particles. There's nothing solid here, nothing consequential. Nothing as fully formed and complete as a real memory would be. Just impressions. And they're solitary impressions—the games children play to occupy themselves when they're alone. She can recall nothing.

She starts the car, drives past the house one more time, slows down. A curtain twitches in the front window. A pale face peers out, sees her watching, disappears. A child's face. There are no clues here. She drives home.

She calls Ed from home. 'So,' he asks, 'is it her? What does the solicitor say?' His voice is calm, careful, they have not spoken since the night before.

'The solicitor doesn't know for certain,' Susan tells him, 'but he thinks it could be her. She's got nothing that proves it—no documents or anything. And she's changed her name—Carly something or other, he said. But she says she's Karen.'

'What do you mean she says she's Karen? Anybody could turn up and ...'

'Hold on, Ed.' Susan's voice is remarkably even. 'She says she's Karen and he says she seems to have a ... a surface knowledge at least about the family.'

'Oh?'

'You know—names, important dates, that sort of thing. She knows all that. And Mr Hamilton, Howard, says there's a certain resemblance. Going by the photograph I gave him, anyway.'

'Oh.'

'And anyway, Ed, there'd be no real reason for an impostor to turn up—you know Howard worded the notice so there was no mention of any inheritance. She doesn't even know about the money yet.'

'Well, she mightn't know, but it'd be easy enough to guess, wouldn't it. Why else ...'

She switches the phone to her other ear. Takes her time.

'Hello ...? Susy? Are you there?'

'Sorry.'

'I just asked what happens next. What did he say? The solicitor. How do we find out for sure if it's her?'

'I meet her.'

'Shit.' she can hear his indrawn breath, can imagine his sudden realisation.

'Listen Suse, don't you think it might be best if we got an independent solicitor? I've got nothing against this bloke, but he's not ours. I know that Derek knows someone good, and I've a few clients who'd be happy to take it on. Maybe we could set up a meeting between the solicitor and this Carly woman and me. Keep you right out of it.'

'Ed,' Susan's voice is firm, her back straight. 'I'm meeting her. Alone. She's my sister.'

Her sister.

Ed

Ed watches the five o'clock news with his parents. There's an old clip of Ronald Reagan, standing behind a podium somewhere, answering questions easily, smiling his affable smile. 'Thank Christ he's gone,' Ed comments at the end of the report. 'Jesus. Just imagine—the fate of the free world was in that halfwit's hands. A bloody movie star. Says something about America, doesn't it?'

'Says what, exactly, son?' His father doesn't take his eyes from the screen, doesn't wait for an answer. 'All that education, and you've still got no bloody idea.' Ed opens his mouth, but closes it again. His father's a good man, and an intelligent man, but not terribly sophisticated when it comes to politics. He's not exactly right wing, but he's certainly no leftie. There's no point in arguing. Susan looks up from the card game she's playing with Stella and Mitchell and catches his eye, smiles sympathetically.

His mother gets to her feet. 'Well,' she says with a little sigh, 'I'd best start serving out. The meal won't put itself on the table, will it?' There's no answer to this, they all know better. 'I'll be needing you shortly, Ed,' his mother murmurs as she makes her way to the kitchen, 'for the carving.'

Ed always enjoys this fortnightly meal with his mother and father. He feels guilty that he doesn't have more time to spend with his parents, despite living nearby. He does speak to them on the phone during the week, and occasionally calls in for Saturday brunch after his morning surf with Derek, but worries that this isn't really enough, that they would like to see more of him and the kids, that the fortnightly visit smacks of tokenism, of a duty discharged. His parents never complain—of course—and they seem to be keeping themselves reasonably busy in their retirement (overseas holidays, veterans golf tournaments, visits to shows, casinos, clubs ...), but he's convinced (despite Susan's rolled-eyed assurances to the contrary) that these excursions are just time-fillers, diversions from their empty nest. He worries too that his father's professed lack of interest in the current running of the company—though he's still a shareholder, he hasn't called in more than half a dozen times in the last year, and no longer asks about the bank balance—is just a smokescreen for a profound, and perhaps repressed, grieving. Ed feels guilty about feeling guilty, too (guilt being such an unproductive emotion, and surely only appropriate when there's a conscious dereliction of duty). And it isn't a duty anyway (is it?) when he so thoroughly enjoys the time spent eating and talking; the inevitable game of cards. Susan might sigh with relief when they're safely home again, the fractious, overindulged children tucked up and asleep, but not Ed. Never Ed.

The carving of the leg, however, is one ritual that Ed doesn't particularly enjoy. His mother frequently takes this opportunity to have what she terms a good heart-to-heart with her son:

which usually means a not-so-subtle nag session or the laying of a few carefully concealed barbs. Tonight his mother pauses in her serving and looks gravely at Ed.

'You're getting a little podgy, Edward,' she says. 'You should go without gravy and potatoes tonight, and not serve yourself so much meat. You don't want to end up looking like your Uncle Frank now, do you?' She puts her arm around his waist and squeezes him affectionately—making it impossible for him to take offence.

Ed says nothing, waits, intuiting that the underlying purpose of tonight's chat hasn't yet been revealed. He's almost certain that she's not really interested in his few excess kilos. Ed has been steadily gaining weight over the last twelve months—he's had to go up a trouser size, and his shirt collars are getting a little too tight—but this is the first time his mother has made any mention of it.

'Is there something wrong, darling? Is something bothering you?' She has resumed her serving, has asked her question in a manner that Ed, from long experience, knows is cunningly deceptive in its casualness. 'It's not like you, Eddy, to let yourself go like this.' She goes on, 'You seem—well frankly you seem a little down, darling. Depressed. Depression's a terrible strain on the waistline.'

Ed murmurs something noncommittal, keeps carving. Then: 'God knows you've got good reason, darling. All those changes you've been making at the factory—all that work!—and that horrible mortgage and now there's this upset of Susan's to deal with—this will of her mother's. I suppose that's what's worrying you?' She asks her questions with such earnest motherly concern that if he did not know her better it would be possible to misconstrue her motivation, to mistake it for the real thing.

He smiles brightly, steadily. 'I've just been eating too much, Ma, and not getting enough exercise. It's no more complicated than that. It's purely physical, nothing psychological.'

'Oh, don't be so silly, Ed. I can tell when you're not happy. I'm your mother, remember?' She picks up the tongs, slaps a single slice of meat onto each plate. 'Why can't you ever admit that everything's not perfect? What are you trying to prove? Your father and I have had our problems, I've never tried to hide them—they're a part of every marriage.'

Ed spoons the peas carefully, stays silent. He is not quite sure what she's referring to here, is floundering, as he always has, in the wild subterranean currents of his mother's emotions, but senses that this conversation is probably about Susan. He knows that his mother has always had something of a problem with his wife, though she's never admitted it and is probably not even conscious of her behaviour. He supposes it would have been the same regardless of who he married—though he does recall her being quite taken with the first girl he went out with at college, a fellow business student—Angela—who was tall and vivacious and exceptionally well groomed, and went on to make a fortune working the stock market.

'You spend far too much time worrying about other people's problems, Ed,' his mother says now. 'You'll wear yourself out. I know what I'm talking about, believe you me.'

Ed, on the other hand, doesn't know what she's talking about and isn't sure that he wants to. He tries diversion. Flattery. 'God, this is good gravy, Mum. Susan uses packet stuff, but it's just not the same, is it?'

His mother's face lightens. 'These modern girls just can't cut the mustard when it comes to cooking, can they?' Her smile is coy, almost a smirk. 'Perhaps I should write out a recipe for her.'

Ed is vaguely ashamed of his disloyalty, but it has had the desired effect.

'Two potatoes, Ed?' his mother asks brightly. 'More gravy?'

Ed is not told the truth about Karen until two weeks before the wedding and he is so hurt by Susan's behaviour, the confected story—a lie!—her humiliating lack of trust in him, that he considers (only fleetingly, it's true) calling the whole thing off.

They have been flat hunting—unsuccessfully. All they can afford (if they are to remain in the beach-side suburbs of their childhood) with their combined student allowances and Ed's pitiful paycheque, are dark and dirty cockroach-infested studio apartments. Ed's father has offered to convert their double garage into a self-contained flat and though Ed is becoming gradually more inclined to accept the offer, Susan remains stubbornly, and to Ed's mind unreasonably, opposed.

'But it looks like we mightn't have any other options, Susy,' he says. They are sitting in a seedy cafe on Manly's Corso, drinking cheap coffee and arguing.

'There are plenty of options, Ed.'

'Yeah, like what?'

'We could get share accommodation near college. We don't have to live around here, y'know. We don't have to live near your family.'

Ed ignores the suggestion and goes straight to the heart of her remark.

'I don't see why you always have to bring my family into it, Susy. Sometimes I think you just don't like my family. You don't, do you? Why not admit it?' Susan says nothing, stirs sugar into her coffee.

'Anyway,' he adds sulkily, 'It's not just my family. Your parents live here too. Surely you want to stay nearby?'

'No, Ed.' Susan ignores his last comment, speaks softly, deliberately. 'There's nothing for me to admit. It's not that I don't like your family. It's your mother—who doesn't like me.' She smiles, briefly. 'Your mother thinks I'm not good enough—not clever enough, respectable enough, or even pretty enough for her little darling.' Ed is suddenly ashamed. Tries to take her hand. 'Oh, Suse,' he begins, but she shakes him off.

'No, listen Ed. Your mother thinks I'm not good enough and that my family's worse. Don't think I don't get what's behind all those innocent little questions about Gillian and Dad, those sly comments about my mother. And the way she always brings up stories about missing teenagers: "I expect the stepfather's murdered her." I don't know why she doesn't come straight out and accuse Dad of murdering Karen.'

'Accuse your father of *what*, Suse?' Ed is completely bewildered by her digression. 'What *are* you going on about? What have missing teenagers got to do with your dad? Why would she think your father murdered Karen? She died of meningitis. Didn't she?'

But Susan has her head down, is staring into her half-empty cup of coffee, is studiously avoiding his eyes.

Ed clamps his hand around her wrist, shakes it to get her attention. 'Susan. What's going on?' He feels a strange knotting sensation in his bowels. 'Did something happen to Karen, something you haven't told me about?' He is surprised that his voice sounds so normal. His throat is unaccountably tight and it's an effort to breathe normally. 'Susan, is there something you haven't told me?'

Ed weeps a little when she tells him, feels his eyes fill and has to dab at them with his coffee-stained serviette. He is saddened not just by the enormity, the tragedy, of the particular events—the story itself seems half-familiar—the teenage girl missing on formal night, the searches, the uncertainty, the ultimate presumption of her death in some brutal manner. This is all pathetic and worthy of tears, but it is the manner of Susan's telling that really discomposes him. The way she sits up straight in her chair and looks him in the eyes as she speaks, the detached, matter-of-fact manner in which she relates the story. The way Susan shrugs when the tale is told and says: 'It was a long time ago, Ed. I was very young. I can truly barely remember her now. It's not important anyway,' she concludes. 'Not any more. Not to us.'

Not important! His brave girl.

It's only later—lying alone that night in his lumpy childhood bed, unable to sleep—that Ed wonders why it is that Susan hasn't told him before this. He can understand, excuse even, the uncomplicated, frequently told lie, proffered at the outset—when they were little more than acquaintances, really, when the relationship was tentative, its future uncertain. But why hadn't she revised the story earlier? Let him know before this? Why had she kept up the lie? He finds it hard to believe Susan's claim that it doesn't matter. Her sister's disappearance, or as Susan insists, her death, was surely a defining moment of her childhood, hardly incidental. It had, after all, led to her parents' separation, her mother's decline, her madness. He wonders too whether such an omission, such evasion, such an unwillingness to share, should be considered treacherous, traitorous (or is he being melodramatic, oversensitive?), a betrayal of their commitment. Of their love.

And just before he floats off into dreams of floods and tidal waves, Ed wonders—and this is the first and indeed only moment of doubt that he will experience for many years—Ed wonders whether his mother might not be entirely wrong, wonders whether she might not have her reasons. Wonders what it is exactly he's getting himself into: marrying Susan.

Thinking about it later, Ed has to admit that his mother (why is it so frequently the way?) is right. He *is* worried. Nobody has actually asked Ed what he thinks, how he feels, not even Susan. And why would they? It's not his problem. But if anybody were to ask him how he felt about the situation and Ed were to answer truthfully (which, being Ed, he most probably would. To the best of his ability, anyway), he would have to say that he is not happy, that he feels decidedly unsettled by the turn of events, even anxious, though he's not quite sure why.

So unsettled is he feeling that—and this is unusual, perhaps without precedent—Ed's work is suffering. Though he is getting through each day's appointments, though he is still selling enough to keep Derek and the boys working late most afternoons, though he is not being noticeably inefficient or slapdash, he knows that for the past month or so (since his mother-in-law's death, that shocking will) he has been functioning way below his optimum level, that he is lacking the spark, the taken-for-granted creative impulse that usually drives him. That he is on automatic pilot, so to speak.

These last few days he has left work early. Usually he likes to spend an hour or two in the office every afternoon. Finalising designs, conferring with Derek on the next day's check-measures, double-checking the production plans. But these last few days he has driven straight to Manly, parked the car under what remains of the Norfolk pines and spent an hour or so just watching the surf. He should, he knows, go home: spend the extra time with his children, with his family. But he's not up to that. He needs this time alone, meditating, contemplating. Wondering.

'Listen to this, Suse.'

They are lying in their first shared bed, in their first shared home—a rented flat in Dee Why. It is past lunchtime and outside it is probably a glorious summer's day, but they have only been married for three weeks, and are determinedly keeping the curtains drawn, the telephone unplugged.

'What?' Susan is lying on her side, tracing dreamy patterns on Ed's back. Ed is reading. Ed is always reading.

'Listen,' he says. He reads aloud. '*Often trauma experienced in childhood is never resolved. Adults, in a well-intentioned effort to shield the child from what they see as unnecessary pain, frequently fail to properly discuss those issues that can have a serious and deleterious effect on the child. Issues such as death, divorce, family dissension. These may be repressed by the child—who has no way to make sense of them—only to resurface in adulthood as depression or unspecified anger or violence.*' He turns around to face her. Keeps reading.

'*But it is never too late to begin remedial treatment. Talking through such issues, even in adulthood, can help to alleviate symptoms of depression.*'

Ed marks the page with his finger. 'You see, Susy. We really ought to talk about it. If you don't, it could come back one day—resurface—take over your life.'

Susan prises the book out of his hand, drops it over the side of the bed.

'Susy! I was reading that.'

She pushes him back against the pillows.

'Ed,' she says. 'I know all about that stuff. I've read all that psychobabble. Had to read it. I'm a nurse, remember.'

'I know you know, but I really can't understand why you won't talk about it. It isn't right. It isn't healthy.'

She straddles him, pins his arms above his head.

'Unhealthy, eh? Let's play doctors, then.'

'Susy,' he says, 'why won't you be serious? I really think you need to, to confront ... to confront this ... the ... past.' He's grinning now and his breath's coming fast and shallow.

'Oh, I am serious Ed. You know I am. But first I think we need to confront *your* pain.' She lowers her haunches, tightens her grip on his wrists. 'You just tell her where it hurts, Ed, and Sister Sue'll fix it for you.'

He doesn't spend much time out in the factory these days. Years ago, when he was at high school and needed the cash, his father had given him a part-time job: three afternoons a week and on Saturday mornings he'd worked in the factory as a general dogsbody. His elder brother Derek had already left school and was part way through his apprenticeship. At first Ed had just been given tasks like sweeping and tidying the benches, or had been sent out to bring back the men's smoko orders—bacon and egg rolls, custard tarts, bottles of Coke, cigarettes. It hadn't taken too long before he'd been given more responsible tasks: the foreman, a patient middle-aged man, had taught him to use the edgebander, then to nail up a cupboard, and finally, despite his mother's protestations, he'd been allowed to cut up board on the beam saw. He was methodical and conscientious, and managed the work easily. But he knew that he didn't want this—the endless menial tasks, cutting, gluing, screwing, the sawdust, the polyurethane fumes, the vulgar lunchtime conversations ... Ed had other plans for his life. Big plans. And they didn't involve being a trained ape in his father's factory.

It had been Susan who'd persuaded Ed that it was an opportunity not to be lost. He'd been working for a sportswear company in the city, running their PR and marketing. It had been an interesting enough job, with opportunities to move up and away—the company had offices in the UK and Malaysia—but somehow he'd become bored. 'There's nothing substantial, nothing *real* for me to do,' he said, 'It's too big—I'm just a cog in a wheel.'

She'd made the suggestion, initially, as a kind of a joke; 'Why not work for your dad, Ed? Derek seems to enjoy it.' And initially Ed had taken it as a joke—just imagine him, Ed—swapping his Country Road Workwear for KingGees and steel-capped boots, sitting out with the blokes in the dusty factory. It was after a conversation with his father—who'd bemoaned the way the kitchen industry and the market itself had changed, that he'd begun to think into it seriously, to see the opportunities and possibilities on offer.

'You can't even hire people these days, Ed, to do the measures. They want new cars, want twenty per cent commission, want to be called designers. Want bloody letters after their name. They're all wankers—think they're bloody architects. And then the bloody architects are even worse. Jesus. Ten years ago you'd just turn up with a tape measure and a scrap a paper. Now all the women want to gasbag about colours, and finishes; want to know which way the shadows of their fucken door handles will fall at particular times of the day, or whether they can get a consistently coloured timber that looks like plastic but isn't, how much the new kitchen will increase their market value, whether the new kitchen will help little Henry get his place at Kings ... I don't know if I can handle it much longer, son.'

Ed had thought about it for a few weeks. He'd spoken to Susan, discussed his ideas with Derek, then rung his father.

'You want to do what? You want to work here? In the factory? You?'

Ed had explained that, no, he really had no desire to work in the factory, but he was convinced he had a guaranteed way to help his father get out of the sales side of the business, and to increase productivity and profitability at the same time. It would be a win-win situation.

It had taken his father a few weeks to get used to the idea, and several years to stop laughing at Ed and his flaky theories, until eventually, inevitably, the company's profits did begin to increase. Ed knows he can't take full credit for this: the Sydney housing boom had certainly contributed to their success, along with the more recent renovation madness that had swept the suburbs. Ed's innovations have been significant, of course: he has made sure they've kept pace with the boom, that they've made best use of new technology; they have invested in up-to-the-minute computer design programs, the latest spray equipment, edgers, saws, cutting-edge hinges and drawer runners. Their presentation and marketing procedures have been significantly enhanced and streamlined, their terminology has been updated: customers have metamorphosed into clients; salesmen and women have become designers (as much for the benefit of the clients' egos as the designers'); cupboards are discrete storage units; benchtops are work surfaces. But Ed is convinced that the major factor in their transformation from back-street budget cupboard factory to boutique bespoke kitchen design and manufactuary, has been his insistence (in the face of considerable scorn) on the development of a 'kitchen philosophy'—a coherent statement of their corporate mission. Ed's revolutionary 'idea of the kitchen'—the recognition that the kitchen is not just an assortment of little white boxes, but the symbolic centre—the heart—of all family activity and harmony—now informs every facet of Middleton and Sons' dealings—from manufacturing the most humble refuse and recycling containment station, to advertorial in glossy architectural digests.

And now Ed does believe—he believes passionately in what he does. He knows that his long consultations with women (in the main it is still women that he deals with, though this is gradually changing) about their kitchens' design, about their choices of finishes and appliances, is not really about that at all; or not just about the obvious material construction and configuration of the fittings, but that it also involves some revelation of their essential being; of the way they think about themselves, conceive of their family life, their place in the world. Few and far between are those clients who continue to regard the kitchen as merely an efficient space for preparing meals—most, if not all, see it as the hub, the centre, of their small universe. It is the room where meals are made and partaken, where discussions are held, homework is done, life plans made and unmade. The colour schemes, the finishes, the design, every tiny element, all contribute towards the making of a good life. In his designs Ed favours an open-plan kitchen—not just a discrete food preparation area, but a space for eating and for living—a space where the entire family can gather together, even if all are engaged in different tasks. He is always faintly depressed when the best design solution he can offer (and he knows that frequently he is providing a solution to other, less tangible problems—the state of a marriage, a career, a parental relationship) is new cupboards in a poorly designed room; that he can't suggest a wall be knocked down here, a window added there, an island bench that separates without division; that he can't provide some more substantial, life-enhancing alteration.

Every change to the business has been made slowly, grudgingly, and against the better judgement of his father, but now, with Mr Middleton Senior enjoying his unexpected early retirement, and Derek and Ed far more comfortably off—indeed, prosperous—than they'd ever thought they'd be; now, finally, the years of effort are paying off and nobody's laughing, no one's scornful. The returns are undeniable.

On Thursday Ed stays back late, catching up, then has a drink at the Brookie Hotel with an old mate. He rings Susan first. 'We're having takeaway anyway,' is all she says. 'Say hi to Phil for me. Have fun.'

Phil—a college friend, now head of HR at a local telecommunications firm—predates Susan by several years and Ed has kept him up-to-date (for counsel—he's a psych major—rather than gossip) on the Karen situation.

'What worries me most,' he tells him now, 'is the effect all this is going to have on the kids.'

'Mate,' says Phil, 'don't worry about the kids. My guess is that like most healthy children they won't give a stuff about your life as long as it doesn't interfere with their television programs, birthday presents, or Saturday morning sport.'

'But what about the indirect stuff? The subconscious emotional stuff.'

'What subconscious emotional stuff, Ed?'

'You know. With Susan. Can't her internal traumas be transferred somehow?'

'Jesus, Ed. You read too much. I'd say the main trauma here is going to be losing a shitload of money—I know that'd piss me off.'

'But imagine how Susan must be feeling—having to meet some woman who's appeared out of—well practically thin air, claiming she's the sister that disappeared—the sister that's been presumed dead for more than twenty years. And not knowing. Not being sure. Surely that'd be a fairly traumatic experience.'

'Ed, it'll be stressful, sure, and certainly unsettling. But traumatic? Come on. What's Susan saying? Is she anxious? Stressed?'

Ed thinks for a moment. 'Well, initially she was pretty shaken, pretty shocked. Now she keeps saying that nothing'll happen, but she seems kind of excited. Expectant.'

'There you go then. You're overreacting, mate.'

'But you don't know Susan. She's, you know, I guess she's been through a lot.' Ed is not sure that he really knows Susan that well, either. To some extent Susan's internal life has always been a bit of a mystery to him, has remained opaque. He's never quite certain whether she takes things as easily as it appears or is expertly concealing a seething pit of insecurities and unresolved anxieties.

But his friend has no such doubts. 'Ed. Relax. It'll sort out. Stop worrying about Susan, for Christ's sake. She's a big girl. She's resilient. She'll cope. Now have another drink, mate, and let's talk about the football.'

Susan

Susan phones to invite her out to lunch. She follows the solicitor's direction to meet somewhere neutral, even though she would be far more comfortable inviting her over to morning tea. Making it easy, making it casual; making it on her own turf. But there's a saying, isn't there, a proverb, something about never inviting an enemy—or is it a vampire?—over your threshold. She wonders whether she should perhaps, when they meet, carry a clove of garlic in her handbag, wear a cross around her neck, as a precaution.

Howard Hamilton has given Susan a telephone number— it's not a home number, but the number of a Kings Cross hotel. She breathes in, makes the call.

'Capital Hotel?' She had expected a direct line, breathes out.

'I'm after a Carly Taylor, I believe she's ...'

'Putting you through.'

The transfer seems to take an age, but even so Susan is unprepared.

'Hello?'

Susan seems to have run out of air. Gasps: 'Is this Carly Taylor?'

'Yes. Who's this?' There is nothing remarkable about her voice. It is low, pleasant. It is not at all familiar.

'It's ... it's Susy.' Susan's voice is full of air now, the words burble out light and fast. 'Susy Carter. Well, not Carter anymore, it's Middleton now. The solicitor gave me this number ... I thought ... he said you'd be ...'

'Susan,' she speaks slowly, almost caressingly. 'I've been ex-pecting your call.'

They make arrangements to meet for lunch the next day. Susan suggests a restaurant in Manly. Karen, Carly will need to catch a ferry over, but it is probably a little simpler for her than for Susan, with the kids to organise ... The other woman agrees, says she'll enjoy the ferry ride anyway. The trip north. It's been a long time. Susan is relieved—she hadn't imagined it'd be this easy.

'I'm looking forward to it, Susan,' Carly says in her low voice. 'Can't tell you how much. I'll see you then.'

Susan echoes the sentiment. Disconnects. Wanders about in a daze for half an hour or so. Collects Stella and Mitchell from school. Ferries them to their various after-school activities. Calls in at Coles to do some last-minute shopping. Retrieves the children, takes them home.

It's not until much later, when she's preparing dinner, chop-ping carrots into the sweet little scalloped shapes that Stella loves, that it occurs to her. Carly called her Susan. It was only when she went off to college (part of every adolescent's quest to remake themselves, she guesses now), that she started to in-troduce herself as Susan, to be known by her full name. Before that, all through her childhood, her family—her mother, her father, Karen—called her Sukey. Occasionally she got Susy or even Sue. But never Susan.

She is helping the children with their homework when Ed gets home from work. He opens a bottle of wine, pours two glasses, sits down at the table with them. Susan smiles her thanks, goes back to Mitchell's sums.

'Well?' Ed looks tired and anxious.

'Well what?'

'So did you talk to her?'

'Uh huh.' She can see that this conversation, like all their conversations lately, is taking on certain characteristics. 'Sixty, Mitch. Half of sixty.' Reluctant, half-hearted, frequently dis-tracted on Susan's part.

'Well?' Increasingly frustrated, even a little desperate on Ed's.

'Well what? Stella's reading is coming along so well, Ed. Show Daddy, Stell.' He listens patiently to his daughter's halting, but enthusiastic, narration. Then, quietly, urgently:

'Oh, come on Susan. Was it her?'

'I guess so.'

'What do you mean you *guess* so? Couldn't you tell?'

'I don't know. We only spoke for a few minutes. She was just a voice on a phone.'

'So what did you say?'

'Nothing much ... We arranged to meet.'

'Where?'

'A restaurant in Manly. For lunch.'

'When?'

'Who are you going out with, Mummy?' This from Stella, who misses nothing.

'Just a friend, darling. No one you know.'

'Oh.' And is easily satisfied. Unlike her father.

'When?'

'No, Mitch. Count down properly. Seventeen minus nine. Seventeen, sixteen, fifteen, fourteen, thirteen, twelve, eleven, ten, nine, eight. The answer's eight.' It is becoming increasingly evident to Susan, even at this early stage of his schooling, that Mitchell has inherited her own stubborn resistance to all things mathematical, and is particularly obtuse when it comes to all but the most basic problems of subtraction. 'You can use your fingers if you have to, darling.'

'When, Susy?'

'Tomorrow.'

'Mum? I need help again. Eighteen minus twelve?'

'Ask your father, Mitch. I've got to get dinner.' It is not hard to find an excuse, easy to short-circuit any discussion. There are always things to do. Ways to keep busy.

'Try counting up, sweetheart,' she can hear Ed, patient man, contradicting her earlier instruction. 'Count up from twelve, not backwards, it's much easier.'

She realises, and not for the first time, that for Ed, everything—even absence—has its positive side. That Ed will always manage to find a way to count up instead of down.

Susan waits until Ed has gone to bed, pleads interest in a late night television show—she'll be a little while yet, don't wait up. When she hears him settle, the low growl of his snoring a guarantee of his unconscious state, that he won't wander out with anxious enquiries, she carries a chair into the hallway, climbs up and drags the box from the top shelf of the cupboard where it has been stored for years. It is taped up, the cardboard sagging and faintly dusty. She untapes the box, there in the half-dark hallway, takes out each item, slowly, hopefully: the books and trophies, the certificates, the trinkets and the beanie—but they hold no answers, no memories, no meaning.

She takes out the manila folders. The first is crammed with yellowing newspaper cuttings, all dated in a neat hand, the page numbers noted. She reads through them carefully, every one. But they hold no surprises; she remembers all these details so well.

Teen Vanishes, shrieks the front-page headline from the *Sun*. *Eighteen-year-old Karen Michelle Brown disappeared last night en route to her high school formal ... Searches are being conducted.* Almost half of the page is taken up with Karen's smiling face—a copy of the same school portrait Susan passed on to Howard Hamilton, but black and white, blurred, grainy. *Friends and neighbours are being interviewed*, reads the next day's article—this time relegated to the second page. *Grave fears are held for the girl's safety.* On the third day (page six), some new evidence has come to light: *Mrs Edith Lamprati—an elderly neighbour who lives only several blocks from the missing girl's home—recalls seeing a girl answering to Karen's description at around 7.30 pm on the night in question.* 'Though it's a little hard to be sure,' she qualifies later in the report, '*all the young girls look alike these days ...*'

On the fourth day more evidence: *A school friend of the missing girl (who does not wish to be named) claims she had seen Karen with a man in a red car a few days before her disappearance. She is currently being interviewed by police.*

After this, nothing but an occasional mention. *New evidence comes to nothing* (page eleven); *Grave fears for missing girl.* And a month later, the final report: a small paragraph (page eighteen): *All leads to teenager's disappearance go nowhere. Police say file to remain open.* After that, nothing.

Susan slips the brittle clippings back and opens the second folder. This contains copies of the police files. She vaguely remembers reading through these reports years ago, and knows that they contain nothing of any interest, but at this stage Susan is willing to look for signs anywhere, everywhere, between lines if necessary. As she lifts the stapled sheets from the folder two photographs slip out. They are tiny black-and-white prints, two-inch squares, with a white rim, strangely old-fashioned. They look like cut up studio proofs, though neither one has been stamped or dated. The photographs both show the same baby girl, around nine months old, propped up to sit, dressed in a pale crocheted dress, her bootie-clad feet peeping out cheekily. In one photo she laughs, clutching a wooden elephant. In the other she is empty-handed, intense, one chubby finger under her chin. In both she looks plump and gummy and content— just as a baby should be. She is not at all familiar. Susan turns the photos over. *Karen Michelle Brown, Melbourne, March 1958* is pencilled on the back in her mother's neat handwriting.

Susan studies the photographs carefully, but the smudgy features, tonsured head, sticking-out ears, could belong to anyone. She opens the clippings file again, takes out the top cutting, with its grainy photograph. Karen at eighteen. She compares the two—but there's no evident resemblance between toddler and teen. She studies the teenage Karen's face carefully, she tries to imagine the girl in the photo twenty years on—but knows that from this point almost anything's possible. Susan thinks of herself as a teenager: physically slight, dark blonde hair, regular, if unformed, features—her grey eyes a little too widely spaced; nose short and straight; lips with their hopeful upward curve. Her thirty-year-old self is consistent with her adolescent self, if not entirely predictable. And there's no doubt she's still reasonably attractive, if rounder. But she knows from experience that it could be quite different. She's seen girls she was at school with become almost unrecognisable over the past ten years—some ravaged by all varieties of unhappiness and abuse, impossibly aged, others, ugly ducklings grown into unexpected grace, beauty. There is an almost infinite number of versions, possibilities for Susan to imagine. Karen's blonde hair could have grown darker with age, or could have been lightened; her nose could have lengthened, been broken, could have thickened over time; her ordinary, perhaps slightly oversized, lips could be newly defined by outlines and lipstick, or could have developed a cigarette smoker's pucker; her averagely sized, averagely spaced eyes could be tired and puffy, bloodshot, or could be kohled and coloured and mascaraed.

She could be anyone now. She could be anyone.

Ed

Routines give him pleasure. There is such satisfaction—no, it's more than satisfaction, it's almost a feeling of joy (but a peaceful, uncomplicated, steady joy rather than the eddying, unsettling variety)—in doing the same things, in the same way, at the same time. Take waking, for instance. Ed no longer needs an alarm clock; he's been waking at six during the week for so long now that he wakes always on the dot, just in time to witness the changeover from 5:59 to 6:00 on his bedside clock-radio. He stretches twice, flexing his way up his body: legs, torso, arms, neck. Then kisses Susan on the back of her neck (occasionally, very occasionally elsewhere, if she's so disposed) before bouncing, yes bouncing, up out of bed and into the day. He eats the same breakfast in the same order. Coffee fruit juice muesli toast.

After breakfast, a shit then a shave—generally in that order. Kisses the kids twice on the forehead and a still-sleepy Susan hard on the lips. Squeezes her bum or tweaks a nipple, and then off he goes to the factory. Every morning he greets Moira with a coffee from the deli across the road and some cheeky, cheery banter.

He knows that most people find such routines unbearably depressing—proof of their own inconsequence, their mundanity, their mortality. But not Ed. Ed likes the idea that when he grows old, these days will be almost indistinguishable from one another—that such insignificant rituals will provide a history, a continuity, in much the same way that the seasons and their endless cycles provide humanity with a framework for the passing of time.

He has often thought himself lucky that he and Susan—an organised woman—have been able to so comfortably coordinate their separate schedules. They generally have dinner around seven o'clock, and get the children into bed by eight. Most nights they share a bottle of wine, talk, watch television, read. Some nights they play cards, or a board game, maybe even attempt the *Herald*'s cryptic together. Once or twice a week they hire a video. Most nights, at around ten-thirty, Ed will yawn, stand up and stretch. 'Big day tomorrow,' he'll say. 'See you soon?' Usually Susan, absorbed in a movie, book or whatever, will just nod absently. 'Uh huh,' she'll murmur, 'G'night.' And he'll clean his teeth, and cross off another day on his bedside calendar before sliding into bed and just as easily into sleep.

But sometimes (he's averaged it out to be 1.6 times a week over the past twelve months—down a little from the previous year's average) his wife will look up and give him a certain look (how to describe it: tender? Lascivious? Suggestive? Inviting?) and on these nights he'll wait until that particular, most enjoyable ritual has been executed, before crossing out, marking off another ordinary extraordinary day.

But tonight is different. Tonight Ed has lain awake, waiting for his wife. Ed has read somewhere that admitting uncertainty, particularly before the uncertainty develops into something more serious, is a sure way not only to clear your own conscience, but to open a relationship to new meanings, potentially better ways of being. He has, he thinks, discovered the source of his anxiety, and has decided to gird his loins, make a clean breast of it. Who knows what positive outcome might result.

'I have an admission to make,' he whispers when, at 12.55 am, Susan finally climbs in beside him.

Susan turns towards him, sighing.

'What is it, Ed? This admission.'

'I hope it's *not* her, Susy. I really hope it's not.'

She sits up. Fumbles in the dark for the bedside lamp. Switches it on. Ed screws up his eyes, momentarily blinded.

'What do you mean you hope it's not her?'

'Well, it's going to be messy, isn't it? Emotionally, I mean. If it's really her. For you.'

'It's going to be messier still, Ed, if it's not her, don't you think?' Susan pulls the blankets up around her shoulders. From Ed's angle she looks lumpy, neckless.

'Why don't you just admit it, Ed—it's the money you're worrying about, isn't it?' Her face is puffy and sour.

'No, Susy, really. It's you. It's not just the money.' He touches her on the shoulder. She turns away, switches off the light.

He lowers his voice, makes it sorrowful, pleading. 'Hey, Susy. Sweetheart.'

She lies down heavily. Sighs.

He tries again. 'I just don't want to see you get hurt. That's all.' He stretches his arms out, goes to pull her to him, but she has moved too far away. He murmurs her name one last time, rolls over, closes his eyes, counts sheep.

On the afternoon that Susan is to meet her sister, Ed takes Mitchell and Stella to Taronga Zoo. They are Zoo Friends, so it is no big deal, they visit the zoo regularly, have done since the children were babies, but still, zoo excursions with their combination of pleasure and learning are, to Ed's way of thinking, a first-class outing. They did the African Animals last month, so this visit (and it's about time) they're doing Australia. Ed gives Mitchell the map.

'It can be your responsibility, Mitch, to lead us to the platypus.'

'But I don't want to see the platypus, Dad. And you never get to see them, anyway. They're always hiding. It's a dumb exhibit.'

'I want to see the seal show, Daddy, not the Australian animals. They're *boring*.'

'I want to see the monkeys, Dad, and the elephants.'

'We'll go see the platypus first, guys. And then we'll see.' Ed tries always to be firm but fair. He is determined that his children will never have any cause for complaint (or lawsuits), that when they look back over their childhood they will remember (and appreciate) this as being both a happy and enriching time. Firm but fair. 'Now lead the way, Mitch.'

Not that Ed has any real reason to complain when he looks back on his own childhood. Oh, there were the usual difficulties and disturbances, all the expected childhood traumas, but nothing major, nothing of any lasting significance. And since Mitchell and Stella were born, Ed has found that he understands, more and more, those things he'd found inexplicable as a child. He remembers, for instance, his resentment at what he regarded as his mother's irrational dislike of one of his particular friends, Sam Maiolo, when he was in third grade. Whenever Sam came home with him after school—to play at the park, or go bike riding—she would make him wait out on the verandah while Ed changed out of his uniform. She warned Ed never to share his drink bottle or to eat food from Sam's lunch box. He was forbidden, on pain of being dispatched, forthwith, to boarding school, to visit the Maiolos' home. He understands now, of course, that his mother was protecting him, Ed, in the only way she knew how. Sam and his parents were recently arrived Italian migrants. Ed's mother had heard rumours of a smallpox outbreak amongst the Italian community (unfounded of course, but still). Ed can't imagine that he'd ever manage such a situation in quite the same way, but is glad that his suburb is affluent enough now to make this a non-issue—the only immigrants who settle here are doctors from Hong Kong and Singapore, or the odd American IT wunderkind.

When they finally find the platypus exhibit (by way of the South American monkeys—Mitchell maintaining that he's been looking at the map upside down), they discover it's closed for cleaning. Ed is disappointed—he likes to watch the strange submarine pups snuffling about in their gloomy aquarium—but the children are delighted, race off down the path that leads to the elephants.

'We don't need a map anyway, Dad,' Mitchell crushes the photocopied page into a ball, 'there are signs everywhere.' He tosses it at the nearest bin in passing. It misses, but he doesn't look back. Ed sighs, picks up the paper, follows the signs.

No, Ed's childhood was remarkable only for its lack of serious trauma (and perhaps, he thinks, it was this very absence of problems, of hang-ups, that initially made him attractive to Susan, and continues to cement his relationship with his wife). His parents were not wealthy, but they were certainly comfortable—his father started his working life as a high school science teacher, but, a keen and capable weekend carpenter, he eventually (after a small seeding loan from his own father) called it quits and established his initially tiny kitchen business. His mother, a primary school teacher, stayed at home after her children were born, going back to part-time work only when they'd reached high school. He has his brother, Derek, who is three years older—to whom he is very much attached, despite their profound differences—and a sister, Pam—six years his senior, unmarried, unhappy—who he tolerates. His family had moved house only once during his childhood—and that was to a bigger house in the same beachside suburb. The Middletons had holidayed two weeks every year at the same caravan park on the Central Coast; spent another two weeks on his (adoring) grandparents' Bathurst property. Ed had been doctored for years by the same physician who'd delivered him; he attended the local primary and then high school and still has friends he's known since kindergarten. Ed knows how lucky he was, how lucky he is; knows that his upbringing was exemplary in its solidity and stability—a picture-postcard suburban childhood.

'Oh God. What is *that*?'

'Oh, that's gross. I think I'm gunna spew.'

'Don't say "God", Mitchell, and spew is not a nice word, Stella. Vomit. Say vomit.' Ed follows the children's disgusted gaze. One of the elephants has a monstrous vine-like tangle of vessels dangling from its rear. They are so heavy, so low, that they almost drag on the ground.

'It looks like intestines,' Mitchell says. 'God, Dad, do you think its intestines have come out?'

He searches for an explanation. 'I think they're blood vessels, kids. They're called, um, haemorrhoids. And I think the elephant might be pregnant. Watch its stomach.' The animal's huge belly ripples, contracts. 'See.'

'Oh, *g-ross*.' Mitchell simulates severe retching.

'Imagine having a baby elephant in your tummy,' Stella giggles. Then: 'Ugh. I think I'm gunna spew, again.'

The stability and consistency of his early years has, or so Ed believes, made him the strong (but not hard), confident (but not insensitive), motivated (but not hyper-dynamic) individual that he is, and so he tries hard to reproduce (though it is such a different, such a difficult world) the same environment for his own two children. He and Susan have moved house only once since their marriage—and not at all since the children were born. Ed sees this consistency as a kind of insurance policy.

Though he has never seen any real evidence of neurosis or instability in Susan's behaviour (she does occasionally cry for no apparent reason, and she did once throw a chair at him), he knows that significant emotional disturbances (and God knows that Susy has had her fair share of these in her own childhood) can be repressed and then transferred, invisibly and insidiously, in a type of psychic slow-release, to those most receptive of creatures—children.

So Ed keeps a watchful eye on his precious offspring. He loves Susan, no mistake and certainly no regrets, but his children, his children are the wellspring of his being. They are his future; his posterity. He is a hands-on father. He conscientiously attempts to monitor his children's levels of self-esteem and bolsters them when necessary. He helps them with their homework when he's home, and takes them to their various sporting venues on the weekends, where he shouts (not too loudly and always encouragingly) from the sidelines. He has taught them both to bodysurf, to respect the sea; they're both enthusiastic members of the local surf club's 'little nippers'. He makes the space to take them out during their school holidays—to the movies, ice-skating, to museums and galleries. Thus Susan is given the necessary down-time from the children, substantial Self Space, and Time Alone; while Mitchell and Stella receive plenty of Quality Time with their father—such time being the one thing, he has to admit, that he feels was lacking in his own otherwise idyllic childhood.

Today Ed is a little distracted, not as focused as he likes to be, as he *should* be, on the children and their experience. He is worried about Susan's meeting with her sister—thinks that this might be the event, might be the trigger, so to speak, that will release Susan's pent-up grief and anger, and he is concerned not only for Stella and Mitchell, but for himself. He follows the children along the path that leads to the cafeteria. They are hungry and have refused the ham sandwiches and bottles of cordial he's prepared. (*Boring. Just like school. We want chips. Hotdogs. Milkshakes. Coke.*) Ed tries hard to stop worrying, wonders how he can transform all this negative energy into something positive, into something more productive. He decides that after lunch they will go back to the platypus exhibit. Perhaps it will have reopened. He's firm. Firm, but fair.

Susan

The cafe—it's a restaurant really—is right on the wharf. It's a big, airy place, all stainless steel and polished timber, an impersonal place, good for business lunches, or meals with distant relatives. Susan has requested an outside table. That way if the whole thing becomes too awkward, too painful, they can at least watch the water, the ferries, the endless stream of people. That way they'll have an excuse, or maybe even an opportunity, for silence.

When the waitress comes Susan is alone. She orders coffee, then changes her mind.

'A bottle of champagne? You're sure about that then?' The young waitress is tall, brunette, cool.

'Yes.' Susan smiles apologetically.

'Anything to eat, yet? Or do you want to wait for your friend?'

'No. Yes. She should be here soon.'

'Okay.' The waitress tucks her pencil and pad away, starts back inside.

'Oh, sorry. Miss? Miss? Excuse me a minute?'

The girl turns back, thin eyebrows slightly raised.

'I'd be grateful if you'd look out for my sister. She might go inside first. Perhaps you could tell her I'm outside? She won't know.'

'What does she look like?'

Susan thinks of the girl in the photograph. What does she look like? The waitress is waiting, would sigh or tap her foot if she could.

'Don't worry,' Susan is apologetic again, 'I'm sure she'll work it out. It'll be fine.'

'Just the champagne, then?'

'Just the champagne.'

A woman walks into the restaurant alone. She is fortyish, tall, dressed casually but expensively in pale jeans and a white silk shirt, her blonded hair cut fashionably short. Susan stands up nervously as the woman looks around. She is just as Susan imagined her, just as she dreamed her. She waves, but the woman doesn't see, so Susan hurries inside. The woman is walking confidently towards an elderly couple who greet her brightly from the rear of the restaurant. The waitress follows, her pencil at the ready. Susan slinks back to her outside table, pours herself another glass of champagne. The bottle is nearly empty. Her hand is shaking. She will have to catch a taxi home.

'Are you Susan?'

Her hair is blonde—not the golden colour Susan remembers, but peroxide blonde, dark at the roots—and straggles limply to her shoulders. Her face is thin, and pale, fine lines are etched about her eyes and mouth. Her lips are a violent magenta slash. Susan scrapes her chair back, gets unsteadily to her feet. The woman is small—much smaller than Susan remembers, or expects, she's probably no taller than Susan herself. Her worn black jeans are slung low on her hips, a grimy white t-shirt ends a few inches above her bellybutton. She has a tattoo around her upper arm, and a gleaming silver stud in her nose. Susan stands there stupidly, just looking at her. She doesn't know what to do, what to say.

The woman smiles. One of her front teeth is badly chipped. 'You'll catch flies, Sukey,' she says, 'standing there with your mouth open.'

When Ed and the kids get home Susan is sitting at the kitchen table, trying to work out the *Herald* wordsquare:

N	E	C
P	E	D
I	T	E

Ed puts a video on for the kids, comes back into the kitchen. He kisses Susan on the mouth. Recoils. 'Jesus, Susan! You didn't drive home, did you?'

'No. Yes, I did.' Sighs. Lies. 'I didn't actually drink that much ... two glasses, maybe three. But early, before she arrived. She was very late.'

Susan looks back down at the paper. The letters lurch and dance about the page. She tries hard to focus, but they don't make any sense; will not form a word.

TENICIPED

CEPITINED

Ed boils the kettle, makes coffee for them both. The smell makes her feel slightly queasy.

'Well?' He pulls out a chair, sits down heavily.

'I just can't get it.'

'Not the word.' He tugs the newspaper away impatiently. 'Don't be thick, Susy. What happened? Was it her? What was she like?'

'What happened?' Susan would like to be very blunt, to tell him everything. Even the part where she got pissed, then vomited in a public toilet and drove home very slowly.

'Well,' she says instead, 'you know. We had lunch. We talked.'

'Susy. Is it her? Does she seem like she could be Karen? The way you remember her? What's she like?'

'Oh.' Susan thinks for a moment, decides to keep it simple. 'She's small. Blonde. Had pâté for entree. Lobster for main. Drinks red wine. Likes animals and small children. She's okay.'

'That's all?'

'What do you want?'

He waits, counts ten. Tries again.

'Did you ask her, Susy? Why she left. What happened?'

'No.'

'You didn't ask her? What did you talk about, then?'

'Nothing. I don't know ... It was just chat, Ed. Nothing deep or meaningful. We didn't bare our souls or dredge up our dreary past. We talked about the weather, the price of eggs ...'

'Well, how will you know if it's her if you don't ask her about all that? You've got to sort it out. You're the only one who can.

It's not a joke, Suse, there's hundreds of thousands of dollars at stake here. Money that we could use.' He slams his cup down on the table, grabs the newspaper and pretends to read.

'If you'll give me a chance, Ed,' Susan's tone is suddenly edgy, serious. 'I'll tell you why I didn't ask her about any of that.'

'Okay.' He folds the paper, puts it down. 'I'm sorry. Why?'

'Because I'd have known if it was Karen. I'd have recognised her, and I didn't. I'm not interested in that woman's past, Ed, because she's not my sister. She's not Karen. She can't be.' Susan hasn't cried yet, and she's determined that she won't. Not here. Not now.

'Shit.' Ed is looking worried. 'Are you sure?'

She sniffs. Nods.

'I'm really sorry.' He frowns. Taps his fingers on the table. Then: 'Did you ring the solicitor, Susan? You'd better ring him, hadn't you, in case he's drawn up the documents or something. He'll still be there, won't he? D'you want me to do it?' He heads over to the phone. 'I'll give him a call, shall I? Best to get it over with.'

'Whatever.' Susan reaches for the paper, turns back to the puzzles page. Tries to focus on the wordsquare.

'Howard, g'day. Ed Middleton here. Susan's husband ...' Ed's voice is low, expressionless. 'Sorry to bother you so late, but ...'

Susan tries writing the letters out in a line this time.

PECEDTNEI

'You might be fairly confident, but Susan's certain that it isn't her.'

She writes the word *cent*. Then *cede, dent, deep, pent*.

'You said it yourself, mate: Susy's the only one who'll know. And she's a hundred per cent certain.' He's speaking loudly now, pulling irritably at the phone cord.

She writes *decent*, and then she has it. Writes it out in thick black capitals.

DECEPTION

'Jesus. You've got to be joking. She's changed her name, the DNA's not conclusive, she's got no ID, Susan says it isn't her—how could she take *us* to court? ... What do you mean Susan didn't even talk to her? Of course she talked ...'

She checks her answer, matches letter to letter, but it doesn't work—there's no O, an extra E.

Ed disconnects. He stands by the phone, watches his wife intently. Susan is gazing, just as intently, at her puzzle.

'Susan,' Ed's voice is soft, gentle. 'Suse. Is there something you'd like to tell me? About today?'

She says nothing. Checks each letter carefully, though this time there's no need. This time she's certain.

'Susan?'

This time the puzzle contains no answers, no signs or mysterious correspondences.

'Sue. Howard Hamilton says you didn't even speak to this woman. That you ran away.'

She stays silent. Writes down the word.

'Susan?'

'I've got it! It's not *deception*. It's nothing like it.' She holds up her carefully printed answer.

'Susan?'

'Centipede, Ed. It's *centipede*.'

'I don't get it, Susan,' Anna is already puffing, her face is pink and damp with exertion. 'How can you know? It's been more than twenty years. People change. You couldn't possibly know at a glance.'

On Tuesday mornings Susan and her friend, Anna, walk. They choose any reasonably long stretch of coastline between Manly and Mona Vale, a different beach each week, and walk for an hour or so. Usually they tramp through the soft sand, which is hard work, but today (traversing the stretch between Collaroy and North Narrabeen) they tread close to the water, where the sand is packed and firm and the walking's easier. This way the talking's easier too.

'It isn't her, Anna,' Susan treads heavily, for emphasis. 'I just know it.' It's a blustery day and the waves are breaking, dumping sand and weed close to the shore. The women have to speak loudly, shout almost, to make themselves heard.

'But Suse—you've always said you can't remember Karen anyway. What makes you so certain now?'

'I just know. Karen *couldn't* be that woman.'

'I think you don't want it to be her.' Anna's step is faltering.

'What? Why wouldn't I want it to be her?'

'I'd say you don't want her to come back.'

'For Christ's sake,' Susan says, 'You're as bad as Ed. Don't be ridiculous. I spent half my life wishing for nothing else; why wouldn't I want her back now?'

Anna stops walking altogether, looks her in the eye. 'I think you don't want her back because you don't want to have to think about all that.'

'About all what?'

'You know—the past. Whatever happened. It's perfectly understandable.'

'Oh it is, is it?' Susan starts off again, walks furiously fast.

'Don't get the shits,' Anna pants when she catches up. 'I'm only trying to work out why you didn't even speak to the woman. You've got to admit that it's pretty weird, Susan, running away like that.' Anna's voice is crisp. Her statements blunt. She's got no time for hysterics and no stomach for bullshit.

'I haven't got the shits. And I didn't run away. It just wasn't her. Okay?' Anna looks like she's ready to argue, but thinks better of it.

'Okay,' Anna says gently. 'Okay, Susan.'

The two women walk on without speaking. Susan has picked up her pace, is power-walking now, has overtaken her friend. She is looking straight ahead, and not at the surf.

'Watch out!' Susan hears Anna call, but a moment too late. A small wave crashes over her knees, soaks her shorts, splashes up over her waist. She doesn't hesitate, wades on through the weed and water, regardless.

At first Susan visits her mother every week. The home is full of elderly people suffering varying degrees of dementia, but it's clean, well kept, the staff cheerful, professional. Her mother is initially pleased to see Susan on her visits—she's never sure who she is of course—sometimes she's her daughter Karen, the famous film star, on a flying visit from Hollywood, at other times she's her long-dead cousin Marjory. 'Marj,' her mother will say, 'you're looking so old, dear. I can't imagine how you got so old so quickly. You certainly got your father's bone structure. And you're not like Aunty Wil, are you—she was no beauty, either, but she never did let herself go.'

Other than Aunty Di, an old friend of her mother who comes to see her once or twice a year, Susan is her mother's only visitor. Her mother's only connection with the world. She had never realised, as a child, how strangely isolated her family was—neither her mother nor father had siblings, they had both been orphaned and, due to some feud, there was no contact with aunts, uncles, cousins. Susan wonders now whether, initially perhaps, it had been a recognition of their mutual solitariness that had brought her parents together. (Susan can half-understand the attraction of it—she too can exist quite easily without others, has never been one for team sports, or committees, has only one or two friends that she can be bothered seeing on a regular basis.) Despite the best efforts of Gillian's family—her parents, her three siblings, though geographically distant, had forever been ringing, sending parcels, visiting whenever they could—her father had always maintained a slight distance from his enthusiastic new in-laws. Gillian had almost always travelled back alone to visit them. It wasn't really until she'd met Ed that Susan began to understand the possibilities of family life—the benefits of such a close family—as well as the constraints, the irritations; and to identify the deficit in her own upbringing. But perhaps that's what attracted her to Ed, she thinks now, that difference. That easy accommodation of other people's desires, others' claims. She finds it difficult, certainly, to be so needed, to be so wanted, to have someone who wants to open her up, as it were, as if to see inside her, to look at parts of her that she doesn't ever look at herself—but there's no doubt that she finds it appealing too.

After the children were born Susan had considered taking them with her on her visits to the nursing home. She'd rehearsed her introduction: 'Look, Mum,' she'd have said, 'these are your grandchildren. Your daughter's children. Three generations. Imagine that.' She had wondered whether evidence of her own humanity, of her genes existing in perpetuity, would be of some benefit. But the doctors at the home were sceptical, didn't think that anything would help, though they didn't think that it would hurt, either. Ed was adamantly against such a visit—her mother's condition had begun to deteriorate seriously, her behaviour had become increasingly erratic, she was occasionally abusive—and he didn't want his babies exposed to any sort of danger. Though Susan felt that he was overanxious, that there was no real threat—only perhaps her own distress—she didn't press the point. Her mother never met her grandchildren.

Susan continued her own visits, once a month, and then once every few months; watched her mother's slow disintegration. Eventually her mother lost the power of speech altogether, and was confined either to a chair or a bed all day. She no longer responded to anything—not voice, or touch, or even food. Clad in nappies, relying on the physio's manipulation of her limbs to keep them from atrophying, being spoonfed purees and attached to an IV drip to keep her hydrated. There didn't seem to be much point to such an existence. But she lingered on, as if her body was for some reason bent on denying its reality, determined to ignore the all too obvious hints given by her long-gone mind.

Her mother's funeral had been a terrible lonely affair. Only a handful of people attended the non-denominational service at the crematorium chapel: Ed and Susan; Anna (though she'd never met her); Aunty Di; the solicitor and a representative from the nursing home. Aunty Di had been the only one who'd shed any tears, had sobbed conspicuously into her large lace-edged handkerchief, shoulders heaving. The pastor had been kind, well-intentioned—but even so, his service contained very few references to the reality of the life that had once been Susan's mother's, or the person she had been—after all, he had another funeral to do in half an hour. What could Susan herself say about her mother? What could she remember? What could anyone remember? There was no one left who had really known her. She had wished, all through the service, that her father had been there—he at least would have known something of who she was. Who she'd been. His own funeral had been very different, he'd had a few good friends, colleagues; there'd been some sense of recollecting, even celebrating, a good life. Later, at the wake, she'd heard stories about her father that made her realise how little she'd known of him. In death he'd become somehow bigger than the man she'd known—his life had taken on a much greater significance than she'd ever expected. In death her mother was smaller, less significant, diminished. A pathetic scrap of humanity.

Susan had tried hard to cry at the funeral, but she'd already been grieving for years and felt as if she had no tears left. Afterwards, she'd invited Aunty Di back for lunch. They only talked about her mother briefly, almost guiltily, but Di could shed no light—she'd been her friend only for a short time, and couldn't really remember much about her—their lives had been connected by school, children, by a neighbourhood, and very little else.

Ed

This time Ed has insisted they visit the solicitor together. Hamilton had been his mother-in-law's solicitor only during the last—the lost—years of her life, and Ed is certain that this man is somehow responsible for the ridiculous will, that he has conjured this woman who says she is Susan's missing-presumed-dead sister, that—despite what Susan says to the contrary—he is a slippery sort of fellow, shonky and conniving. He has checked with the Law Society, and the man is registered and evidently above board, but still, Ed is suspicious, wants to make sure they are not being conned, cheated.

Ed knows that Susan is irritated by his company, wishes him elsewhere. But he is resolute, immovable. 'I'd really rather do this myself, Ed,' she hisses as they wait in the small reception area. 'You're being too aggressive. You'll get his back up. It's not his fault, Howard's only doing his job.' He tries to hiss back, but she ignores him. 'Why don't you wait in that cafe downstairs, have a cup of coffee, a hot breakfast? Go on. It's not too late.'

But it is too late. Hamilton's office door opens and the expensively suited solicitor ushers an elderly woman to the front desk. He has a brief word with his secretary, then turns to Ed and Susan, walks toward them smiling, his hand outstretched.

'Susan. Hello. How are you? And you must be Ed.' Ed stands and takes the proffered hand. The man's grip is firm, his skin cool and dry. 'Are you people hungry?' he doesn't wait for a reply. 'Let's talk about this over coffee.'

Ed is disappointed. Other than a slight six o'clock shadow, the man is the model of the suburban solicitor. He's a little younger than Ed would like (of that indeterminate age, somewhere close to middle), but perfectly respectable looking.

He turns to his secretary. 'I'm taking Mr and Mrs Middleton downstairs for breakfast, Virginia,' he says. 'Be about half an hour. I'll bring you back something. A pastry? Coffee?' Howard Hamilton is hardly Ed's idea of a con man.

'So,' the solicitor says, 'So what's the problem, Sue? Why are you so certain that she isn't Karen? Fill me in.' They have spoken only about general things—Ed's work, the traffic, the perpetually escalating value of Sydney real estate, while the man gulped down his late breakfast.

'Look,' Ed says before Susan gets an opportunity to answer. 'Look, if Susy says it isn't her, then it isn't. Don't hassle her. Don't make her feel guilty.' Ed knows he sounds like a belligerent child, but he can't help himself. He is consciously reducing his fat intake and the sight of the solicitor's eggs Benedict (Ed has ordered a skim-milk latte, toast and Vegemite, no butter) has been almost more than he can bear.

'Ed,' Susan pats his hand gently. 'It's okay. Howard's not hassling me. It's fair enough that I explain, don't you think?'

Ed says nothing, blows on his coffee.

'You do understand that I've got nothing at stake in this, Ed,' the lawyer chips in. 'I don't get any sort of commission. I don't get a percentage. I get paid for my time, nothing else.' The man is looking at him intently. 'This is a will, not some sort of legal challenge.'

'Yes. I know. It's just ...'

'I do understand that there's a great deal of money involved—that you and Susy stand to lose a substantial amount if this woman is who she says she is. I'm sorry, but the terms of your mother-in-law's will are quite clear, and I have a legal duty to ensure her wishes are carried out. I'm working for your mother-in-law—her estate, at any rate—not you and Susan. And certainly not Karen.' He smiles widely as if to take the edge off his words. But Ed has been wounded, doesn't respond.

'Anyway,' Susan sounds slightly impatient, 'We're here to talk about this woman, aren't we? This Carly? And why I don't think she's Karen.'

'You're right as always, Susy.'

Ed wonders if this man always takes such an intimate tone with his female clients—*as always?—Susy?*

'So tell us, Susan—okay if I take some notes?—Why do you think she's an impostor?'

Susan

Impostor.

It's such a portentous, such a weighty word. Such a serious accusation. Suddenly Susan realises that she can't tell him why with any certainty at all. And certainty is what's needed here, isn't it? Such a grave accusation. What she wants to tell him is that it's not the shape of the woman's nose or the colour of her eyes or the line of her jaw; that it's not the set of her mouth, or the sound of her voice; that it's not the hair or the jeans or the tatts or even the stud in the nose that matter. She wants to tell him that hands and feet and height and even bone structure don't mean much. That really, all these physical attributes don't seem to add up to anything. That it's just not so simple.

'She's too short,' Susan says instead. 'Karen was much taller than me. She was *tall*.'

'Susy.' Even Ed looks slightly disgusted. 'When you're eight everyone's much taller than you are.'

Howard consults his notes. 'The woman's 161 cm,' he points out. 'That's not something you can fake. It matches.'

'But there's no saying that Karen didn't keep on growing, is there. Plenty of women keep growing well into their twenties.'

'There are probably some women who do, Susan. But there are plenty more who don't. And then there's all the other physical indicators. Her eye colour, face shape, her nose and mouth—they're all within an acceptable range—and any differences are consistent with the ageing process.'

She tries again. 'But you could make almost anyone fit within that range. She doesn't look anything like Karen. She's too thin, for one thing. And she's too ... too hard-looking. Karen didn't have that pinched look.'

'It's been twenty-odd years, Susan. And I don't believe she's had an easy life. People change.'

'*It's not her*. People don't change that much. Karen could never have become that woman. I know.'

'Is there any other reason, Susan? Have you got anything—more concrete?' He pulls up his sleeve, glances at his watch.

'I just know it's not her.' She looks at Ed, but he's busy reading the menu.

'Susan. Ed.' The solicitor's face is solemn. 'I really can't find any legitimate reason to doubt this woman—physically it's more than possible that she's Karen, and as far as her knowledge about your family goes—well frankly, Susan, I'd say she knows a fair bit more than you. You need to consider that if this goes to court it would be very expensive—things like this can go on for years. And they have been known to consume entire estates. I think you need to arrange another meeting with this woman. You have to talk to her.' He packs away his notes, motions to the waitress.

'I don't want to meet her again,' Susan sounds childish even to herself.

'You have to meet her again, Susan, either way. If this ends up going to court you'll have to be able to give some reason why—you'll have to be able to defend your position.'

She wants to tell him that it's not her position—that it's the position of her gut, her heart—and that those things are not (why should they be?), *not* easily defensible.

'Listen,' Hamilton taps his pen rhythmically against the table, 'how about we set up an interview, but with me present this time. Perhaps meeting on your own for the first time was a little confronting. Perhaps if I were to be there—a third party—I could—facilitate the conversation, so to speak. And mediate if necessary.'

'Oh, I don't really think your presence'll be necessary, mate.' Ed blusters, 'I'll be there next time.'

The solicitor looks uncertain. 'I don't really know that that's a good idea, Ed,' his voice cautious, soothing. 'Solicitors can be almost invisible—impartiality and all that ... We're used to these sorts of situations.'

'But this is a family affair, and Susan may need my support. I don't see ...'

'Ed,' She sounds his name as firmly as she can, 'Howard's right. You really don't need to be there.'

He goes to argue, pauses. Forces a smile. 'Whatever you want, darling.' He picks up the menu again.

Susan makes a decision. 'We'll try again tomorrow then. In your presence, Howard. Morning tea at my place. Ten-thirty. *You* can contact her.'

'I don't know that your place is such a good idea.'

'My place.' There is a principle involved here, though Susan's not quite sure what it is.

Hamilton purses his lips, sighs and shakes his head. Then breaks into a surprisingly boyish grin. 'Okay then. Your place.'

Susan takes a deep breath, tries to smile back, is defeated by gravity.

That night she dreams she is back at college. She is sitting in a small lecture theatre, has written *Nursing 101: Human Anatomy* in large letters on her open foolscap notebook, is listening avidly. But the lecturer isn't the fussy little man she recalls—a dapper little doctor with a well-groomed goatee, famous for his garish bow ties—but the solicitor, Howard Hamilton, dressed bizarrely in a Pierrot costume, his face painted white, several large black waxy tears adorning his cheeks.

'You will find the heart,' the Hamilton-clown lisps, in a high-pitched faux-French accent. 'Right here.' He pulls down a chart. 'Beneath the ribs, between the lungs.' He taps on the diagram with a thin golden cane. 'The blunt edge of the heart rests on the diaphragm, leaning a little to the left. The heart is not, as organs go, large: only five inches by three. Roughly the size of a fist.' He pauses, says conversationally, 'You know, I've always thought it a pity that the vampire's most vulnerable organ isn't the kidney, say. Or even the lungs, the large intestine, the skin. With the heart, you see, there's such a wide margin for error. However,' he shuffles his papers together, glowers out over the podium, 'by the time I've finished with you lot, you will all know precisely where the heart lies, will be able to drive that wooden stake, or shoot the required silver bullet, with one hundred per cent accuracy.' He pulls on the cord and the chart cracks back. 'Right?'

The students begin to file out, but as Susan packs her books he beckons to her. She moves towards him reluctantly and he hands her something. It takes her a moment to recognise what it is he's offering: a miniature revolver, inlaid with mother-of-pearl, lies in the palm of his hand; three silver bullets resting beside it. 'I think you might need these, Sukey,' he says, and now the clown is Ed, not Hamilton, 'I think you might be needing these very soon.'

This is how she imagines it:

The woman (she will not, cannot commit to the intimacy of a name), the woman (and it is that same woman from the restaurant, only thinner, cheaper looking, harder) follows her into the kitchen. Her impractical high heels—or, no, scuffed elastic-sided boots—sound on the tiled floor. Howard Hamilton is already there, waiting. He stands, shakes her hand. He has already met her, of course.

Or perhaps he hasn't arrived yet, the two women are alone. Just the two of them. Susan invites her guest to sit down at the kitchen table, to take a seat. The woman sits. But doesn't she first ease out of her shiny leather jacket? Yes. She is wearing that same stained white t-shirt underneath. Or is it a black t-shirt this time? Yes. It's black and it's tight, and exposes her taut brown midriff. There's a silver ring in her bellybutton today, it catches the light. Or are there two rings, copper, slightly green-tinged? There's a metallic jangle as she hangs the coat over the back of her chair. Keys in her pocket? Or is it an uncapped needle and spoon? She leans back easily into the creaking leather—or straddles the chair between her thin denim-clad legs. Says: *Yes tea would be lovely, just what I need, such a lot of traffic. Milk and two sugars, please.* Says no to tea but would like coffee. *Black.* Would also like a whisky. *No water. No ice.* A silence (awkward?) while Susan boils the kettle, busies herself at the kitchen bench. Not silence but a strained conversation between the woman and Howard Hamilton about the weather (unseasonably wet, typically dreary?) or between the two women—about bus routes and ferry timetables and how far it is to the local mall and is the children's school nearby? And what are the little ones' names? And *fancy that, a nephew and niece and what about hubby? Can't wait to meet them all. Instant family.* No. The water boils loudly and nobody speaks. Safer.

Susan puts a plate of Tim Tams in the centre of the table. Or homemade patty cakes (with icing and sprinkles?), orange and poppy seed friands bought from the local deli. Pours coffee for the woman and tea for herself. Carries the cups, mugs, glasses to the table. Steady hands, no spills. Or does she leave a trail, her hands shaking? Takes the seat directly opposite. Pulls out the chair at the head of the table, Ed's chair, sits adjacent to the woman, who sips her tea delicately. Or blows noisily and slurps, dunks the Tim Tams, leaves a brown ring on the waxed table. Downs her whisky in one gulp. The two women drink in silence (what to say? where to start, who will take the initiative?) then suddenly look up at the same time; their eyes meet.

In her imaginings it is at this point that the events are suddenly clear, without alternatives. It is at this point that the woman will sigh and get to her feet. *It's no good*, she'll say (and despite the deep, throaty reality, her voice will be high-pitched and plaintive, a little girl's voice), *I can't do it. I'm not your sister*, she'll say sorrowfully as she struggles back into her coat. *I'm sorry. It was the money*, she'll say as she sidles down the hallway, *I just needed the money. I'm truly sorry*, she'll say when Susan opens the door for her, *to have caused you all this trouble. All this pain. It was the money, you see. It was always the money. I'm not your sister. Your sister's dead.* And Susan will feel sad for the woman, not angry. She will feel sad for the woman but happy for herself. Will be infused with warmth and understanding. Will feel generous, even magnanimous. Full of pity for those whose sorry lives lead them down such paths. *I forgive you*, Susan will say, placing her hand on the woman's bowed shoulders. *I forgive you.*

When the woman (not her sister, never her sister, how could she be? Karen's dead. Dead) has finally gone (and Susan stands watching her shuffle sadly along the street, watches until she's out of sight), she will lean heavily against the closed door for a moment and then head straight for the fridge. Will pour herself a glass of wine and down it in one gulp. Will pour another.

That would have been so much simpler. Upsetting, perhaps, for a short time, but later, a story to eat out on. A story guaranteed to elicit gasps of disbelief, maybe even a few laughs. But nothing that would upset the course of their neat and tidy, their *simple* lives, nothing to scar the psyche. Not an event that would have changed anything. (Oh, maybe Susan would have drunk a bit too much that night, cried a little, been comforted, supported by Ed in his textbook way; maybe they'd have made love, with Susan too drunk to really enjoy it, and Ed guilty in his pleasure, concerned that perhaps he'd taken advantage.) But the overwhelming reaction would have been of relief. Oh, not just about the money, but the lack of complication. The lack of change.

Anyway, it's a nice scenario. Neat. Karen stays dead. Life goes on much as it did before. Nothing changes. End of story.

But Susan knows that life never happens the way we imagine. The way we plan.

It is the woman from the restaurant, but she is dressed differently this time, is hardly recognisable. She wears a tailored skirt and jacket, and her hair has been cut tidily. Her make-up is conservative, her lips coloured, but barely. For a moment Susan wonders whether she is the same woman. But when she speaks, her voice low, slightly tentative, she knows. 'Susan?' This is all she says, but this is all she has to say. It is that same low smoky voice from the phone. From their brief meeting. 'Susan?' Unmistakable.

'Hello,' Susan's voice is shrill, jagged, edgy. 'Come in.' She doesn't wait for the woman to enter, but turns and walks back up the hall. There is the click of the closing door, then the soft tap-tapping of footsteps behind her. By the time the footsteps reach the kitchen Susan has her back to the door, is standing at the sink filling the kettle.

'Coffee?' she asks without turning, without looking at her guest. 'Or tea?'

'Coffee,' the woman says. 'Thanks.' Susan hears the scrape of a chair, a faint rustle and a sigh as she is seated. 'Nice place you've got here.' Susan says nothing, spoons instant coffee into earthenware mugs, waits for the water to boil. The woman tries again. 'Good position too. Lots of light. You'd never find this kind of thing where I'm living.'

'Milk?' Susan asks. 'Sugar?'

She places a cup in front of the woman, carefully angling her head so as not to look at her. Not to meet her eyes. Susan takes the seat at the end of the table, as far away as possible, stares into her cup. There are things she wants to say, needs to say, things that must be said, but somehow she is frozen, speechless, voiceless. The coffee, she knows, would give her some courage, some heat, but her hand, both her hands, have begun to tremble, and she doesn't dare lift the cup. She wishes desperately for the presence of somebody, of anybody else. Hopes that Howard Hamilton will arrive early, but has no doubt that he'll be punctual. 'Half an hour,' he'd said. 'I'll give you half an hour alone. That should give you time to break the ice. Sort things out a little.' Obviously trying to avoid the anticipated emotional scene. Tears, recriminations. He needn't have worried. Susan is paralysed.

Finally it is the woman who breaks the icy silence.

'I realise that this must be really shocking for you, Susan. Mr Hamilton told me that you'd always thought I was dead. I'm sorry if I'm disrupting your life,' her deep voice is measured, calm, confident. She doesn't sound sorry. 'But I *am* Karen. I am your sister.' She pauses, as if expecting a response, but Susan is still incapable of speech, cannot even lift her head.

'Susan? Please. This is hard for me too. Please,' there is a slight break in her gravelly voice. Then somehow she is right there, kneeling by Susan's chair. 'Sukey,' she says softly, and the woman's arms are around her, surprisingly strong. Susan is rigid, unresponsive. 'Sukey,' the woman gives Susan the slightest shake, 'It's okay. It'll be okay. I promise. Sukey?'

What happens next is the stuff of daytime soaps, of

melodrama. Weeping, laughter, protestations of disbelief, of delight. Nothing that can be recalled without simultaneously sniffing and wincing. By the time Howard Hamilton arrives— half an hour, maybe an hour late—who cares? Who remembers? Anyway, he has timed it well, clever man that he is, the champagne is flowing and Susan has a sister again.

A sister.

Ed

Susan calls just as he's preparing his monthly 'Recent Achievements, Future Goals' presentation to the staff.

'It's her,' she says gaily. 'It's Karen.' Just like that. No introduction, no gradual admission, not even a greeting.

He is astonished by her change of heart, amazed that after all she's said of her certainty about the woman's imposture, her own determination to end the charade, that Susan's decided that yes, indeed this woman *is* her sister, no doubt about it. He is bewildered by her obvious elation too—Ed would have sworn that her sister's possible return had not excited her in the least. That she had in fact rather dreaded it. And he is somewhat annoyed that she has chosen to give him such momentous news over the phone. Susan knows how this puts him out. Today of all days.

'It's her,' she says again. 'It's Karen.'

'What do you mean it's her, Susan? We've just been up half the night discussing the fact that it's not her, and what you're going to do about it.' Ed's head is aching, his limbs are heavy from lack of sleep. He has had to send Moira, his personal assistant, out for drops for his bloodshot eyes. His tongue is thick. He likes to get at least nine hours' sleep the night before a presentation. But the matter was pressing, and a resolution wasn't arrived at until the early hours (three, four o'clock). A reaction, practically a speech, was prepared, rehearsed. 'We've just been up half the night working out how to get rid of this bloody woman and now you're telling me it's her?' He can hear his voice rise, feel his heart pound. 'What's going on, Susan?'

'I'm sorry, Edward. Sorry to bother you. But I thought you'd want to know.' Susan's voice is flat now, steely, cold. The elation gone.

'Oh, Christ.' He doesn't know what else to say. Runs his hand over his face. Sits down. Says wearily: 'So what next? If it's her.'

'It *is* her, Ed. I'm certain of it.'

'Oh Christ.'

'Look, I have to go. Howard's leaving—I'd better see him out.'

'Susy?'

'Yes,' impatient now.

'It's really her? Really your sister?'

'It really is.'

Ed's presentation goes badly. He stumbles over figures, forgets the pertinence of particular points, is unable to answer several (*simple! simple!*) questions put to him by Derek. Even the overheads refuse to focus. He tries not to notice Moira's raised eyebrows, the soft snigger of the foreman as he leaves the room, but it's impossible to ignore.

He leaves work early that afternoon. He goes straight home.

He can hear their voices from the hallway. Susan's, light, familiar tones; then another female, but lower, darker. Unknown. There is the sound of laughter. The unmistakable smell of cigarette smoke wafts along the corridor. He guesses that one of Susan's friends is visiting, is staying for coffee, and he is annoyed. (Why today of all days? And why are they smoking inside?) He pokes his head through the kitchen door, intending only to give the briefest of hellos, then take himself off somewhere (the beach, the pub) to think. But when he looks into the kitchen it's not his wife he first sees. It's another woman. A woman he doesn't know. And it takes him a moment (one second? two?) to realise that this is *the* woman. (He had imagined a girl. A schoolgirl.) His wife's sister. Karen.

Susan

Karen is perched on a stool in front of her dressing table (pale veneer, kidney shaped, once their mother's) applying make-up. She's getting ready to go out: a party, a dance. Susan sits very still on the bed behind her, watching her sister's reflection in the mirror. Karen expertly traces a heavy blue line around her eyes. Her mouth is open just a little, the tip of her tongue flickers occasionally at one side of her mouth. Susan follows the path of the pencil in the mirror. Her jaw slackens, mouth opens. Her sister pauses, grins at Susan's reflection. 'You'll catch flies, Sukey,' she says, 'if you don't watch out.'

II

Carly

It's the kind of story the women's magazines love.

Imagine the headlines:

Sisters reunited: Mystery disappearance solved after twenty years!

Or:

One woman's joy: 'They told me that my sister was dead!'

And then the photographs: the two women dressed in their best casual clothes (a little too tight, a little too new); their faces made up, hair carefully styled; embracing stiffly; smiling uncomfortably, unnaturally for the camera.

And then to predict the story's slant, that's simple, too: first the details of the disappearance (more photos—unfocused family snaps; freckly, gap-toothed school portraits) followed by the years of fear and grief and resignation. And then (only two paragraphs later) the prodigal's return—the surprise, the joy, the catching up, the memories, the lives finally shared.

And best of all, in conclusion, the ultimate happy ending: the anticipation of a continuing relationship. *'She's like my best friend already,' says one sister. 'It's as if she's never been away, as if I've known her forever.'*

'It's fantastic,' responds the other, 'the way she's accepted me, taken me in, made me a part of her family.' Then, squeezing her sister's hand for emphasis: 'I won't be going anywhere. Not for a long time. Not ever.'

Leave it at that and you have a good solid story that will leave readers feeling pleasantly teary, agreeably moved. As if they've got their money's worth.

Just as long as they don't wonder too much about the detail, the bits left out, the story that lies between the lines. What happens next.

Especially what happens next.

It's best to keep these stories simple.

Susan

She's late for lunch.

The barbecue was Ed's idea. 'You really need to have some sort of welcome for her, Suse. Not too formal—but still some sort of proper acknowledgement of her return. It's such an odd situation, surely it'll help to have some sort of occasion to ease her ... to ease you both back in?'

A barbecue is not Susan's idea of ease—she'd much prefer to start with quiet informal get-togethers—morning tea, lunch, family dinners, even a walk along the beach, a swim, but she knows there's no point in arguing, after all, it won't hurt too much. Ed's always been big on ceremonies: before they'd married she'd seriously suggested that they just elope, cut out all the fuss and bother, have a party later, but Ed had been shocked, had insisted that they have a more or less traditional wedding, that it was necessary to mark the day, to declare their love, their new allegiance, publicly, and Susan had reluctantly agreed. Then, when first Mitchell and later Stella were born, Ed had insisted on holding naming days for both children (Susan had baulked at the Presbyterian christening ceremony his mother had eagerly anticipated). He'd invited all his family, his friends and most of the Middleton employees to a huge spread (served by caterers), had supplied champagne, several kegs, organised and made speeches, the whole shebang, and though neither of the children had really appreciated their earthly welcome (being at that stage of life either asleep or attached to their mother's breast), Ed had had a wonderful time.

Ed always has a wonderful time on such occasions. He loves parties. At social gatherings—especially his own—he is often to be found at the centre of a small group, maybe two or three friends or colleagues, holding forth on subjects dear to his heart. These are many and endlessly changeable and Susan knows them well, having been privy to their evolution: the place of men in a post-feminist world; fatherhood and family; rising property values on the lower north shore and the impact of this on the middle classes; the value of public education to society as a whole ...

His ideas on all these topics have developed through long wine-fuelled sessions into what is almost a sermon, so detailed and logically structured is the ineluctable half-hour (give or take a few minutes) disquisition. Ed likes to lean when he talks, so he can usually be found with his hip pressed into the barbie, or casually, easily, one leg crooked against a tree. But this casualness is treacherous, even the experienced are deceived into thinking a quick chat about a more trivial this-and-that might be possible. The inexperienced nod and snort and make polite efforts to end the conversation, those who know Ed well resign themselves, assume an interested expression, grit their teeth and endure.

He wears himself out; rather like a child at a birthday party. Susan knows that at the end of most gatherings she's quite likely to find Ed asleep somewhere—never drunk, but exhausted—on a couch or in a quiet corner, snoring softly.

So Susan bows to the inevitable and arranges a Sunday afternoon barbecue. No big deal, she tells her bemused sister over the phone. 'Just a casual thing, meat, salad, bring a friend if you want, say around twelve o'clock, even earlier if you like. If you've got nothing better to do.'

'Yeah, okay,' Carly laughs, 'I don't have a friend handy, but I'll bring a bottle of something will I? You do drink don't you?'

But on the day, two o'clock comes and still the guest of honour hasn't arrived. Susan's had the salads out, the table set, the potatoes in the oven for hours; the kids are whinging—they're starving, though they've eaten bowls of nuts and crisps, hacked into the cheeses. Ed's whining too. He drove in early to the fish markets, brought back mussels, salmon cutlets, kilos of prawns; he has his chef's apron on and fired up the barbie. Despite Susan's best efforts to distract him (she has kept him well supplied with drinks and nibblies and soothing conversation) Ed is getting edgy: his cheeks have a slight pink tinge, his expression is taking on a particular and familiar set (righteous? disapproving?); he pulls at his shirt cuffs, mutters about consideration and respect (how difficult is it to make a phone call?); threatens to start without her. Susan, bolstered by their recent meeting and the bottle of champagne she has already consumed, feels light, unworried, indifferent. Her sister will turn up—she's sure of it.

Ed had wanted to invite a few other people—his parents, Anna and her husband Tom, Derek and his wife Cathy—but luckily, as it turns out, Susan had managed to talk him out of it. (*Think of Karen ... Carly, she's barely even met me, and you want to expose her to the entire family menagerie!*) Susan's one exception had been the solicitor, she'd invited Howard Hamilton on impulse—though now she's really not sure why. He did have a previous engagement, he'd apologised, but he'd be nearby, so would call over in the late afternoon.

Karen, Carly (to call her Carly seems awkward, but no more awkward than Karen) does turn up, of course, but it's close to three and she makes no mention of her lateness, no excuse and no apology (Oh, how Susan envies such casual—or is it studied?—carelessness), just brushes Susan's cheek with her own and hands her a bottle, then advances on Ed (who is simmering by the barbecue) her hand outstretched, her smile wide. Susan can't hear exactly what she says to him, but she can see Carly's friendly handshake, her large gestures, the gradual lightening of Ed's face, his eventual unchecked smile.

She is pleased by Ed's almost immediate capitulation to Carly. (*She's a great girl, Susy*, he whispers to her in the kitchen later, *a terrific girl!*) After his initial brief meeting with her he'd seemed doubtful (*for some reason she reminds me of my kindy teacher*, he'd confessed, *a bit stitched up, slightly scary*) and it seems to her utterly right—both desirable and appropriate—that Ed should be so charmed. After all, Susan observes in her suddenly sentimental state, there's no doubt that her sister has set out to be, and is, remarkably charming. Oh, it's not the sort of charm that manifests in the painfully obsequious and ingratiating behaviour that Susan remembers thinking constituted womanly good manners (*oh, what a wonderful room/baby/lunch; do let me help you make that/carry those/clean this*) and that she now knows is gush, though she occasionally (and somewhat shamefully) succumbs involuntarily to her early instincts. No, Carly's is a far more sophisticated appeal. Ever-so-slightly offhand; subtle and insinuating.

Susan has always considered herself reasonably attractive (a pretty enough girl, and she's worked hard, hasn't let herself go), but she feels herself dowdy, almost matronly beside Carly. Everything Carly does—the clothes she's wearing (she's less conservative today: not quite the same look as their first disastrous meeting at the restaurant—though it's a similar style. Today she's dressed all in black: jeans, t-shirt, boots, everything's tight and vaguely worn, it's probably op shop, and not at all the sort of thing that Susan would ever wear, but on her, on Carly, it's right); the way she walks (head down, all her movements unhurried, loose, graceful); the way her streaky hair, fashionably untidy, falls across her face (only to be ignored); the way she involves herself physically when she listens—stretching her long neck forward—all this seems to Susan to be just right. And somehow enviable.

Then there's her talent for conversation or, to be more precise, her flair for encouraging conversation, for asking the right questions—though none of this, Susan notices, is directed at her. She had hoped for some moments alone with her sister, had imagined another cosy tete-a-tete in the kitchen, or some comfortably banal chitchat about this and that, would even have been satisfied with time spent in companionable silence, but Carly seems to be avoiding all such contact. Instead she has played totem tennis with Stella and Mitchell—who are immediately won over by her unexpected clumsiness—and then acted as Ed's barbecue assistant, standing by his side, ready with the tongs, taking charge of the caramelised onions, the mussels. When they finally eat—and it's past four by that time—Susan finds herself sitting at one end of the rectangular table, leaving Carly and Ed opposite one another in the middle, the children having willingly agreed to eat inside, in front of the television. Susan, who is well into her second bottle now, pleasantly sozzled and really beyond playing the good hostess, is also beyond conversation, is content to listen as she eats. She feels weepy, uncharacteristically sentimental, feels strangely privileged to witness her husband and new sister's undeniable rapport.

Says Carly (her plate pushed to one side now, her chin propped casually on clasped hands):

'So you have your own business, Ed? The kitchen industry? It's always appealed to me—the thought of having my own business, but then I guess it appeals to most people. Not being beholden, not relying on others. Being your own master, more or less. But I guess it's like any job—the glamour eventually wears off?'

Says Ed (leaning forward, mirroring her posture, his expression earnest, thoughtful):

'Well no, actually. Personally, well for me anyway, the glamour—the excitement—never wears off. I don't think it's the job, necessarily, I know that plenty of blokes who're in a similar situation get pretty fed up and bored with the whole thing. But I don't really ever get bored: my gran always used to say that only boring people get bored, and I reckon there's some truth in that. That's my attitude to life in general. Sometimes, when things get *too* easy, you might have to create your own challenges. You've got to always set goals for yourself, to try to extend your possibilities, to reach for something that's slightly beyond your capacity ... It's like exercise, isn't it? When it stops hurting you have to go further, harder, faster ...'

Says Carly (with an admiring shake of the head, a respectful tilt to her lips):

'I can't imagine how you've managed to do all that and have kids as well. It's not that I don't like kids, but how do you find time to have any sort of *life*?'

Says Ed (leaning back, stretching, smiling benignly):

'Quality time. That's our secret, isn't it Suse?' (Susan smiles, nods, pours herself more champagne, breaks open the last mussel.) 'My father, for instance, was real old-school. You know, home from work at five-thirty, sit down and read the paper, *leave your father alone boys, he's had a hard day.* He gave us the odd belting, made us help him out in the garden on the week-end, cleaning bricks, burning off. Then we were working at the factory when we got older: cleaning, edging, stacking. I grew up not knowing him, and him not knowing me. Not as a person. We didn't have a real relationship, couldn't communicate, could never really talk about the things that matter. Our relationship's only really improved since I joined the business—he's been more or less forced to communicate in a meaningful way— we've had to talk, had to get to know one another. But it's taken more than thirty years to get here ...

'Now, me and my kids, my family, it's different. Susy's home most days and the one day that she works I leave work early, so the kids are always straight home after school, and always one parent available. And then most other days I'm home early enough to help Mitchell with his homework, to read to them before bed, tell them about my day, explain that I'm working hard for *them* as well. For their future. The weekends are their time. I take them both to the beach on Saturday mornings, when it's warm enough. They paddle, play in the sand. Then maybe we'll see a movie, go out to lunch—McDonald's, Pizza Hut, a cafe down in Manly, wherever. Have a quiet sit down and a good talk. Find out how they really feel about things—it's important, you know, to get below the surface of things. That's what parenting's all about. It's not just about being there, is it Suse? It's about making that time count, every minute of it, making it really count. Establishing a close relationship ... Quality time. That's what makes a strong family unit.'

Another aspect of Carly's charm, it appears, is patience.

Ed doesn't hog the conversation, however, he's a better host than that; and he's curious, intrigued by this woman, wants to know a few things. 'So, where do you live?' he asks her, 'What do you do?'

All the questions that are in urgent need of an answer. Susan had planned to gently interrogate her sister herself during the afternoon. She'd intended to question Carly about their shared past, to perhaps discover the reasons for her departure, at the very least to find out where she's been, what she's been doing since. But now she leaves the questions to Ed, and they're not quite the right questions, of course, or at least he doesn't phrase them the way Susan, the way a sister, would. But even so, Susan's slightly disconcerted by the fact that at the end of the meal she still can't quite piece together even a rough chronology of Carly's life. However hard she tries to make some sort of a story, some sort of cohesive narrative, there are more gaps than facts, and she is left with more questions than answers. From the bits and pieces that Carly lets slip (and they are slips, Susan feels sure of this, her sister has an almost uncanny ability to slide away from any direct examination—even the most innocent enquiries about her past are expertly deflected) all Susan can be certain of is that Carly's life has been difficult.

To Susan this ability to remain somehow mysterious, a little opaque, is the most potent of all Carly's charms. Potent, and it occurs to her momentarily—though it's a thought that dissipates just as quickly as it materialises—maybe just a little dangerous.

At five-thirty, just as Susan's finishing washing the good glass-ware (she answers the door pink-gloved and dishclothed, her face damp and shiny with steam), Howard Hamilton arrives. He seems curiously unfamiliar on this Sunday afternoon—dressed in civvies: Levis and joggers and an old black t-shirt, his dark hair untidy, curling wildly. She offers him beer, wine, but no, he says, he'd prefer coffee, really, and he sits on a stool at the island bench while Susan pulls off her gloves, prepares the coffee. Ed and the kids have taken Karen (it's so hard to remember!) have taken Carly for a walk down to the beach, she tells Howard when he asks where everyone is. And yes, it has been a successful day, she adds before he can ask.

'My sister—' (she giggles a bit over the word) '—arrived a bit late, but she's certainly made up for it—she's fitting in really well. We're all—were all over the moon, it couldn't be better.'

Hamilton nods his head thoughtfully. 'That's good.'

'Yes, it's very good. Perfect in fact. The kids, Ed, me. Every-one's happy.'

Like Ed, she remembers to reciprocate. It's possible that this man has his own life, isn't just concerned with her own. 'And you,' she asks brightly, as she passes him his coffee, 'have you had a pleasant Sunday?'

'We-ell—yes,' he stirs in a teaspoon of sugar, frowning. 'We-ll no, not really. I've just been visiting my old man. He's in a hospital near here. Actually, it's a hospice. I take my mother over twice a week to visit him. The whole thing's pretty har-rowing, really, but you'd probably know all about that. There's not much left of him, he's doped up with morphine, can barely speak. I don't think he's got long to go.'

'Oh, that's so sad ... so hard. And your Mum? Is she coping alright? Does she have someone staying with her?'

'My youngest sister's living at home. She takes her when she can. Then there's my eldest brother, he lives nearby ...'

'And you live nearby, too?'

'Oh, no. I grew up here, but I live in Woolloomooloo,

Brougham Street. Haven't managed the move back since uni—and probably won't now. Though I still miss the surf ...'

'And you're married? Kids?' Susan's genuinely interested now, not just making polite conversation. She wonders how it is that despite so much contact with professionals—doctors, lawyers, accountants, dentists—she so frequently regards them as being somehow untouched by the everyday world, never really imagines them as having families, a life, an existence beyond the office. Wonders whether it's her or the professionals, or both: perhaps it's necessary to maintain a certain distance when such an intimate knowledge is required—from both confider and confidante.

'I'm divorced. I've a six-year-old daughter, Maisy, but she's with her mother, in Melbourne. I see her in the school holidays. You know how it works.'

'Oh, God. That must be bloody hard.'

He shrugs. 'They've been gone for five years now, my ex has since had another two kids. You get over it, I guess.'

'Not really.'

'No, of course not really.' He smiles, stands up. 'So, how about I help you finish the dishes while I'm here.' He grabs a tea towel.

They stand companionably at the sink, their only conversation to do with what goes where. She knows that it is probably the effect of too much champagne too early in the day, but suddenly Susan finds herself mesmerised by the efficient elegance of his movements; he dries the dishes expertly—in contrast to her own clumsy, indifferent washing. She stops and watches, fascinated.

'What?' He pauses. 'Are you alright?'

She wonders whether she is actually alright. 'I'm not sure. It's all a bit bewildering, all a bit much, I guess ...'

One end of the kitchen window curtain has come loose, has fallen off its track. It billows out in the breeze, and the fabric brushes over her face, sticking to Susan's damp skin. She pushes it back, ineffectually, with her damp rubber-clad fingers. She grapples with the glove, while Howard moves closer, peels the gossamer-light fabric away almost absently. 'It must be difficult,' he says slowly, 'I hadn't really thought too much about it. How do you become sisters again—after twenty years?'

'Yes, how do you? I've had all this time to think about it. Years really. It's not like I've never imagined it. But I just don't know—what to do. How to handle it.' She sighs, relieved that she's said it, but amazed that she's admitted her doubts to a virtual stranger.

'I don't think there are any guidelines—it's not a very usual situation is it? There are probably counselling services—people who help with adoption reunions. Maybe that's as close as you'll get—I can find out ... if you like.' He sounds doubtful, and as if he's making conversation, babbling.

'I suppose ...' Susan stops mid-sentence, can't recall what she was going to say, has unaccountably lost track of the conversation.

They both stand quite still, saying nothing. The curtain billows out again and Howard's fingers brush hers as they both move to push it away. Their fingers tangle (hers red, a little puffy with heat) and stay together for a long moment. Then, inexplicably, it is more than just their fingers intertwined, it's arms, legs, lips, tongues. Susan is the first to pull away. She turns back to the sink, plunges her hands into the greasy lukewarm suds. Says briskly: 'I wonder if you wouldn't mind clipping that curtain back into its runner, Howard? It's annoying—and I can't quite reach.'

Ed

He likes Carly from the first.

It could be said that Ed is inclined to like everyone. It's only fair, he feels, to take people at face value, to take them at their own estimation—and though this has brought him unstuck occasionally over the years (particularly in his line of work, where face value is generally worthless), in Ed's personal, in his *intimate* relationships, it is an attitude that has always proven useful, beneficial.

Still, he likes this woman. Carly. His new sister-in-law. He likes—well it's hard to locate precisely what it is that he finds so appealing. Carly possesses, despite being thin, a certain voluptuousness, a sensuality that's absent from her sister, a sensuality that he finds intriguing, enticing, though she couldn't, in all honesty, be called good-looking—or at least they're not the sort of looks Ed generally admires. Usually he's attracted to well-groomed women, fashionably (but not flamboyantly) dressed, wearing sufficient (but not excessive) make-up. And given a choice he would have to say that he prefers women's hair long; long and tied back. He's a sucker for an elegant low slung ponytail, or even a librarian's demure chignon. But Carly displays none of his customary preferences. She's about forty and still dresses like a student: worn jeans, t-shirts, big clumpy boots. Her hair is cut to her shoulders, badly styled, and is streaked blonde at the tips with darker roots. Her ears are pierced not once, but three, maybe four times, and she sports a small silver stud in her nose. He can see no trace of make-up. No trace of a bra either. It's not that he's looking, not exactly, he's never really been a tit man (he has grown to love Susan's little mounds, not quite a handful, drooping slightly from pregnancy and breast-feeding, but round, soft), nonetheless he can't help noticing that her breasts sit freely under her thin shirt—without any evidence of swing or sag. It's not a style Ed generally approves of (geriatric rock star, a kind of down-at-heel Paula Yates)—it's untidy, with the mildly disreputable shabbiness he associates with the inner city, and on anyone else her age he'd call it affected, pretentious, mutton-dressed-up-as-slightly-spoilt-lamb, but Carly—well, somehow Carly can carry it off. He reckons that Carly has earned the right—after all (from the little he can gather, anyway), she's lived a life that's almost impossible for him to imagine, and her appearance is perhaps a natural, a physical manifestation of her experience.

He likes her voice. Low, breathy, slightly gravelly. A smoker's voice, as Susan has pointed out, and even that's okay, though generally he abhors cigarette smoking. Especially in women. But Carly rolls her own, and suddenly (though he's seen it done countless times before) he finds the whole process strangely fascinating. The way she rolls the tobacco quickly, expertly, between two fingers, without even thinking about it. The flicker of her pink tongue—efficient, but sensual—along the thin paper.

He likes her eyes. Blue. Changeable. One minute pale, opaque; the next translucent, full of light, the colour of the sky or the ocean.

He likes her calm. Susan is calm too, but hers is such a practical calm—she is matter-of-fact, efficient. And she's quick, reactive. Carly does nothing, says nothing in a hurry. She occasionally pauses mid-sentence—as if she's reflecting, reconsidering, even as she speaks. Her smiles break slowly, are careful, measured. He'd noticed a similar ponderousness in various of his friends during their pot-smoking days, but Carly's eyes are bright, focused. All her movements are, he thinks, graceful, and they're certainly not the awkward twitches and blunderings that come from being stoned.

He likes the way she is with the children. She's not at all how he remembers any of *his* aunts—kind, but distant, not quite approachable, except in an emergency. Carly talks to Mitchell and Stella as if they're adults—there's no patronising here, no adult superiority, and though he really doesn't approve of bad language around kids, they don't seem to notice with their new aunt. He can't see that she'll be a negative influence in any way.

He likes the smell of her too. Musk, vanilla, he's not sure, will have to check with Susan. Though on second thoughts maybe he'll ask Carly herself. It might be a nice gift for Susan—her birthday's coming up—a change from her customary floral scents.

All things considered, Ed's rather pleased with his new sister-in-law.

He insists on accompanying Susan when she next meets with Howard Hamilton, though she tells him to go to work, that she'll be fine, she can handle it, she doesn't need him holding her hand. Susan doesn't actually tell him that it's none of his business, but he senses that she'd like to. He manages to shrug it off, to not take offence—she's not really been herself lately, and it's no wonder—and he restrains himself, limits himself to a simple statement to the effect that he's coming no matter what. That she needs him there to (and here he clears his throat delicately) protect her interests.

'Oh, for Christ's sake, Ed. It's Howard Hamilton's job to protect my interests.'

But Ed knows that's not so: 'The solicitor's there to protect your mother's interests, Susan. The interests of the estate. Not yours.' Ed doesn't tell her that he still doesn't trust that greasy solicitor—is aware that for some reason (women!) she has taken to him, has, perhaps, been *taken in* by him. Nor does he mention (perhaps he doesn't realise) the fact that part of this eagerness to accompany her is tied up with the prospect of seeing Carly again. Though it's not like Ed to deny such an impulse. Not at all like Ed.

Carly is already comfortably ensconced in Hamilton's office when they arrive. The solicitor stands when the secretary ushers them in, but Carly stays seated, though she smiles and says hello to Susan, who returns the greeting a little too coolly to Ed's way of thinking. He knows his wife was slightly put out, slightly hurt by her sister's failure to talk to her during the weekend barbecue, but as he has already, none-too-diplomatically, pointed out, Susan was half-pissed by the time Carly arrived; she was scarcely able to remember her sister's new name, let alone conduct a meaningful conversation. Now he directs a slightly too-warm smile in Carly's direction, to make up for Susan's obvious remoteness; he proffers his hand, and it seems to him that she grasps it eagerly, that she clutches it the way an exhausted swimmer might grab onto a buoy, and that the smile she turns on him as he takes the seat next to her is understanding as well as grateful. Carly is dressed differently again today, though he's not sure what it is precisely that's changed. Is it the way she's done her hair? He can't be certain but thinks perhaps it looks more stylish somehow; artfully tousled rather than unkempt, uncared for. Or is it the blouse: silk, unbuttoned just enough to allow a tantalising glimpse of cleavage? Whatever it is, she looks different, more conservative, younger somehow, and even more attractive. She leans towards him, her hand still loosely in his.

'I really want to thank you for Sunday, Ed,' she says in an undertone. 'The barbecue. It was great. You were great. So warm, so welcoming. I know this is difficult for you both,' glances briefly at Susan who is talking quietly to the solicitor, 'but it's difficult for me, too. Difficult and ...' suddenly she seems lost for words, her fingers tremble slightly in his, 'difficult and wonderful. To have a family again ... after all this time.' She sighs and drops his hand, leans back in her chair, turns away for a moment as if to compose herself, then back again, smiling weakly.

Susan

She is careful that there is no particular consciousness on her part. Susan is cool, collected, and willing (indeed, more than willing, desperate) to let the whole episode remain what it undoubtedly was. The outcome of some sort of momentary derangement on both their parts. An aberration. An uncharacteristic act of no great significance committed under duress and the influence of alcohol. Meaningless. Best forgotten. Already forgotten.

It appears that he too has put the incident out of his mind. Howard—Mr Hamilton—is back to wearing his well-cut suits. His hair is brushed back neatly, his handshake firm, his manner briskly businesslike. It would be easy to think that she had dreamt up the whole incident—but then why would she bother?—this conservatively dressed middle-aged man is certainly not the stuff of the even the most desperate housewife's fantasy. Susan takes the seat furthest from his desk (there are three chairs ranged around his desk, Ed takes the centre chair, the chair closest to Carly) and they exchange pleasantries.

Howard asks Susan in his dry voice if the traffic was bad. She replies calmly that it was okay, that it was better than last time, better than she'd expected. He asks her, without any change of expression, any sign, if she felt that the barbecue, Sunday's barbecue, had been a success. He says he is pleased that Ed has accompanied her again, that it's good that he's made the time, that this—the business side of her—their—mother's will, the sale, the disbursement of proceeds—involves him too.

Susan nods her head, and glances briefly towards Ed who has his back to her, is chatting away to Carly. When she turns back Howard Hamilton is frowning at her, the skin on his wide forehead puckered quite alarmingly. She says nothing, stares back uncertainly.

'Well,' he says finally, holding some papers towards her (his wrists jut out awkwardly from his well-made shirt; they are surprisingly thin wrists, the bone knobbly through the skin like a child's). 'We may as well start. I'd like you to read through this document first and then sign on every page, where I've indicated. This first document is to verify your positive identification of your sister ...' The tips of his fingers brush against hers (so contrived, so cliched) as she reaches for the paper.

His fingers tell her that he hasn't forgotten. His fingers tell her that neither has she.

Ed

The solicitor seems to have concluded his tete-a-tete with Susan, and is speaking loudly, is addressing the three of them, though Ed only half-listens.

'The two of you need to sign these documents and then we

can get the house on the market ...'

On Sunday, Ed had been looking hard for a family resemblance between the two women, had failed to find any physical similarities, but had eventually come to the conclusion that there was a particular personality trait they shared: on first meeting it'd seemed that Carly displayed the same sort of self-sufficiency, an admirable and singular toughness, that his wife possesses. But now it seems that he was mistaken, that Carly's tough exterior is only a veneer, a shell.

'... be certain, but I've had advice that properties of this sort are extremely easy to move—they may even have an interested party already ...'

He had no idea she was so soft, so unsure. So vulnerable.

'... and then another six weeks before the disbursements ...'

His sister-in-law doesn't remind him of his kindergarten teacher anymore, and Ed can't imagine why she ever did.

Carly

She is surprised that it is so easy. That the tears, the sighs, the show of grateful vulnerability, aren't more difficult to affect, to manufacture. That occasionally these emotions seem real even to her. She is surprised too that their response—the obvious concern, the generosity, the solicitude, the nauseating sincerity of it all—is so gratifying.

She thinks she could get used to it, she thinks she really could.

Ed

It is Ed who initially suggests that Carly move in with them.

'It'll be a fantastic opportunity for you two girls to catch up, get to know one another,' he says. 'She can have Stella's room—it'll be a useful experience for Stell and Mitch, a good lesson—having to share—before they're too old.' Adds: 'And it'll be good for Carly to be part of a real family again.'

The positive aspects of such a move present themselves rapidly and he continues to enthusiastically argue his case, though Susan has said nothing yet, has made no sign of dissent. 'The experience will be good for the kids too. And easier, surely, for Carly, it can't be healthy living in the city—it's so unsafe.' He grimaces at the thought of those grimy streets, dingy motel rooms, the untold and unknown dangers lurking in every dark corner. 'What do you reckon, eh, Suse? Shall we offer to make a home for your sister? I don't mean permanently, just until all the money stuff's sorted out. Whadda you think, Suse?'

He imagines Carly's response to the offer of sanctuary—her grateful surprise, the shedding of an overwhelmed tear or two, his own solicitous response. Imagines, too, the three of them sitting under the wisteria in the warm spring evenings with glasses of wine, the kids playing contentedly on the lawn, or already asleep; the glance and shimmer of their conversation. It makes a pretty picture. He doesn't notice—though once he would have been alert to her every mood—the worried frown that passes briefly over Susan's face, her momentary hesitation, hears only her reply: 'I was thinking the same thing. Why don't you give her a call?'

To Ed's satisfaction, Carly doesn't hesitate.

'I'll bring my stuff over tomorrow, will I?'

They move the children in together. Clear out all Stella's drawers, the wardrobe, her desk. Susan changes Stella's pink floral quilt for a darker, deeper plaid.

Carly arrives late the next afternoon carrying two green garbage bags. All her belongings, she says. It takes her only ten minutes or so to unpack, to arrange. When Ed looks into the room, later, he can see no evidence of the new occupant. There are no photographs, no casually strewn clothes and shoes, no personal odds and ends. There's not even a ripple in the surface of the bed covering. It's as impersonally tidy as a vacant motel room.

Susan

Susan knows that there are some days (weeks, even months) when it seems she's just going through the motions—days when everything is done on some almost unconscious level that requires nothing of her, where everything from early morning yoga, to consoling a temporarily friendless Mitchell after school, is accomplished without thinking, automatically, without any reference to a deeper self, a self who's touched by what's going on. On these days it's almost as if that deeper self is absent, has gone elsewhere for refuge, is in hiding.

After Carly reappears, after she moves in, such days are few and far between.

She could say that once Carly moves in life goes on pretty much as before. Susan still walks Mitchell and Stella to school at the same time every day. She still has the house to maintain, her one day of work, her walks with Anna. Afternoons, there's the children's homework and music and sporting practice to oversee. Shopping on Thursdays, tennis on Tuesdays, meals to prepare. Ed heads off to work, comes home, visits his parents on Wednesday afternoons, surfs and jogs—the same as always. Theirs is essentially the same busy existence that's replicated all through the Sydney suburbs, regular to the point of monotony. On the surface at least, life does go on pretty much as before. But in every respect that matters, in every respect that will resonate in the future, life has changed.

The nights, for instance—where once it was Ed and Sue, their comfortable old conversations—now it's Carly and Sue, Ed maintaining a tactful distance when he sees the two of them, intent over a glass of wine, a cup of tea, talking, talking, always talking.

It is all they do in those first few days. It seems to Susan that there is little time for anything else. Ed, the children, it seems that the everyday routines of her ordinary existence have become peripheral, shadowy, insignificant. For a while at least, they seem part of another life, another world—and she is surprised and a little annoyed that they themselves, the children in particular, don't seem to have understood this properly, that they still continue to demand her attention, her consideration.

She is bursting with questions about the past—Carly's, her own—and finds herself bursting with explanations too. She doesn't know where to start.

'Tell me about you,' Susan says. 'Tell me. I need to know.'

Hard, Carly tells her, her life has been hard, tough, but no details, please don't ask, you don't want to know. Drifting, going nowhere. 'There's not much point in doing anything much,' she says to her sister, 'if you've got no one to share it with. No one to care.'

Carly had been waitressing at a cafe in St Kilda and she'd seen the notice, serendipitously, while she was scouring the papers for a new job. The notice had been placed in a small local paper, on the same page as the 'positions vacant'. It had given her something of a shock, seeing her name like that. She hadn't used it, hadn't even *thought* about it, for years. She contacted the solicitor almost immediately—didn't give herself any time to consider, to think into it. She'd acted on impulse, without considering the consequences, the repercussions. Which was pretty much the same way she made all her decisions.

'But this time it was the right thing to do,' Carly says. 'And I'm so glad I did it.'

'I'm glad too,' Susan takes her hand, squeezes gently.

Sister.

Carly

She stays quiet about the past. This is extraordinarily difficult in the face of Susan's constant dredging up of memories, her anxiety to know what really happened, what they were really like, who they really were.

There's so much she doesn't remember, such huge gaps in her knowledge, that really it's easier, it's *safer* to stay silent, to shake her head and sigh, to murmur indistinctly: 'You don't *really* want to know,' or 'Oh, but it was such a long time ago Susy, why does it matter now?' or to simply change the subject.

Ed, of course, homes in on Carly's discomfort, champions her. 'Come on Suse,' he says to his wife, who's excited by some vague recollection, intent on exploring some new hypothesis. 'C'mon Suse, lighten up. Leave your poor sister alone.' And while Susan blushes, suddenly confused and guilty, Carly will reward him with a grateful fluttering smile. At these moments she is all defenceless uncertainty, and Susan a blundering bully.

At other moments, alone with Susan, she'll show a harder, sharper edge. 'Look, Suse, I don't want to go there,' she'll say. 'Let's talk about the weather. The children. Politics. The price of eggs. Anything. Anything but the fucking *past.*'

She could, she supposes (and at times she is sorely tempted), she could make it up—who can contradict her?—but really it's better this way. To remember little and offer nothing. It *was* all such a long time ago, after all.

And the little she does tell them about her past is always basically the truth. Oh, sometimes a name will be changed, a place, a time. But on the odd occasion that she reveals anything about her life, she sticks as closely as she can to the real story.

When all's said and done, it's easier.

Susan

'Tell me about you,' says Carly.

'After you left ...' Susan starts awkwardly. She doesn't really want to mention those first days that followed Karen's, that followed Carly's, disappearance; knows that it's all too painful, and she can't really remember, anyway. So she goes on from there, summarising, glossing over. She recounts the little she remembers clearly of those first few years: her parents' divorce, her move with her father to Manly, the arrival of Gillian, their mother's gradual decline, her madness. Carly listens politely, but asks no questions, seems mildly bored, as if Susan's discussing people she's never met, never likely to know. Susan had expected something more (what?—some sign of guilt, of contrition? some recognition of her own contribution to their mother's sad existence?) but she listens unmoved, gives no indication that these people, these stories, have any real connection to her. Eventually Susan gives up.

'How come you don't want to hear all this stuff?' she asks.

'It's history,' Carly shrugs. 'It's over. It's irrelevant. These people don't mean anything to me anymore. But tell me about you,' she says, 'tell me what you've been up to.'

'What I've been up to?' The casual phrase makes Susan, makes them both, laugh. Catching up. They're catching up.

Some part of Susan knows that there are things you don't tell strangers, parts of your life you shouldn't offer up to people you have just met, even if the stranger is family. Even if the stranger is your own sister. She can see that there are things that should be kept private, or at any rate should only be revealed slowly, cautiously, as a relationship progresses. She guesses that those books Ed is always quoting would counsel caution, taking it slowly, building up a natural, an organic rapport—would advise against taking emotional risks, against leaving yourself vulnerable—but she doesn't care.

Susan wants Carly to know who she is, and wants her to know why. She wants intimacy. Instantly. She tells her sister everything. *Everything.*

In the mornings Carly sleeps in, is never up before ten, emerges only after the children and Ed have gone. Pads to the kitchen in her t-shirt (why don't Susan's breasts sit so pertly?—she's ten years younger, after all), stretching and yawning, demanding coffee in her huskier-than-usual morning voice (oh her demands are gentle, polite, never seem demands, but they are). Then sits sipping noisily, lights her first cigarette (though it could be her second, there have been times when Susan's caught a whiff of stale tobacco in Carly's bedroom, in the bathroom) and sits for half an hour or so, saying little, before she takes herself off for her shower.

Most days Carly stays home—curls up in the lounge reading magazines, watching television, drinking coffee. She rolls cigarette after cigarette. Occasionally forgets herself, and ashes on the carpet, flicks her butts out the window, or leaves them, smouldering, on the windowsill. Susan invites her to come when it's time to pick up the kids, to do the shopping, to join her and Anna's beach walks, social tennis, to go out for lunch. No thanks, Carly says, she's fine, she's happy here, would rather not. Is content just mooching around for now. She's generally finished her mooching by the late afternoon, is up and alert by the time the children get home, ready for drinks and conversation by the time Ed arrives. She doesn't help cook, never even offers: most nights Susan prepares dinner while Ed and Carly sit at the kitchen table drinking and chatting, helping the kids with their homework.

Very occasionally Carly leaves the house after lunch. Comes back around dinner time, sometimes after. There's a particular expression Susan begins to recognise—a tight-lipped smile, one side of her mouth slightly downturned—that indicates Carly's disinclination to answer any questions. After the first few weeks Susan stops asking her where she's going, when she'll be home.

In a way it is as if Susan is the older sister, Carly the younger.

After a while Susan begins to feel rather annoyed, tangibly put out by Carly's inactivity, her secrecy. It's a good feeling, this, Susan thinks. It means the reality of their being sisters is beginning to sink in, proves that this is a real relationship. Flesh and blood. Or 'blood and gore' as Anna frequently describes her own relationship with her younger sister. Anyway, Susan says nothing, makes no mention of her irritation—it is the sort of thing she knows most siblings routinely experience—that such petty aggravations are stewed over for weeks, and eventually erupt in a huge and ultimately purifying conflagration. But she can't afford any such explosion. Not quite; not yet. So she keeps her feelings to herself, doesn't even mention them to Ed. She enjoys her irritation. She savours it. She has a sister.

The question has been scratching away between the two of them since Carly's arrival, but Susan hasn't been able to bring herself to ask—somehow it seems impertinent, an intrusion—until now.

'Why did you leave?'

The two women are alone together, Ed retiring early with a book—and, for the first time, fortified by the best part of a bottle of wine, Susan is brave enough to ask, feels she has the courage to bear the implications of Carly's answer.

Carly says nothing. Seems to shrink a little, huddling into the lounge. Her face closes up—eyes narrowed, lips compressed. She shakes her head, gives a slight smile. The meaning is clear.

'Oh, no,' Susan shakes her head slowly, a little drunkenly. 'You have to tell me. I need to know. That one thing at least.'

Carly leans forward in her chair. Looks at her sister intently, 'Susan, you really don't need to know. Believe me.'

Susan really does need to know, but lets Carly change the subject anyway. This time.

Carly

Why?

Susan thinks it's important to know why. Thinks that it will tell her something essential; that it will explain everything she wants explained: about the past; about her parents; about herself.

But she knows that Susan's wrong.

Knowing why won't tell her everything. Really, it won't tell her anything at all. Nothing she wants to know, anyway.

Why? It's a question that can never really be answered, though Carly will have to make some reply eventually. There's no way around it.

Susan

'Read us a story,' the children cry at bed time. 'Read us a story, Carly!'

Mitchell and Stella adore their new aunt. Her sister makes no fuss, bears no gifts, seems to Susan to be quite cool with them, but still, they think she's wonderful. She watches from the doorway as Carly picks desultorily through the selection in their shelves. She takes one of the children's favourites, *The Mousewife*, sits cross-legged on the carpet and begins to read:

'Wherever there is an old house with wooden floors and beams and rafters and wooden stairs and wainscots and skirting boards and larders, there are mice. They creep out on the carpets for crumbs, they whisk in and out of their holes, they run in the wainscot and between the ceiling and the floors. There are no signposts because they know the way, and no milestones because no one is there to see how they run.'

She reads haltingly and, without any expression, follows the words with her finger. It's as if she's rusty, hasn't read for years. Susan is surprised, has assumed that Carly, like her, would be a fluent reader. One thing she does remember clearly about their mother is her attitude to schoolwork—that she expected and encouraged Susan to read well. Halfway through the next sentence Carly tosses the book over her shoulder. 'Bo-ring,' she explains to the surprised children. Mitchell claps his hands.

'We've readed that one a zillion times and I'm sick of it too,' he says, desperate to be agreeable.

'But you will read us something, won't you, Carly?' Stella is more cautious, doesn't want to miss out, be forced to go to sleep early.

'I don't know,' Carly frowns. 'I couldn't see anything very interesting. Nothing I'd want to read ...'

'*Awww.*'

'So how about I tell you a story?'

'A real-life story?' Mitchell is wary. Ed specialises in what he calls real-life stories—they are long and, from a child's perspective, extremely convoluted. They are somewhat lacking in momentum and almost always have a moral. *Bo-ring.*

'Oh—it's not real life, exactly,' she says. 'More like a fairytale.'

'A fairytale?' Mitchell's face falls. 'I hate fairytales. Fairytales are for girls. Fairytales are really boring.'

'Oh. It's not about a fairy—it's about someone way more exciting than any boring fairy. Someone different to anyone you know.' She pauses. Waits. 'Do you want me to tell you?'

'Tell us, tell us, tell us,' chants Mitchell.

'Yes please,' says his big sister who is always polite.

'Once upon a time,' she starts, 'there was a little girl who lived with her mother and father and four brothers and six sisters in a tree house in the middle of a great rainforest. Now this little girl was a very ordinary little girl who in nearly every way was exactly the same as every other little girl. She had two legs and two arms and two plaits and five fingers on each hand and the proper number of teeth and exactly the right number of freckles on her nose that was exactly the right sort of nose for a little girl to have and right smack in the middle of her normal little round face. This little girl was so ordinary a little girl that sometimes even her mother got her confused and called her by the wrong name. This little girl whose name was Rose was sometimes called Daisy and sometimes Barbara and now and then Jane and once in a while Sally or Trish or Erica and occasionally her mother would call her all seven at once—would call her Daisy Barbara Jane Sally Trish Erica—Rose. Because these were the names of her sisters (all of them older and taller) and this is the sort of thing that mothers who have too many children sometimes do.'

She pauses for a breath. Susan wonders at Carly's transformation, from halting reader to consummate storyteller. The two children are sitting straight up in bed, their eyes wide, breath held. Susan has never, whatever the story, however entertaining, known them to be so obviously rapt, so spellbound.

'Well,' Carly continues, 'what do you think it is that's so extraordinary and exciting about this perfectly ordinary little girl? What could it be that makes her so different?'

The two children make excited guesses:

'She's got an extra toe?'

'She can fly?'

'She's a *nalien*?'

'She's a genius?'

'She knows all her times tables?'

'She's a zillionaire?'

'She's never naughty?'

'She's a terminator?'

'Your mum should be able to tell you,' Carly looks Susan's way. 'It's a story that our mother used to tell me when I was little like you—and then when your mum was little, I told her.'

'Tell us Mummy! Tell us!'

Carly waits, smiling.

Susan has no memory of any bedtime storytelling sessions—in fact she can't remember being told stories by anyone other than school teachers and Benita and John on *Playschool*, and whichever way she turns it (is it Goldilocks in disguise, an embellished Cinderella, a tale from the *Arabian Nights*?) there is nothing at all familiar about this tale. She would like nothing better than to participate in this story, to add her memories to her sister's, to be part of some fine bedtime storytelling tradition, but she can't. She has no idea why this little girl is different—for all Susan knows, this little girl could pack shelves in the local supermarket. She is as intrigued as the children.

'Mum's probably forgotten.' Stella is scathing: 'Mum always forgets everything and says it's all because of us.'

'But not stories,' Mitchell corrects her. 'Even Mum wouldn't forget a story. Not even if she had *namnesia*.' Such faith.

Eventually Susan shrugs, admits defeat. Carly raises her eyebrows, smiles gently (reproachfully?), turns back to the children.

'This little girl,' she tells them, 'this little girl can become invisible.'

It is not such a big deal, and it's not that Carly says anything, but Susan feels she has failed an important test. There are an almost infinite number of stories with infinite variations, after all. Surely to forget one is not so extraordinary.

'I don't trust her.' Anna is never one to mince words, though her bluntness frequently provokes hostility.

'You've barely met her, Anna. Why don't you trust her?' Susan is panting a little. The king tides have begun and the water has cut deeply into the shore all along the stretch between North and South Curl Curl. All the firm sand is under water and to walk and talk requires considerable effort. 'What is there to not like?'

'I don't know, Suse. There's just something about her that doesn't ring true. All that silence about her past. She can't really have forgotten everything. And what about the last twenty years? What's she been doing? Why can't she tell you? I wouldn't trust her, Suse. There's something a bit off about her.'

'What do you mean, off? She *is* Karen. All that's been established.'

'I don't mean that. I'm sure she's your sister. That's not what's bothering me.'

'Then what? What *is* bothering you? It's been fantastic having her. She's great. With the kids, with Ed.'

'She's trying too hard.'

'Trying too hard? Oh, Jesus, Anna! How can she be trying too hard? We're all trying hard. She's my sister. We're the only family she's got—the first family she's had for twenty years.'

'Oh, Susy, how do you know? You really don't know anything about her. She could have three husbands and six kids stashed away somewhere. She hasn't told you *anything*.'

'Anna,' Susan's jaw is suddenly tense, her eyes sting. 'Anna, it means a lot to me, too, you know. To have her back. To have a sister.' Even to her own ears, Susan's words sound stiff, defensive.

'Oh, God.' Anna takes hold of Susan's arm and gives it a friendly squeeze. 'I'm sorry Suse. I didn't mean to upset you. I just worry. Sometimes you're so good at not seeing things.'

Susan shakes Anna's hand loose. Digs her heels in. 'Let's turn back.'

'Already?' Anna sounds bewildered. They are only halfway along the beach, have barely begun their walk. But Susan insists that she has had enough fresh air and exercise for one day. They turn and trudge back. They avoid each other's eyes; don't speak.

Ed

When his mother pulls herself up with her customary sigh, and heads off to dish out the dinner, Carly, despite discreetly desperate shakes of the head from both Ed and Susan, offers to help. And when Mrs Middleton inevitably declines—'I'll call Ed in presently to help me carve, that's all I expect'—Carly follows her out into the kitchen anyway. Susan shrugs and turns her attention back to the television, but Ed is stricken, can imagine the—at best—frosty treatment she'll receive.

His mother has already told him over the phone, and in no uncertain terms, what she thinks of Carly, who she has only met once, and briefly: 'A nose-ring, well, alright, a bolt, a stud, whatever you call it! She's a middle-aged woman—she's older than your sister, Ed!—it's disgusting. And her messy hair. Her clothes. Ridiculous. And Stella tells me ...' Ed silently curses (for the very first time) the open nature, the honesty that he has always considered his daughter's most appealing trait. 'Stella tells me she has a tattoo on her buttock. The one on her arm is bad enough, but her buttock!' She spits the word. 'And how does your six-year-old daughter know that about her aunt, Ed? Can you tell me that? What sort of a woman is she, son, to have living in the house with your children? I don't care if she's Susan's sister. If she *is*.' Her doubt about this point is clear. 'You say you don't know anything about her, but I'll tell you something—and it's as plain as the nose on my face. Do you know what I think? I think she looks like a drug addict. A drug addict! And it's not just me who thinks this, Ed. It's your father too. And Derek and Cathy. We can all see it. What sort of influence, what sort of a role model can she possibly be? Oh—and the diseases, Ed. AIDS, hepatitis, gonorrhoea! Don't you imagine for one moment that I'm ignorant of these things. I read the papers. A drug addict! How could you?'

Anxious, he gives it a few minutes, then saunters into the kitchen casually, prepared for the worst.

But what he finds is completely unexpected.

Carly is carving the leg—expertly—and his mother, his mother is actually laughing at something Carly is telling her. Tongs poised above the steaming vegetables, pressures of high office momentarily forgotten. His mother is shaking with laughter, her cheeks are pink with pleasure, her eyes glitter. His mother is laughing so exuberantly that it takes her a moment to notice Ed, who is standing uncertainly in the doorway. When she finally sees him she points the tongs in his direction and says merrily, 'You didn't tell me your sister-in-law was such a funny, clever girl, Eddy. And such a carver.' She grips Carly's shoulder, shakes it affectionately, 'My goodness—what a treasure.'

Ed looks at Carly who is still carving demurely, then back at his mother, who is wiping her streaming eyes on a tea towel and who says, 'Now scoot, Edward, we'll be out soon. I want this girl to finish her story ... and it's not one that can be told in front of a man, is it darling?'

His mother turns her back on him, and he has no option but to leave the room, wondering what has been said, and astonished by his mother's use of the endearment. *Darling.* She has never once called Susan anything but Susan, has never even called her Sue. He has noticed that, quite frequently, his mother fails to call his wife anything.

Later that night, lying in bed, Susan asleep beside him, he goes over those moments in the kitchen. He is simultaneously amazed and pleased by his mother's reception of Carly. He has always wanted his mother to approve of his friends and, though he knows he should be getting over this at his stage of life, is always disappointed when, invariably, she doesn't. He wonders whether this is an indication that at last, after ten years of marriage, his mother is beginning to accept Susan. Perhaps Carly will be the one (so unlikely!) to bring the two women together. To break the deeply frozen ice.

He wonders, too, what it was that Carly told his mother. He can't remember the last time he saw her laugh. Not with such uncomplicated pleasure, anyway.

Ed recently read an article that discussed the benefits of living in an extended family situation—how another adult can provide not only a new perspective, but also a space free from the sometimes overpowering intensity that is part and parcel of the nuclear family. That what's referred to in the jargon as an 'outside-insider' (or should that be 'inside-outsider'?) can help deflect conflict, dissipate tension. And that this can benefit children as much as adults. The conflict thing has never been an issue in his little family—so far all their relationships have been uncomplicated, easy, untroubled—but he has no doubt that Carly's perspective has opened them all up somehow, has let in, metaphorically speaking, light and air. It has exceeded his expectations—this addition to their family. This expansion of their intimate circle.

Since Carly's moved in, Ed feels himself changed, his skin loosening, feels himself becoming more susceptible, more responsive to new impressions, new sensations. He feels that he understands his family better. In their interactions with Carly, who treats them in a way that's unguarded, equal, offhand without being unkind, he sees his children anew—as people with their faults and foibles, rather than as precious and perfect beings, to be somehow removed and protected from the real world.

And his wife. Susan. To see her relationship with her sister develop—they're such close companions already—is a wonderful thing. So different to Ed's relationship with his own sister. And even with Derek. Susan's been granted the one thing that's rarely available to siblings—a fresh start. For the first time there is someone in his life whose familial loyalty is to Susan—and not him. And for the first time Ed has someone—another woman—with whom he can discuss his wife without feeling he has been in any way disloyal. Gillian's too distant—geographically and emotionally—and Ed's mother and sister are unlikely to proffer the necessary sympathy. There's Anna of course, but friends are different and Anna, in particular, tends to laugh at Ed, refuses to take him seriously. He can't imagine she would ever want to talk to him about Susan, senses that Anna would always know better, would pooh-pooh his perspective (if not be actively hostile). Now, if he ever needs such a confidante, he has one. He has Carly.

The article he'd read also mentioned the possible drawbacks of the extended family environment—the ganging up, the manipulation, the increase in family tension, the interference, the constraints, but he's certain that they've managed to escape these pressures, these difficulties. It takes a particular type of person to create such situations. And they're none of them that sort of person. He's sure of it.

Susan

Carly points out things that her younger sister doesn't see. Things she's never considered; that she doesn't want to consider, but, Carly insists, they're things Susan really ought to see; should consider.

The two women are walking through a local reserve with the children, late in the afternoon. They troop past a toilet block. Mitchell tugs on his mother's hand. 'Mu-um. I have to pee.'

'Well, go on,' Susan says, pushing him towards the men's. 'Just hurry.' He skips up the steps, narrowly missing a man who is exiting.

'Hold on, Mitch,' Carly calls out of the blue. 'Come back.'

The man looks up at them briefly, then hurries past, head down, hands in pockets.

Mitchell trots back obediently. 'What's wrong?'

'I wouldn't go in there,' Carly says. 'They're really dirty. Disgusting. Go behind a tree. It's much more fun, anyway.' The child is only too happy to comply, rushes off into the bush before Susan can interject.

'Carly, what ...?'

'Wait a minute,' she smiles slightly, 'and I'll explain.'

'Watch,' Carly looks towards the toilet block. 'There should be another one.'

'Another what?' Susan doesn't bother to hide her exasperation, her impatience.

'Shhh. Look.' A second man exits the toilet block, this one middle-aged, red-faced. He rushes away in the opposite direction.

'See,' Carly's smile is broad, satisfied. 'I was right.'

'Right about what?'

'God, Susan. Where've you been? It's a beat. Not a nice place for a little boy.'

Mitchell runs out of the bush grinning, fumbling with his fly. 'I weed on my shoes, Mum. I couldn't help it. They're all nice and shiny but.'

'What's a beat?' Stella asks.

'Just walk quickly, kids. Let's hurry up.'

'Like a drum, stupid,' Mitchell answers his sister. 'It's when you bang.'

Carly laughs, but Susan grabs the children's hands and holds them tight. Walks fast.

Another day a young woman rushes up behind them as they're walking down to the school together, pushes past without looking up or excusing herself. Carly watches, eyes narrowed. The woman is young, tall and thin, unnaturally pale, slightly stooped. She's wearing a short black skirt and leather jacket. Chunky heels.

'On the game,' Carly says, 'and on the gear.' She looks like a young university student to Susan, no different to any other.

'Around here? I don't believe you. How do you know that?' she asks her sister. 'How on earth can you tell?'

Carly rolls her eyes. 'How d'you reckon, Susy? I saw it in a movie once?' she knocks lightly on Susan's skull. 'Use those brains, honey. It won't hurt. Really it won't.'

One weekday when Ed is in town for a design conference, the two women catch the ferry to Circular Quay to meet him for lunch. The ferry is unseasonally crowded and Susan sits next to an elderly man, chatty and interesting. Interested. They talk about the weather, about the water, move gradually into more personal territory. The man, who introduces himself as Peter, asks Susan about the children—how old they are, their interests. He was a child psychologist, he tells her, is retired now, but still finds children infinitely interesting. He misses the everyday contact, the access into the singular child's-eye view of the world. He has none of his own—his wife couldn't—a minor tragedy. Though he makes every effort—once he realises that the two women are travelling together—to include her in the conversation, Carly does not speak to him. She sits across from Susan, feet splayed out casually, reads a magazine. Looks up every now and then. When Susan takes out her wallet in order to show the man a photograph of Stella and Mitchell, Carly drops her book, and as she leans forward to pick it up, knocks Susan's wallet out of her hand. 'Sorry,' she smiles sweetly at her sister. 'So clumsy.'

'A bit of big sisterly advice,' Carly offers as they disembark.
'What?'
'Don't talk to blokes like that about your kids.'

'What do you mean? He's a child psychologist. He was genuinely interested.'

'Child psychologist, my arse,' Carly snorts. 'I just hope you didn't have your bloody address showing in your wallet.'

'What do you mean? What's my address got to do with it?'

'Fuck, Susan. That bloke is a rock spider.'

'A rock spider? What are you talking about? What's a rock spider?'

Carly rolls her eyes. 'A pedophile, Susan. A bloke who likes sticking his prick in very small spaces.'

A woman in front of them turns, glares. 'Do you mind?'

'He's probably had to go for a wank after what you've been telling him about your two.' Carly is unrepentant, her voice louder.

'Shut up,' Susan hisses. 'Just don't say another word.'

'Sorry, lovey,' she says brightly, 'hate to spoil the party and all that, but this is the real world.'

The real world. Susan wonders why her sister is so suspicious. Wonders why she considers such sordid behaviour, such a squalid world, to be the real world. The more authentic world. She wonders, but doesn't dare ask. The truth is, she doesn't really want to know. Susan is certain that the world she inhabits is just as authentic. Just as real. And she wants her world to remain benign, doesn't really care what's lurking beneath. And even if the harmony of her existence is some sort of a facade—just a fantasy of comfort and ease, order and security that's camouflaging chaos—well, she doesn't want, doesn't need to know *that* either.

'Come on, Sue,' Anna says, 'normal people don't do this. Just up and leave their lives without a backward glance. How long has she been staying with you now? Four weeks? Five? She must have had another life. Why won't she tell you about it?'

It's Mona Vale Beach today and an easy walk—high tide early this morning and the sand packed hard and flat. The two women can walk fast and talk.

'Maybe there's nothing to tell me, Anna. She says she had no one. Nothing. Some crummy job in a cafe. What sort of a life is that? It's not really worth going back to, is it?'

'That's exactly my point. What sort of a person really has no life? She must have had something—a job, a car, a flat. Friends. A lover. Something.'

'It's not my business.'

'Why isn't it your business? Surely you've a right to know who she is?'

'When she wants to tell me ...'

'You'll be there? Christ, Sue, you're starting to sound like Ed. It's not normal. She's become too much a part of your life—too instantly—and you still don't know anything about her.'

'She's my sister!' Susan can feel her face heating up, knows it's not just exertion.

'Oh. So she's your sister. So what? Where's your common-sense gone, girl? You know what? From the outside, from where I stand, it really looks like she's using you. She's living with you, eating your food, I don't suppose she does anything to help, does she? Or pays for anything? Does she take the kids to school, cook dinner, clean the bathrooms? No? And I'll bet you've lent her money, haven't you? She's sucking you in, Susan, and I don't know why you can't see it. If she was an ordinary sister you'd have told her where to get off by now. Believe me—the whole situation—it's not normal.'

'I wonder,' Susan manages eventually, 'what exactly "normal" would be, under these circumstances. And how is it that you can make such a call anyway; what experience have you had, Anna, that makes you such an expert on my situation?'

She breaks into a slow jog, overtakes her friend, who shouts after her:

'I don't need experience, Susan. I don't need experience to see what's happening. You've got to ...'

Susan takes off, sprints, can hear only the wind of her own speed, the rush of the water.

Ed

'She's just a bubble burster,' Ed hisses. 'Always has been. She's always sticking her nose in, interfering. Someone ought to sort her out. Tell her once and for all to keep her opinions to herself. You can see why poor old Tom hits the bottle from time to time.' He manoeuvres his arm under his wife's back, pulls her over to his side.

'But Ed,' Susan draws away from him, wriggles into a sitting position, hunches over her knees. 'What she says isn't completely untrue. Carly's told us nothing about herself. She avoids answering any questions I ask. She straight out ignores me if I mention anything about the past. About Mum and Dad.'

Ed sighs and sits up beside her. 'Susy. Honey. We've talked about this. You've got to give her space. Give her time. Her past might be too painful to discuss with just anyone.'

'But I'm not just anyone, Ed, I'm her sister. I just wish she'd tell me why. That one thing at least.' He can tell that she's hurt, gives her a brief comforting hug.

'C'mon Suse. Think of it from Carly's perspective.'

'Oh, Ed. I have. I do. I really do, believe me.' She slides down and pulls the blanket up to her chin. 'I just think Anna's got a point.' Her voice is muffled. 'I think Carly's hiding something.'

He stays where he is. Wide awake now. Indignant. 'Jesus, Suse, I really thought you'd be a bit more loyal to Carly. To your sister. You should be telling Anna where to get off, not agreeing with her.'

Susan says nothing. Rolls onto her side away from him.

'She's your own flesh and blood, Suse. Your trust should be absolute, unconditional. The way you trust me.' He pauses for a moment, adds, 'The way *I* trust her.'

'She's not your flesh and blood, Ed,' Susan mutters. 'She's not your sister.'

No, she's not his flesh and blood. Not his sister. As he slides down beside Susan and grapples with her rigid form, he thinks how glad he is that Carly is his sister-in-law and not his sister, thinks how useful he can be to her, psychologically that is, in his role as disinterested observer. How glad he is that he can champion her without challenging other allegiances, without the complications of a shared history, shared trauma.

He cups his wife's breasts from behind, presses his groin into her warmth, feels her loosen, respond, thinks how well such detachment suits him.

There are not words in his vocabulary, and not in the English language either, Ed suspects, to describe the overpowering emotion—a mixture of love and passion and responsibility and tenderness—that he felt when he first held his babies. And although the intensity of those first moments can never been repeated, the quality of his connection with the two children has never diminished. His feeling for Susan has, he is aware, changed over time: he loves her, this is not in doubt, indeed his love for her is probably far more profound than it was in the beginning of their relationship. Even if the once all-encompassing nature of their sexual communion has lessened over the years, this is only because they have reached a higher level; are connected forever by their shared creation. Still, he is not overwhelmed by feeling for her in the way that he once was (those long ago days when his heart would constrict whenever she entered the room, when countless hours were spent mentally undressing her). In any case Susan does not need that sort of adolescent devotion from him—she is strong, self-possessed, self-reliant, would probably find it irksome.

He wonders whether it is partly the knowledge of the children's vulnerability, their undeniable, unspoken need of him that secures, has in fact created—in a neat illustration of the principles of supply and demand—his particular emotional response. Wonders whether what he feels for Carly might not be a similar sensation—brought on by what he knows is her particular defencelessness and vulnerability, the insecurity and uncertainty of her position. Along with her almost unconditional trust in him. It's remarkable how a need can be so easily, so effortlessly and so pleasurably fulfilled. Remarkable how the need can so quickly become mutual. He wonders and marvels at the strangeness of human relationships.

He has never felt like this about his own sister.

Ed has never had a real female friend. In fact, there aren't that many women in his life. Oh, there's his sister, Pam, but she lives a thousand miles away—in central Queensland—and the five-year gap seems never to have closed. She is bossy and critical, and in her presence he is boorish, becomes as callow as she anticipates. There is Cathy, his brother Derek's wife, but with Cathy's interests currently not extending much further than her own ever-increasing brood (she and Derek have four children under six; and a fifth on the way) there's been little opportunity for them to develop any sort of a relationship. Then there are the women he works with: Moira; and the office girl Trudy, who comes in on Wednesdays and Fridays to file, dust and run errands. He also knows a number of female designers and architects, but none of these could be classified as friends; these relationships are only casual, far from intimate, or, in some cases, highly competitive, tinged with vague resentment. They're not friends. There's Susan, of course, but that's different. She's his wife.

But now there's Carly. Despite her official sister-in-law status, Ed has no qualms about thinking of her as a friend also. She displays all the characteristics of a friend. She is easy to talk to, is interested in his opinions, in him. Unlike Susan, who is always busy, always semi-distracted by the children, a meal to be made, an appointment to be kept, who seems always to be walking out just as he's walking in, Carly is available. He can talk to her about anything. Anything. She is familiar with the situation at work—the conflicts, the personalities—and on a few occasions has helped to devise strategies for Ed to deal with Derek, difficult clients, the odd recalcitrant employee. She is genuinely interested in the work he does. Never displays a blank face, or yawns, but interrogates him in her charming way, demands to know more, more, more. Wants to understand. She even—and he is careful here, there are all sorts of loyalties, all sorts of boundaries that can't, that shouldn't, be crossed—listens to his concerns about Susan. And occasionally voices her own.

One night when they are the last up, are sitting at opposite ends of the couch watching television, Carly says, out of the blue: 'You're worried about something, Ed, I can tell. You seem tense.'

'Eh?' (Though now that she mentions it, Ed realises that the left side of his jaw is sore, that he has been grinding his back teeth, clamping down, clenching—always a sure sign of tension.)

'There's something, Ed,' she insists, 'something's really bothering you.'

'No, really,' he gropes for an answer, gives up. 'It's nothing.'

'It's Susan, isn't it?'

It's miraculous, the way she identifies his anxiety, knows what is wrong with him even before he has managed to articulate his concerns to himself. Susan. He shrugs, grimaces, gazes mesmerised as she moves up the seat towards him.

'You mustn't worry, Ed. It's just a phase. All women go through it. It's to do with having children. A friend of mine said that for years after her kids were born she felt nothing for her husband. She hardly knew he was there. That she felt distanced from everyone. Really detached. It's not depression or anything, at least only of the mildest sort. It's nothing serious. She's not going to harm herself. Or the kids.'

Carly is right beside him now, pats his hand gently. 'It's nothing to worry about, Ed. Just one of those things married men have to cope with.'

Ed believes he has read of this phenomenon somewhere or other, a sort of common, low-grade, postnatal depression—but was unaware that Susan was experiencing such feelings. The children, after all, are hardly babies anymore. Thinking back, though, he must admit there have been occasions (more and more frequent?) when Susan has seemed not only down, but switched off, unreachable. Until now he has put it down to a preoccupation with work, or the onset of her period, an influx of mysterious hormones; has offered only a minimal degree of support and sympathy, has indeed sometimes reacted impatiently. Has put it down to an inevitable increase in fractiousness, irritability, the taking-for-grantedness that characterises an enduring relationship like marriage. Has thought it a normal phase of married life. And no doubt this was the very worst reaction he could have had. The sort of a reaction that could only exacerbate any sort of depression.

He assumes that Susan has described her condition to her sister, feels sad momentarily that she has been unable to tell him herself. But really, overwhelmingly, he's simply grateful that she has a relationship with her sister now, an experienced, compassionate, older sister, a relationship that lacks all of the entrenched resentments of the past that he knows tend to bedevil most sibling relationships.

Carly is silently watching him, her hand still lightly covering his. He manages to dredge up a smile. 'Thanks, Carly.'

'I shouldn't have told you. I just thought ...' She bites her lip, looks away.

'No. Oh, no,' Ed turns his hand upwards in hers, grips her fingers tightly, 'I appreciate you telling me, I really do. Now that I know about it I can try and be more helpful, careful. Find a solution, perhaps.'

'Well, I've been thinking ...' her voice suddenly hesitant, slightly shy.

'What? Tell me.'

'Oh. It's not really any of my business. I'm probably being a bit presumptuous ...'

'Carly. No. You could never be presumptuous.'

'Well ... I've been thinking that maybe Susan's the tiniest bit ... bored. That maybe she could do with an extra day or so of work. I've noticed that she's always far more cheerful, far more—alert—when she's had some time ... away.'

'But...'

'Wait,' she squeezes his hand. 'I know you don't want the kids in childcare, you want them to be able to come home and all that—and they can. Remember I'm here now. I can pick them up from school. Help them with their homework. Get dinner ready. Whatever. And I'd be really pleased to be able to do something useful. To make it up to you both. To pay you back.'

Ed is moved, has to clear his throat before he speaks. 'Oh, Carly. You don't have to pay us back. You're part of our family, now. It's our pleasure. Our privilege.'

Carly

At first she is unnerved by their trust. They have no doubts, none whatsoever, none that she can discern anyway. Whatever she says, whatever she tells them, is taken at face value, is believed. Whatever she says is valued. They never question what she does, either. They trust her; they value her.

This is a new experience. New and intoxicating.

Susan

She is pleased but puzzled by Ed's suggestion.

Susan has made this same suggestion several times over the past few years. The temping service that Anna runs generally has trouble filling afternoon shifts—which is the shift Susan already works, prefers to work—and Anna has been begging her to take on the extra work for years now, but Ed has always insisted that her one day a week was sufficient, that they didn't really need the money. That the children needed her, their mother, available to them—the way his mother had been available to him. That the hours after school were probably the most important part of the day. That kids needed to unwind in a secure, loving environment. That they shouldn't have to spend long hours in institutional care. She mentions all this to him now, reminds him of his previous stance, surprised by his inexplicable about-face.

'But the children are older,' he explains (this has never provided a justification before; age, he had proclaimed, didn't matter—a sixteen-year-old was just as likely—more likely—to need to talk over the stresses of the day with a concerned and loving parent). 'It's not so important that you're always around now. And it's different, I won't have to leave work early—Carly has offered to pick up the kids after school, to get dinner ready, whatever we need.

'Anyway, I think it would do you good to get out of the house more,' he doesn't quite look at Susan when he says this, looks slightly off to one side. 'You need to—to re-establish yourself in the world. Make sure you keep up your skills, learn new ones. And you'd meet new people—it'd cheer you up.'

'What do you mean—cheer me up?'

She's perfectly cheered.

She phones Anna. Tells her she's available to work an additional evening a week.

'What's going on, Sue?' Anna sounds suspicious. 'I thought Ed was adamant about you only working that one day. Last I heard he was convinced that the children would become alienated, anorexic, self-mutilating delinquents if they were denied access to their mother for periods of more than an hour at a time?'

'Oh, you know, we just ...'

'And who's looking after the infants, Sue? Don't tell me they're being allowed to mix with the socially-stunted, emotionally-deprived after-school care kids?'

'Oh, shut up, Anna. He's not that bad. And I don't think that he really thinks they are deprived. The after-school care kids, I mean ...'

'Well, who's looking after them? Not Mamma Middleton?

Or has Ed made the business more family-friendly—has he arranged to leave work early?'

'No.'

'Then who?'

'Carly.'

'Oh. Carly.'

There is a long silence.

Then: 'Well, I can offer you a three-to-eleven at Delwood Private.' She's brisk and cheerful as always, but Susan can sense a wariness in Anna's voice, a withdrawal. 'Every Wednesday. How's that?'

They are walking the children to school. It's an easy walk—only a few flat blocks—and for once they are well ahead of time, the pace is leisurely, unpanicked. Stella skips between Susan and Carly, swings her aunt's hand back and forth, chatting away to the two women about this and that, her conversation like a spurt from a little bubbler. Mitchell walks a fair distance behind, stops frequently to examine bits of bark, insects, rocks. Already his pockets are filling up.

Susan takes advantage of a brief lull in Stella's chatter. 'Have you ever wanted kids, Carly?' It's another question she's been longing to ask.

Carly says nothing for a moment, then leans down and whispers something to Stella, who giggles and runs back to Mitchell.

'Sorry,' Susan is embarrassed suddenly. 'Maybe I shouldn't ask.' Although Carly hasn't said anything, and her expression gives nothing away, Susan knows she has somehow transgressed, that she has asked the wrong thing again. She resigns herself to a skilful deflection, an artless non-answer, but Carly surprises her.

'No, that's okay. You just startled me—asking out of the blue like that.' She considers for a moment, then: 'I guess I've never had the opportunity, Susy. No bloke whose gene pool I'd want to share.'

'Oh, I guess it's not ...'

She interrupts Susan's fumbling rejoinder: 'And to be quite honest, Sue, they're a bit of a bore aren't they? Oh, I don't mean yours in particular, but kids in general. A bit of a drag. They get in the way of—of *real* life, I guess.'

She looks over at her sister and smiles widely, as if to take some of the sting out of her words. But Susan's stung. She gropes for a reply, finds none. She turns back to hurry the kids, who've stopped, are squatting in the middle of the footpath, examining a particularly interesting mound.

Just for a moment Susan can't see them, feels her eyes fill, her vision blur. She shouts: 'Come on, you two,' feels her voice reedy, slightly tremulous. 'Hurry up, or we'll be late.' They keep their heads down, ignore her, poking at the mound with sticks now. She takes a deep breath, calls again, more forcefully. 'Come *on.*'

Mitchell gets up reluctantly, but hovers, while Stella skips towards them, her stick waving about dangerously, breaks into a run.

'Aunty Carly, Mummy. It's a dead mad-pie. Come and look. It's gross—there's blood and stuff and it's all hard like cement. And Mitch poked out its eyes. Come and see.' She pulls at Carly's hand. 'Come and look, Aunty Carly.'

Carly gives Susan a wry smile: 'Never a dull moment, is there?' and lets herself be led back down the street. Susan follows more slowly; wonders about real life, dull moments, early morning diplomacy.

She tells her out of the blue. Over lunch.

'I left because I was bored.' She says it casually, conversationally. Susan is not prepared; she chokes on her sandwich.

'You were bored?'

'Shitless.'

'That was it?'

'Yep. Sorry, Suse. There are no gory details, no skeletons in the family closet. Your father wasn't hitting me, Mum wasn't treating me cruelly—well, no more cruelly than most mothers of teenage daughters did back then—I didn't have a secret lover, I wasn't a drug addict. I didn't even mean to leave home. I set out for the dance, walked to the corner, kept walking. Didn't come back.' Carly butters a slice of bread, layers on ham and cheese, bites down hungrily.

'You were *bored*?' Susan shakes her head, can't quite fathom it. All the pain, all the waiting.

'Uh-huh.' Carly's voice is muffled, her mouth full. 'It's as good a reason as any for leaving home, isn't it? And better than some I can think of. I was just a pretty ordinary teenager, Susan. I just wanted to be left alone, y'know? Nothing complicated.' Swallows. Adds clearly, almost jauntily: 'So there you go, Susy. Now you know. Satisfied?'

Karen is going to see *Picnic at Hanging Rock* with her best friend Julie. Susan begs her and begs her and finally Karen agrees to take her along. The child is overjoyed, but her mother is not so happy. 'It's not a children's movie, is it, Karen? It looks a bit too frightening for Susy. I don't know.'

'Please, Mum. Please.' Susan is desperate. She's not that interested in the movie—though the pretty girls in long white dresses she's seen in the ads are appealing. But there's the ferry across the harbour and then the bus to the cinema; there's chips and Fantales and Coke and maybe a hamburger after. 'Please. I promise I won't get scared. I'll close my eyes if it gets really scary.'

'She'll be fine, Mum. We can always take her out if she gets scared.'

'Well, you take good care of her, then. Take good care of my baby.' Mum reaches down to give her a hug but Susan wriggles away, impatient to get going.

'I'm nearly nine, mum. I'm a big girl, not a baby.'

Her mother smiles, chucks her under the chin.

'Ah, but you'll always be my baby.'

It's a windy day and the usually calm harbour waters are choppy, and get gradually rougher as they chug between the heads. The ferry dives and plunges from side to side and Susan clings, terrified, to her older sister, convinced that they are going to capsize, to drown, to die. Karen prises the child's fingers from hers and tells her that she is to go with Julie, that Julie will take her upstairs. 'It's not as rough up there,' she says.

Susan grabs hold of Karen's shirt. 'But what're you going to do? Can't you come too? Please come.'

'No. Now, go on, off you go,' she says firmly. 'Julie'll look after you.'

Susan lurches up the stairs with the older girl, holding on hard to the rails. Even Julie looks a little worried, her face pale and slightly green. When they reach the top Susan forces herself to turn and wave to Karen, but her sister is standing in the gangway facing the sea and doesn't notice. She isn't holding on to anything, but braces herself, legs apart, head back, at one with the surge.

'Just sit back and close your eyes,' Julie croaks when they finally make it to a vacant seat, 'and then you won't see the boat move. You'll feel better, believe me,' she says, squeezing her own eyes shut, 'if you can't see what's happening.'

Susan has to keep her eyes closed tight, or peer between spread fingers through much of the movie, too, which is not about a picnic at all but about something terrible and terrifying and unknowable that takes the schoolgirls away or sends them mad. She tries to grab Karen's hand occasionally, when she's really scared, but Karen's like the girls on the screen, entranced, lost, transported. Mouth open, eyes shining, she pushes Susan's fingers away, irritably.

'Leave me alone,' she hisses, when Susan's desperate hands can no longer be ignored. 'Will you just leave me alone.'

Susan leaves the decision until the last minute, makes a sudden detour, doesn't tell her sister where they're going. Pulls up outside the empty house. Sits for a moment, breathing.

'What are you doing here? I thought we were going straight home?' Carly sounds vaguely peevish, put-upon.

'I just thought I'd like one last look before it's sold. The real estate guy said I could meet him here at two, he's showing someone through. We're fifteen minutes early, but I found a spare set of keys anyway.'

'Look at what?' Susan has worried that Carly might be angry, or unwilling. She seems merely bewildered.

'At the house, Carly. Mum's place. Our place. What else would I mean?'

'Oh, yeah,' she says quickly, 'the house ... I thought you meant something else as well.'

Susan walks down the hallway, pushes open the first door on the right. 'Your room, Carly.'

The room is empty, just a small square space with a sheet-covered window and worn shag pile carpet. Like the rest of the house this room smells sour—a combination of cat piss, unwashed clothes and stale food. Their mother or the tenants?

'Don't you remember, Carly, your beautiful dressing table? Right here. God, I was so jealous. Mum wouldn't let me near it after you left. Had it taken away. Carly? D'you remember?'

Her sister is silent, makes no reply, but Susan can't help it, she is desperate for a response, for some confirmation of shared memory.

'And that bedspread you had. Covered in pink roses. It was quilted—you know, I can almost feel the pattern. Remember how you used to fold it back so carefully? You showed me once. Three folds down then two across. I thought you were so clever. God. I'd forgotten all about that. Funny isn't it?'

'Hilarious.' Carly smiles vaguely, stands fingering the dusty sheet, then thrusts it aside, unlatches the window. 'God, this place is stuffy,' she says, pushing at the bottom sash. We should open everything up.' The window is reluctant, shrieks. 'Let in some bloody air.'

The agent, a sleek young man in a too-shiny double-breasted suit, arrives before his clients and is immediately overcome by a fit of sneezing, is unable to greet Susan in a dignified manner. Carly's open windows have stirred up months, maybe years, of dust. He walks quickly through the house, handkerchief at the ready, peering and tapping, scribbling now and then in a notebook he produces from his inside pocket.

'We haven't actually shown this place yet,' he explains. 'These'll be the first lookers. Glad you're here. You might be able to tell me a few things.' He trails along in Susan's wake as she walks through the house, asking occasional choked questions. ('When was the wiring last done? The plumbing? The gutters?') In the back bedroom, Susan's old room, he interrupts his scribbles, frowns out the window.

'Who's that out there?' he asks. Carly is wandering about in the garden, absent-mindedly breaking off twigs, rubbing leaves between her fingers.

'That's my sister,' she tells him.

'Your sister? Truly?' He shakes his head, disbelieving.

'Truly. Why?'

He moves closer to the window. 'God,' he mutters, 'I could have sworn ...' He turns back to face her. 'Sorry,' he says, 'but it's just that she looks like someone ...' His cheeks are slightly pink, his voice creaks slightly. 'I ... er ... met once. But it couldn't be her.'

'Well,' Susan says, 'maybe it is ... but she's been away for years. We've actually only been reunited recently. It's been amazing ...'

He interrupts. 'What did you say her name was?'

'Carly.'

'Carly?' He breathes out heavily. 'Carly. Christ.' He starts up his coughing again.

When Susan introduces them in the front garden, he shakes Carly's hand quickly but is unable to look her in the eye. Carly doesn't seem to notice, gets straight down to business. 'So?

What's the verdict? How much?' she asks. 'And how quickly?'

'Houses here are selling fast, it's a desirable suburb. The surf. The laid-back atmosphere. It's still seen as being family-friendly, the local shopping centre's big enough, but intimate too, if you know what I mean. There's a sense of community.' He directs his reply to Susan, still avoiding Carly's gaze.

The house itself isn't great, he tells them, but it isn't too bad, and if they wanted to give the interior a coat of paint and a good clean it'd be beneficial. But even in its current state he'd expect a sale somewhere around the early eights, purely because of the enormous block. The home could be knocked down—it's perfect for flats, dual occupancy ... They could get more if they changed their minds and were willing to go to auction.

'What do you mean by early eights? Eight one? Eight five? Eight thirty? And how long?' Carly's voice is brusque, impatient.

'Eight forty-five, I'd say. Six weeks. But, really, you should consider an auction.'

'Oh,' she says slowly. 'Oh. But we don't want to go to any of that fuss, do we Suse?' Carly's voice has lightened considerably, is casual, cordial. 'We just want to get rid of the place as quickly as possible. It's not the money. The money's not important.' She turns to her sister for confirmation. 'Is it, Susy?'

'No, not important at all,' Susan's echo goes unheard, she may as well not have spoken.

The man's attention is all with Carly. 'Money's not important?' He's looking at her directly now. Is looking hard. 'I haven't heard that line for a while,' he says. 'Not for quite some time.' He runs his fingers through his too-shiny hair, smirks unpleasantly.

'I don't suppose you would,' Carly smirks back, 'doing what you do. You can't run a car like that,' she gestures towards the flashy black BMW that he's parked in the driveway, 'on hot air, can you? And it isn't a line, anyway, mate; it's the truth. There are some people out there,' she adds helpfully, 'who don't do lines. You should try to remember that.'

Carly

It is a shock, a big shock, to meet someone she's known from her previous life. It wasn't something she'd counted on, not something she'd expected, but in the end not something to get too anxious about. There are plenty of ways to persuade people to keep quiet. And all sorts of payments, not all of them involving money.

Not all of them unpleasant.

Ed

'What will you do with the money?'

'What will I do?' Ed is surprised by Carly's question. He never asks questions about other people's money—considers this one of the most personal of personal questions—and a vulgar one at that. Ed knows that talking about one's own financial situation is equally taboo: that this can only be construed in one of two ways: either bragging or, what's worse, complaining.

'Yeah. I mean it's not like you really need anything, is it?' Carly yawns and stretches her arms behind her head. Surveys the room. 'You've got everything you could possibly ever need. All the material things.'

Ed looks around, trying to see it through a stranger's eyes, the eyes of someone who hasn't much in the way of personal belongings. Ed doesn't consider himself particularly materialistic, as being overly concerned with accumulating things, but he supposes that this would not be obvious to everyone. They do seem to have an overabundance. Good cars, quality clothes, a decent stereo, two televisions, a personal computer, an SLR camera, a pile of videos, mountain bikes, a substantial collection of books, an oversupply of children's toys.

The house itself: oh, it's nothing flashy, a 1930s brick bungalow, but it's solid, respectable, comfortable, and (his heart still contracts with pride when he turns into the drive) it's his.

Theirs. Inside, everything is neat, clean, in good working order. The kitchen with its sleek, high-gloss colours, granite bench tops, mid-range European appliances, is efficient without being merely utilitarian. The lounge room with its Persian rugs, chintzy sofas, his favourite Heidelberg School prints on the walls, is warm and welcoming as well as tasteful. The bathrooms (two shared; one ensuite), newly renovated, are unpretentiously stylish. The bedrooms are cosy—as bedrooms should be—and are kept in order: beds made, clothes and toys packed away, with built-ins for this purpose. There is no peeling paint, no worn carpet, there are no holes in the walls, no door handles hanging loose. And Susan is a committed and talented house-wife, the house is clean as well as tidy: there's no dust, no grime, no cobwebs or cockroaches. To Ed it is just as a home should be—simple, comfortable, harmonious—but he can imagine that to someone like Carly it would seem fantastically luxuri-ous—like a home out of one of the glossy magazines.

'I guess we do have more than we need,' he says thoughtful-ly, 'but they say you can never have enough money. For long-term security.' Then in answer to her question: 'I guess we'll pay off our mortgage. Maybe we'll take a trip overseas. Or buy a four-wheel-drive and head into the centre for a month or two. I wouldn't mind a dinky little Bose stereo, or a bigger television. Maybe we'll use some for private schools when the kids get to high school—it depends on whether they get into the selectives. I guess there'll be enough left over to invest. Maybe enough to get some sort of decent return ...' Ed pauses, is momentarily ashamed of his obvious acquisitiveness. When there were peo-ple starving. 'What about you?'

Ed is breaking his own rules now, has never even summoned the nerve to question his own parents' financial situation. He's certainly aware of how much he and Derek paid their father for additional shares in the business, but as to the rest he's in the dark. He supposes his father has a substantial super fund—hopes so anyway. But with Carly the question hardly seems out of place or intimate. And anyway—she asked him first.

'Oh, I don't know. What I'd really like is what you have, a big old house like this. But I won't have enough for that, will I?'

'No,' he is stung by the wistfulness of her voice, 'No, not quite.'

'Maybe a smaller place then. A terrace in the city? Maybe I'll go back to Melbourne. A place somewhere. It'll be better than anything I've had, anyway. And it'll be mine.' She pauses for a moment. 'It's not the stuff, you know. It's not the stuff you can buy with money—the house, the car, the furniture—that's nothing. I guess it's the life that I'd like. A life like yours and Susan's. The whole thing. But it's not going to happen, is it? I've missed out on all that, haven't I?'

'Oh no,' he says, 'don't say that.' Her resignation is suddenly unbearable. Unthinkable. Ed rushes to reassure her. 'Anything could happen, Carly. You never know what's waiting for you in this life.'

She breaks into a grin. 'Never say die, eh?'

Ed blushes. 'I know it sounds corny, but it's true. Anything could happen.'

'Sweet Ed. Susan's a lucky girl. Such a sweet man.' Her smile is gentle, warm, all for him. He feels himself fiercely hot, and for one glorious moment, lost.

Susan

Carly watches her with the children. Just the everyday interactions, nothing out of the ordinary—the constant round of nagging and nurturing. Says: 'You're good at this, aren't you?'

'At what?' Susan is busily cutting a row of paper dolls for Stella, who is jigging up and down, barely able to contain her impatience.

Carly waves her hand around vaguely. 'Oh, you know. All this mother stuff.'

'Oh. That. It's like breathing. Nothing to it.' She passes the concertinaed figures to her daughter, who opens them out slowly, her eyes wide, awed by the unexpected magic.

'Maybe. Guess I just haven't seen it in a long while. Brings things back.'

Susan tries hard to sound casual. 'Reminds you of Mum, I guess?'

'Of Mum? Our mother?' Carly snorts, rolls her eyes. 'You never give up, do you Suse?'

Carly

Some questions she can answer honestly.

Did you ever think about us after you left? Did you wonder about us? Did you miss us? Did you ever regret leaving?

Never. No regrets. No guilt.

End of conversation.

Ed

It's been a long time since Susan came surfing with him. In the beginning, the first few years (was it years, perhaps it was only months, or weeks?) he had taken Susan with him, had tried hard to share his passion with her. Initially, in that first flush of love, she'd wanted to learn, wanted to understand what it was that Ed found so pleasurable—had perhaps even been slightly jealous (Ed's surfing frequently meant early rising, long absences, less time spent together, depending on tides). At first she'd been as eager to learn as Ed was to teach. (Living so close to the ocean— and you've never surfed!) But it hadn't taken Ed long to realise that the wonder of this experience, like so many personal experiences, just couldn't be so easily transmitted, that Susan (and there was no blame attached here, indeed he could only be flattered) was only doing it for him, that she had no—and would never have—real insight into what it meant. What it was. That to Susy it was at best a source of discomfort and boredom, a chore.

She told him she just couldn't see the point: all that effort, all that sitting, waiting, either frying or freezing, just to ride for one terrifying moment on the back of a wave before crashing ignominiously, and sometimes painfully, only to start again. She'd learnt enough—could discuss tides and wave formations, had understood enough surfing jargon to make intelligent comments, informed enquiries.

Ed would never admit it, but in a way he's relieved when Susan's (professed) interest wanes, is happy to leave their shared experience of the beach to the odd weekend swim, family picnics. The beach is his own space, as he sees it, the only space that is his alone, unshared, where he is under no pressure save that applied by nature. It seems only other surfers (mostly blokes) really understand the inherent solitude of the experience—even when they're out there together, sharing the wait, the wave, they're essentially alone.

Ed's love of surfing is almost the only thing in his life that he does not try to analyse. Oh, he buys the occasional surf magazine (just for the photographs, he tells a bemused Susan), and he and Derek discuss technique, exchange the odd story of great waves with surfing mates; but as to what surfing means to him—this he has never attempted to delve into too deeply. Sometimes when he's out the back waiting for a wave, *the* wave, and he is overwhelmed by it all—the sky, the surf, the breeze, his body tingling with an aliveness and anticipation that he feels nowhere else— he imagines that this feeling, of wanting to be part of something rather than insisting, always, on separateness, on control, is what religious types mean by spirituality. That perhaps spirituality requires the sort of merging into a kind of nothingness, the relinquishing of consciousness, the absolute surrender to sensation that he experiences when he's surfing. Ed doesn't ponder this seriously, however, takes it no further. He is afraid that if he tries too hard to understand what the surf means to him, it will evaporate, disappear like his adolescent faith in God.

But now with Carly, it's completely different. He's surprised she's never surfed before—she's a natural, takes to it, like—well, like a duck to water. It seems that in only a few hours—he takes her out on a Wednesday afternoon, and then on the following Thursday, and now, on the Saturday evening—she's up and moving through the water like a pro. Or at least she's surfing competently. He's impressed and tells her so.

'Oh,' she shrugs, 'I guess I've always been good at water sports. Always thought I'd like to surf, but never really had the opportunity. Not much surf where I grew up.'

'You mean once you'd left home?'

'Yeah, well, I mean obviously I could've surfed when I was a kid—I guess we didn't take advantage of it back then. Girls, I mean.'

'No. I guess girls didn't really surf much back then. Different now.'

Ed's surprised by just how much he enjoys surfing with his new sister-in-law. Somehow, Carly's naturally attuned to the unspoken 'rules': she doesn't make conversation, doesn't expect compliments, reassurance. After a while her proximity feels as necessary as the ocean itself. He begins to avoid surfing in her absence—he looks forward to the sight of her black clad fig- ure straddling her board beside him, silent, confident, cool, the wind whipping back her hair. The look of intense concentra- tion when she's paddling in anticipation, the slight triumphant smile when she's up, the bark of laughter, flick of wet hair when she emerges, the rueful humour when she's dumped. For the first time in all his years of surfing, Ed's mind is on other things.

There are confidences from Carly, too. And Ed—who instinc- tively understands her reticence, knowing how reluctant she is to bother him and Susan with the sordid details of her past—is pleased and proud that she trusts him so. He's circumspect, the soul of discretion. He knows that Carly is particularly unwilling to have Susan disturbed, so though it pains him greatly (when has he ever kept anything from his wife?) he doesn't pass on any details. He's certain that she only needs time—that eventually, as she gets to know Susan better, the sisterly confidences will come. Right now, though, it's not a warm and sympathetic ear that Carly needs but a detached, objective listener. It's not the guilt-tinged, complicit, too-responsive sympathy that Susan would offer, but the sort of cool-headed, disinterested compassion Ed knows he can provide.

He has thought himself a man of the world. He studies the paper, watches the news, reads magazine articles. He has a fair knowledge of the harsher side of life; of that other world where events do not run smoothly, where nothing is easy, where life is cheap, where the forces are darker, the consequences harsher. Though his own existence is in some sense cocooned from all this, he has friends and acquaintances—social workers, nurses, doctors, even several police officers—whose stories of a world, worlds, where love and kindness don't exist have occasionally made him reflect on his own good fortune, the immense privileges afforded him and most of his friends and family—perhaps at the expense of not-so-lucky others.

'There's something I should tell you,' she says one night, when they're alone together. 'Living here and you—you both being so kind. Something you should know. About me.'

Carly's muted the television, turned to him out of the blue. Ed's been going through the company's accounts, he looks up at her, blinking, surprised. He clears his throat, makes his voice as warm and reassuring as he can: 'Whatever it is, it doesn't matter. It's not my business. Please don't think you have to ...'

Her expression checks him.

'You should know,' she says, 'you have children, you may want to ... to protect them.'

Ah, God. He imagines HIV, hepatitis.

'Oh, it's not a disease.' As always, she guesses the direction his mind has taken. 'I'm clear of all that—though I hardly know how. I don't deserve to be.'

'Oh, don't say that, Carly. Nobody ...'

'Wait. Let me tell you first.'

He is silent. Waits.

'I guess you know that there's a certain scenario, when a young girl leaves home at such an impressionable age, certain things usually happen. Not just these days, either, it was just as bad—maybe even worse, because it was so hidden, so secret—back then.'

Ed knows. He reads the papers, watches television. He gives a slight, encouraging nod.

'Well. I guess you could say I did everything.'

'Everything?'

'Oh you know, drugs, crime, prostitution ... the whole bit.' She says it so lightly, and Ed tries to take it just as easily, but he is nevertheless shocked, can think of nothing, nothing at all to say. It seems, however, that Carly does not expect him to say anything. She goes on: 'And prison, Ed. I've spent a few years of my life inside.'

'Why?' Ed's voice is strangled, comes out a whisper, 'What—did you do?'

For the first time she appears to struggle. 'Look,' she says finally, 'I'd rather not—there're some things—some things I'd rather not talk about. I just wanted you to know. And to tell you that I'm clean now, completely. That I haven't touched junk for years.' Her smile is crooked, wry. 'But look—if you'd rather I left—hey, it's cool, we're still friends, I'd understand. Just say.'

'Oh, God,' Ed gushes, desperate to make his support clear, he hates to think he's given her the wrong impression. 'Look—I'm honoured—I'm really honoured that you've confided in me. It wouldn't have mattered, you know. You needn't have told me and don't worry, it won't go any further. Not even ...' he gulps, 'not even Susan. I don't—don't care about your past. I know I'm speaking for both of us—Susan and I—when I say that we really love having you here. Having you in our life—part of our family. That we'd love it if you'd stay—as long as you want.' At this point he extemporises, goes beyond anything he's discussed with Susan, goes out on a limb: 'We'd love you to stay longer, even after the house business is all sorted out.'

Carly is transparently, nakedly grateful. And relieved. 'You're such a good bloke, Ed. You really are.' She reaches over, kisses him gently on the lips. Briefly. Casually. 'I can't imagine what I did to deserve a brother-in-law like you. Susan's one lucky girl.'

She's settled back down at her end of the lounge, is aiming the remote, has transferred her attention to the screen, almost before he's had time to react, time to respond. Ed sits upright, his hands gripping one another, his heart pounding. Sisterly affection, he tells himself. Nothing more. He runs his tongue over his lips. Tastes musk, tobacco, pepper. Just sisterly affection.

Carly

Quite often she lets them fill in the blanks. She finds that sometimes it's easier, much easier, to let people believe what they want to believe.

Susan

It's rare that her sister asks Susan anything about her life—she's generally strangely distant—completely uninterested. She's never asked any questions, for instance, about the photo gallery that lines their hallway. Susan has taken pictures down, has pointed out this person, that event. *Here, look Carly, it's Stella, when she was first born; our wedding photo—see how Mrs M has muscled me out of the way, how she's next to Ed in every single shot; here's Mum's school photo—do you remember this?—she was cute wasn't she? Pity we didn't take after her*; but regardless of the content of the photograph, Carly's interest is never more than that of a polite stranger—not that of an aunt, a sister, a daughter. She never starts any conversation with a personal enquiry. So Susan is struck by her sister's sudden interest in her marriage.

'It's fascinating to me,' she says, out of the blue.

It is ten in the morning, the kids have been packed off to

school and Susan is clearing up the breakfast chaos: wiping benches, stacking the dishwasher. Carly is sitting at the table flicking through an old copy of *Who Weekly* magazine.

'It's absolutely fascinating to me—marriage. You read a magazine like this and it's bizarre—eleven out of ten Hollywood marriages fail, and yet they all keep doing it. They're all crazy. What actors do you know who've stayed married to the same person for any substantial period?'

'Well there's ... um. There's Goldie Hawn and what's his name.'

'I don't think they're actually married, but okay. Any others?'

'Hasn't Harrison Ford been married for years?'

'Well, to his second wife. Come on!'

Then—'Oh, I know: Joanne Woodward and Paul Newman.'

'Come on—they're dinosaurs.'

'There's ...' Susan shrugs, concedes defeat.

'Hard, isn't it?'

'Well ... I'll bet there are some we just don't know about.'

'Yeah, but they're obviously outnumbered by the ones we do know about: Roseanne, Elizabeth Taylor. Julia Roberts.' She folds up the magazine. 'Well, you're the expert on happy marriages, Sue. How long've you and Ed been together now—is it more than ten years? So what's the secret? There must be some secret to it, some sort of method to your madness?'

'There's nothing. We ... we just love each other, I guess.'

Carly laughs. 'Oh, come on. Love. What crap. You must have something *on* each other. Something that keeps you together. Some skeleton in the closet.'

'There's nothing like that, Carly. You've got such a dirty mind ...'

'But it's unreal, Sue. Nobody lives this way.'

'What way?'

'This Doris Day life that you lead. Real people just aren't this—this wholesome.'

'We're just average suburban people, Carly. We're normal.'

'Normal? He must hit you.'

'Ed? Hit me? Don't be so stupid.'

'Maybe he's a cross-dresser; a serial killer; a rapist. Maybe he's gay and deep, deep, deep in the closet—with a mother like that, I wouldn't be surprised.'

'Oh, come on, Carly. You have to learn to take people on face value. Not everyone's got something to hide. Sometimes what you see is what you get.'

'Bullshit. There's always something underneath. And if there's nothing—well, maybe that's even worse.'

Later, Susan thinks perhaps there's something to Carly's observations. In some sense she and Ed *are* unreal. Their lives have been relatively easy, their only hardships, their only difficulties so minor they barely register on the scale of possible human suffering. Their life together has been too smooth—Life Lite. Like a fairytale life, a life lived happily-ever-after. Only after what?

And then she wonders vaguely, what happens next?

Ed

On Friday nights, Ed cooks. Susan usually takes the opportunity to get out—sometimes she'll go for a walk in the late afternoon, or a swim; this evening she's at the gym. The kids are in front of the television, Carly's in the shower. Ed opens a bottle of wine, gets started.

He dons an apron, clears the benches, sharpens his knives. First, he chops the vegetables precisely. Broccoli florets are split down the middle so they are all close in size, the stem is completely discarded. Beans are topped and tailed, stringed, cut on the diagonal. Garlic, coriander and chilli are minced and scraped into nifty little ceramic bowls. Chicken fillets have been sliced thinly, the wooden chopping board scrubbed immediately in hot soapy water. The shrimp paste has been carefully weighed. Cucumber has been cut at a regular angle and a consistent thickness. The rice has been measured, sits waiting for the water (measured precisely, boiling to just the right degree).

The tin of coconut milk has been opened, the correct quantity poured into a jug. The oil in the wok is heating up. Ed leaves nothing to chance.

He likes to cook dinner at least once a week. It's important, he feels, to engage in such tasks, not only to relieve Susan of some of the heavy responsibilities of nurturing, but to provide a role model for Mitchell. His own father has never cooked a meal in the kitchen—oh, like most Australian blokes, he's a whiz behind a barbecue, but Ed thinks that it's all too likely that Mr Middleton Senior has no idea how to light his own oven, and that he wouldn't have any idea of what to do once it was lit anyway. Ed is determined that Mitchell gets an entirely different view of the male sphere, that he realises that despite the choices he and Susan have made in regards to public and domestic work, these are not the only options. He wants Mitchell—and Stella—to be flexible, to regard male and female roles as largely interchangeable, to consider neither one nor the other as more exclusive, nor more prestigious.

He has been preparing the Friday night meal since he and Susan were first married. Even so, he has developed no real sense of cooking. He always tries to make something delicious, something different to the general run of workaday meals—not bangers and mash, but an exotic curry, or a rich pasta dish—but no matter how often he prepares, for instance Thai green curry (a family favourite), he still follows the recipe to the letter. Never improvises; never makes even an educated guess. He uses the cups, spoons and scales—measures each portion carefully, double-checks—he is as meticulous as a chemist mixing a medicine. And on the odd occasion that Susan suggests there is something missing, something additional required—an extra clove of garlic, the addition of chilli, salt, tomato paste, fish sauce—he is immovable, refuses to follow her advice, sees it as gratuitous interference, stubbornly continues to follow the recipe zealously.

By the time Carly joins him in the kitchen, the preparation is all done, the ingredients sit neatly lined up along the bench in order of use. Ed turns, pink-cheeked with exertion, and smiles in response to her greeting. 'Wow!' she stands smiling, hands on hips, eyes wide. 'You're so organised.' She has showered and changed—she's wearing striped Indian-cotton pants that flare slightly at the bottom, a low-cut black singlet. Her hair is damp, silky around her ears. Her feet are bare, and Ed notices that her toenails are painted a semi-transparent blue that matches her eyes. She looks younger than Susan, not ten years older. Carly gazes around the kitchen in wonder, gives a great gusty laugh.

'I thought Susan was a bit anal, but you take the cake. My God, Ed, I've never seen anything like it.'

He is not sure about her laughter, knows that in the kitchen he is slightly absurd, his management skills gone mad.

'So what can I do to help?'

'Nothing. You can just relax. Have a glass of wine. I only have to throw all this together now.'

She laughs again. 'Throw? I can't imagine it, Ed.' She stands close beside him at the bench, investigates the contents of each bowl.

She smells good as always, a clean musky scent that he recognises but cannot place, it's quite different to any perfume of Susan's, darker, heavier, it overpowers even the shrimp paste. He is aware of her scrutiny as he pours carefully measured herbs and spices into the waiting blender.

'What're you doing?'

'I'm grinding them into a paste. For curry.'

'Ed. Don't you have a mortar and pestle?'

'Well, yes, I think so. But that's so messy. And I've never done it.'

'Since when has that been an excuse not to do something? There has to be a first time, you know, Ed.' Carly takes the blender jug from his hands, places it gently on the bench top.

'What do you mean?' Ed is slightly bewildered, now she's behind him, unknotting his apron, sliding it up and over his head.

'You just find me that mortar and pestle, Ed, and I'll let you

into a secret. Some of the best meals are the ones that are messiest to make, or the ones you've never made before.'

'But ...'

She places a finger on his lips. 'Shhh. Just watch.'

'Okay. Fine.' He digs around in a drawer, hands over the
mortar and pestle.

Carly empties the contents of the blender into the marble
dish, starts grinding, Ed leans back against the bench to watch.

'It's a metaphor for life, really, isn't it?' She pauses in her
work.

'What? The mortar and pestle?' he thinks quickly. 'You mean
they represent male and female ... organs?'

'No, silly. Not the mortar and pestle. I mean cooking.' Carly
dips her finger into the bowl, touches it to her tongue.

'Cooking's a metaphor? I'm afraid you've lost me, Carly.'

She dips her finger again, offers it to him. 'Well—in the same
way that the messiest experiences, the most unexpected experiences—the things you've never done before ...' his lips part, he
takes the offering, a delicate brush of finger on tongue, '... are so
often the most satisfying.'

Ed chokes, splutters, his throat burns, eyes water.

'Oh, dear. Too hot for you, Ed?'

He shakes his head helplessly, gulps his wine. Carly goes
back to her pounding.

'We'll have to do something about that, now, won't we.'

Susan

'D'you think you could lend me some money, Suse? Just until
everything's sorted out? There are some people I have to pay ...
bills ... and no income, at the moment. You know.'

'Oh God, Carly.' Susan feels immediately guilty, is pained
that her sister has even had to ask. That she didn't realise, didn't
know. 'Of course.' She reaches for her handbag. 'How much?'

'How much can you spare?'

She scrabbles through the bag, pulls out old dockets, telephone bills, letters, finally locates her chequebook. 'How much do you need?' Fishes for a pen.

'A couple of grand would probably tide me over.'

'Oh ... two?' Susan starts to fill out the cheque details, but Carly stops her. 'Not a cheque,' she says. 'I can't do anything with a cheque, Sue. I haven't got a bank account.'

'No bank account?' Enquires without thinking, 'How on earth do you survive?'

Carly raises her eyebrows. 'There are still places where people don't need all this,' she takes in her sister's handbag, the mess on the table, the kitchen full of shiny chrome appliances, with a bemused glance, her sideways smile, 'all this to survive, you know, Susan. Life can be lived without a bank account. Maybe just not life as you know it, eh?'

Susan shoves the chequebook back in the bag.

'I'll organise cash,' she says quietly. 'Sorry.'

Saturday morning has always been Susan's big clean up day. It's not that the house is ever really messy—or even untidy: she's a painfully conscientious housekeeper. (Too conscientious, insists a more relaxed Anna, who once presented Susan with a small beaten copper plaque she had had especially made. *A Tidy House Is The Sign Of An Empty Life*, it read. Though she disagrees entirely with the sentiment, and the implied assessment up of her character—it hangs proudly above the kitchen door, in full view.)

Ed is always a little bemused by the traditional Saturday clean—his mother, he says, never seemed to do such a thing. The house was just always clean. Susan has pointed out that this apparently seamless housekeeping actually requires endless effort. Bathrooms, kitchens, carpets, windows, refrigerators are never actually allowed to get dirty—because they're in a constant state of being cleaned.

The kids are tidying their room—a frustrating and largely

futile process involving a great deal of encouragement and overseeing from Susan, endless reminders, repeated threats (there will be no McDonald's tonight, Stella, if you don't pick up those Barbies) as the children discover items of interest, dress-ups, toys that have been hidden from view, that they are meant to be clearing up, putting away ready for the vacuum cleaner.

Cleaning is not Carly's scene either, and usually she takes herself off for the day, but today for some reason she has stayed behind, has volunteered to help out. She has dressed for the occasion in overalls and has her hair tied back in an old scarf. Ed, after his usual guilty prevarication, has gone for a surf.

Susan does the kitchen and bathroom, while Carly has taken charge of the lounge room, dusting, vacuuming, straightening and realigning rugs and furniture. When Susan passes through the room, Carly is tidying away the teetering stacks of CDs and movies—matching case to disc—that seem to have accumulated on every surface overnight, and is down on her knees in front of the stereo cabinet.

'Jesus Christ, Susan. There's some crap here. This is awful. Unbelievably bad. How can you listen to this shit?' She pulls out disc after disc. Elton John, Toto, Cold Chisel, Simon and Garfunkel, Crowded House, Celine Dion … 'Fu-uck. You should toss the lot.'

'Hey,' Susan pounces on one in Carly's pile—*Carly Simon's Greatest Hits*. 'What about this?'

Carly glances at the cover, makes a face. 'Can't handle that boring crap. Never could.' She pulls out a Pearl Jam album left by Derek after some family gathering. 'Now this I don't mind …' she looks up and sees Susan's face. 'What? What's wrong? What did I say?'

'Don't you remember? That Carly Simon album. I thought that was why …?'

'What? I've told you there's stuff I don't remember. Half my life's a blank.' Carly's voice is brusque, impatient.

'But this is different.' Susan is indignant, insistent. 'I only have this album because it's one of the few things I do remember. About you. That you had this record. You played it over and over again. Sang along. "You're so vain". "Mockingbird". It's not something you'd forget.'

'Tastes change, Sue, you grow up. I don't remember it. It's no big deal.'

'But I thought that was why—why you chose that particular name. Carly. I just assumed you'd named yourself after Carly Simon.' Susan waits. Carly takes a moment to respond, speaks softly.

'Well, maybe that was why I chose the name. In the beginning. I wouldn't know, I can't remember. I just know I can't stand that shit now.' She shrugs and turns away, indifferent. Slides the Pearl Jam disc into the player, turns it up loud.

Carly

Sometimes she's amazed by the ease of it. She has them worked out almost immediately—they're so easy to read, so transparent: she knows when to embroider and when to omit; when to manufacture—and what. When to remain silent. This last especially. It's her particular strength, you could say. She's always been good at improvisation—she's had to be.

Ed

Ed is startled by how easily Susan adjusts to using her sister's new, her preferred, name. It's easy for him, of course, he's only ever known her as Carly, but for Susan, well, he'd expected a few more slips.

Ed takes the whole business of names very seriously. Ever since the births of his own children he's been fascinated by the sometimes eerie correspondence of name and character. His own name, Edward, is an old English name that is generally said to mean either rich guardian or guardian of prosperity. His mother, he knows, had no notion of the name's origin—he was simply named after his great-grandfather, one Edward Robertson, a saddler from Bathurst.

He'd been uneasy with Susan's choice of Mitchell—tradionally a surname, had preferred Matthew—and had only been persuaded by Susan's reassurance that Mitchell came from Michael, meaning 'who is like God' which, though perhaps a little too biblical for his taste, at least meant something. (And that first child—was there anything more god-like, really? Was there better evidence of a supreme being than the firstborn?) Stella—Estelle—had been his choice—and as he'd predicted, as he'd hoped, the name thoroughly suited his daughter's radiant personality, her twinkling soul. Somehow only Susan's name is an awkward fit with her personality.

Susan is an anglicised version of a Hebrew name, a lily, and however hard he tries, however he angles for a correspondence, Ed can't find a connection. He buys his wife lilies, rather than the usual roses, regularly—and in this way has attempted to manufacture a correspondence, impose a connection. His sister-in-law's names—both of them—seem entirely appropriate: Karen, her original, her real name, means pure, while Carly is Latin, means little and womanly, and, when combined with the Teutonic male name, Carl, means strong. Pure. Little. Womanly. Strong. The combination of definitions encapsulates those aspects of Carly that most characterise her, quite miraculously. There's a perfect, an almost divine symmetry.

When as a younger man he'd first investigated the etymology of his own name, he'd been a little disappointed—being defined as a rich guardian is hardly a romantic or powerful proposition, and it wasn't something he particularly aspired to. But as his responsibilities expanded—first Susan, then the business, and the children—he'd felt the weight and significance of the role, and now he can feel himself growing into it, as if fulfilling the requirements of his name. He *is* a custodian, a trustee.

And he's recently come across an extended definition—one

that's less pragmatic, more esoteric. Evidently, Edward is also a guardian of the mists—which is far more suggestive and contains a significance that is still waiting to be revealed.

Susan

Last Christmas, while holidaying together down the south coast, staying in adjoining cabins, Anna had told her about an affair she'd had, years ago. It was late in a boozy evening, husbands and children asleep, the two women sitting alone in the dark.

'It was crazy,' Anna had said, 'and totally unexpected. It was when we were first married, just after I'd had Jimmy, when Tom was still young and handsome and successful—the world his oyster, the world at his feet. But it had nothing to do with Tom himself—or even what I actually felt about him. It was me, I think. And this fellow—his name was Jake, he was younger than me, our mechanic, for Christ's sake, there was nothing to him really, he was a bimbo—but he made me feel—well, something I hadn't felt for a long time. He made me feel desirable. Young—though of course I was young—only in my early twenties. And when it happened,' she says a little unsteadily, 'it just had to happen. There was nothing I could do and no way of stopping it. Even though I knew it was wrong and that I would probably regret it, it just had to happen.'

Susan can remember being shocked, dismayed, and uncertain how to respond. Eventually she'd asked: 'And did you—do you—regret it?'

'The funny thing is,' Anna had answered, 'I don't. Put me back there and I think I'd do it again. Funny, isn't it? I read this report once—they asked some old people in a nursing home what they most regretted in their lives—the most common answer from the old men was that they were sorry they'd cheated on their wives, that it had ruined their relationship, destroyed their marriages—that it wasn't worth it. But for the women it was different—they regretted that they hadn't had affairs.

Regretted their faithfulness ... We're a weird lot, aren't we?'

Susan was not only shocked, but was oddly put out by the confidence, afraid almost. For if such a thing could happen in Anna's world—steady, sensible, focused Anna—what lay in wait for her? Perhaps the fortifications Ed and she had so diligently built up, their insurance against just such an event, wouldn't be secure. Wouldn't be enough.

She has avoided thinking about the incident with Howard Hamilton—easy enough with so much going on, so much to do—so when he rings and says merely, 'Howard here,' Susan has to think hard for a moment.

'Howard Hamilton,' he repeats, 'your solicitor.' Suddenly there is a strange constriction in her chest; a warmth spreads throughout her lower limbs. She angles her body away from the kitchen table, where Ed and Carly sit chatting, sipping Sunday morning coffee, cups the receiver close to her ear.

'Howard,' she says quietly, 'Hi.' Her heart pounds.

'How're things?'

'Fine. Yes. Things are fine. Absolutely fine. Great.' She can feel the gush gradually becoming a babble; pauses abruptly, takes a deep breath.

Hamilton's voice is calm, measured. 'I think it's time we got together again for a meeting. There are a few things we need to discuss, and I need your signature on some documents.' A brisk, businesslike enquiry. 'How are you placed tomorrow morning?'

She doesn't stop to think, to consider. 'That'll be fine.' In fact she has no idea how she's placed; right now it's possible that she has no idea of the word's meaning.

'Say nine-thirty?'

'Yes. No. I mean ... the kids: I'll have to get them to school first. How about ten? Will that be okay?'

'No worries.' Casual, so casual. 'See you then.'

He disconnects before Susan can say goodbye. Before she can compose herself. She keeps the phone to her ear, the line buzzing loudly, for a long moment, returns the phone to its cradle reluctantly. She can feel her cheeks crimson, her ears burn; she keeps her back to the table, busies herself clearing the bench.

'Who was that?' Ed's interest seems vague, cursory.

'The solicitor. Howard Hamilton. He wants to meet me tomorrow morning. To sign some things.'

'Just you? He doesn't need me?'

'No. Just me.'

'You don't want me to come?'

'I don't think so ...' She turns, dishcloth in hand, gives him an encouraging smile: 'Unless you want to, Ed?'

'No, no. I'm sure you can sort it out.' Ed sounds relieved.

'What about me?' Carly asks suddenly. 'Why doesn't he need me? Surely if you have to sign papers, I'll have to sign them too?'

'He didn't say he needed you.' Susan makes her voice as neutral as possible, though she can feel her cheeks hotting up again. 'So I guess not.' Carly is watching her closely, looks slightly amused. 'I've no idea what it's about; what he wants.' Susan shrugs and turns back to the washing up, suddenly flustered.

'Strange,' Carly's voice is low, almost a murmur, 'you must have a good relationship, you and that solicitor. First time I've heard of a solicitor phoning to make an appointment on a Sunday. He'll probably charge you double for the call.'

Carly

They say that sometimes it is only when a cancer is diagnosed that that the cells divide and spread. Left unnoticed and undisturbed, a tumour may remain dormant for years, decades, sometimes only discovered post-mortem and even then not the cause of extinction anyway.

Susan

Before Carly's return she didn't think about her life too much, too intensely. After all, with the two kids, the house, Ed, the garden, work, friends, busy busy busy—who has time to think? And even those rare moments of reflection never involved much in the way of regret. Oh, perhaps she wondered vaguely whether she should have married later, worked harder, been more ambitious, travelled further, that sort of thing. But any doubts, any long-harboured unsatisfied desires were indistinct, fleeting—and probably had more to do with how she felt others saw her than how she really perceived her life. In truth, Susan had come to the happy conclusion that she was an immensely fortunate being. That she had everything she needed. Everything she wanted.

Lately though, since Carly's return, her reflections have become slightly more complicated. She still acknowledges that life has provided her with everything she needs, but how, she wonders, how do we ever know exactly what it is that we want? How do we even know who we are?

Lately she wonders, really wonders, who she is.

When she was younger, surely she was more certain of herself. She thinks that before the kids she was somehow more solid, more substantial. More like Carly—vivid and alive. Now, she feels herself shadowy, like a light that's been dimmed, as if she's not quite switched on properly. She has heard other, older women talk about finding themselves invisible, feeling their own desires swamped by others' endless needs. Her own mother, for instance, was expert in inducing a guilt-provoking awareness of this—of being ignored, taken-for-granted, of little consequence. Susan has thought for years that this was justified in a way—that her mother's personality had required this quenching. Somehow she hasn't noticed her own dimming, her own increasing invisibility. She can't see Ed—or indeed any man that she knows—suffering from this peculiar phenomenon, however. Ed is not fading. If anything, Ed is becoming more and more himself. And it's Carly, she knows, Carly's vivid presence that's made her aware of her own diminishing, her increasing blurriness. She feels like a fading sepia print. And soon, soon she'll be all but invisible.

There are parts of herself, aspects of herself that she can list: she is Stella and Mitchell's mother; she is Edward Middleton's wife; she is a nursing sister.

She is good at all these things, she knows that. She is a loving mother, a good and loyal wife, a conscientious nurse. She tries hard; she does her best. But still she's not sure what it all adds up to.

All of a sudden she isn't quite sure who she is.

She arrives late, flustered as always by her inability to find a park. Howard's secretary looks up from her frenzied typing to give Susan a withering smile, tells her that Mr Hamilton delayed as long as he could, but had another client to see ... if Susan's prepared to wait now, perhaps she can be squeezed in. Alternatively, she can make another appointment, for say, Wednesday week. The secretary frowns at her monitor, jabs viciously at the keyboard. 'Mr Hamilton's a very busy man.'

There is no squeezing. Howard ushers her in with a smile, ignoring his secretary's tut-tutting, the scheduled client's impatience. He offers Susan a chair, and takes the seat beside her rather than the one behind his desk.

'Sh-it.' He sighs as if exhausted, glances at his watch, 'It's only eleven and already I've had enough.' He yawns, grins. 'How about you? Guess you've been going since half past five, or some ungodly hour?'

'Oh, it's not quite that bad, they sleep in a bit these days.' She gives him a tight, polite smile, isn't quite sure how to behave, what's expected, what she wants to happen.

'You forget they grow up ... eventually. Now, I've got you here ...'

She interrupts nervously: 'About the other week—the barbecue. I really want to apologise—I'd drunk an awful lot, and was very emotional to start with. I don't want you to think ...'

'Shhhhh.' He stills her hand, which is anxiously beating a pen against the arm of the chair. 'It's okay, Susan. Really. These things happen. All forgotten. This is strictly business. Just a few more bits and pieces for you to sign. They're for the real estate agent—you're the signatory—not Carly.'

'Oh. Okay.' She feels unexpectedly deflated, disappointed.

'Though, I wouldn't want you to think that I didn't find the—moment—very pleasant ...' he says it so casually, half laughing, but doesn't quite meet her eye.

'No. I ...' Her voice catches. His hand is still covering hers, his thumb absently stroking the soft skin between thumb and index finger.

'Because I did,' he clears his throat. 'And if you, if you ever need, well, anything, really ...'

'Anything ...?'

'You've only to ask.'

Now, here, with this man, Susan feels herself again. Feels more real than she has felt in a long while. When he touches her—even the slightest contact, even a movement in the air between them—she suddenly knows that her heart is beating, her blood is pulsing, oxygen is moving in and out of her lungs. She is aware, for the first time in years—it seems almost as far back as she can remember—she is aware that she is alive.

Ed

He likes to wait up for Susan on the nights that she works. It means he gets less than his required eight hours, but he knows he won't be able to sleep anyway, not until he knows she's arrived home safely. He likes to be there too, just in case she wants, or needs, to talk through her day. To debrief. Though of course she never does.

Like many long-married couples, Ed and Susan have stopped talking. Oh, there's the kids and money and family affairs to discuss, but really talk—somehow they've lost interest. Ed looks back fondly on those early post-coital talkfests, where they'd be awake half the night sharing their every memory, fantasy, ideal—wonders what happened. What changed. Now they're usually both asleep within seconds of hitting the pillow, never mind post-coital. It's almost as if there's nothing more to know. Ed realises that this is what most marriages come to—and that it is, if you stop to think about it, one of the really good things about a long-time partnership. The growing ease of the relationship. Becoming Darby and Joan.

Now, on the nights that Susan is away, Carly waits up with him. He appreciates her company. And her conversation—which is always new, always interesting, always unpredictable. Even when they don't talk, even when they just sit together and read, or watch television, Ed enjoys her quiet presence, takes pleasure in her just being there.

This night, a Wednesday, Susan's second shift for the week, they have hired a video, a French film, a recent release. Ed has been looking forward to seeing it—the movie has had favourable reviews, won prizes, has come highly recommended by the video store staff (who are usually reliable in their judgements), but fifteen minutes into the film Ed has had enough, is exasperated with both plot and character.

'What a sleaze,' he says loudly. The main protagonist is an adulterer, is cheating on his beautiful and blameless wife, and Ed finds it impossible to muster the required sympathy for the man. 'What a dickhead. This is bullshit.'

Carly pauses the film.

'D'you want to watch something else?'

'No, sorry. For some reason it just pisses me off. Blokes like that. Getting away with it! What an arsehole.'

'What do you mean?' Carly seems genuinely interested in

his reaction, rather than irritated by the interruption.

'Well—all that screwing around, and there're never any real consequences for blokes like that. We all want to fuck around, y'know, but some of us just manage to control ourselves. Why turn him into a hero? You know it'll all end up okay. That somehow he'll manage to have his cake and eat it too.'

Ed isn't quite sure why he's so worked up, why on earth he feels so strongly about a fictional character. The moral consequences of adultery are not something he's ever thought into that seriously—why would he?—but it makes him genuinely angry tonight.

'I don't know, I've always thought that it's kind of courageous.' There is a hint of laughter in Carly's voice, but he takes the comment at face value.

'Courage? Come on, Carly—surely there's nothing even remotely brave about doing what your hormones, your animal instincts, tell you to do!'

'No. It's not that, Ed.' She pauses, considers. Then: 'I think it must be like being an explorer, or an astronaut. You're going somewhere new, unknown. You could end up seeing things— your whole life, everything—differently. That's pretty scary. You might find out you're not the person you thought you were. That you don't really want what you've got. I don't mean a serious, a serial adulterer, but a guy like this one. When it's a one-off kind of thing. The guy who loves his wife, but does it anyway.'

He groans. 'That's the most feeble excuse I ever heard. But I'll pass it on. I know a few blokes who'd really enjoy that one. Don't know that their wives would, though.'

Carly shrugs. 'Just a thought.' She hits the play button.

Ed laughs, but watches the film with a slightly different attitude. He wonders whether Carly's speaking from experience.

Adultery as exploration.

He manages to get through almost two hours without once mentioning Carly. To hold out until midway through their fourth beer.

Ed and Phil have discussed the usual things—work, politics, kids, the Wallabies' latest triumph—and have reached that stage of the evening where long reflective pauses are involuntary, and discussions of a philosophical or personal bent, inevitable. When Phil suddenly interrupts his musings on the infrequently discussed positive ramifications of globalisation to ask him how the sister-in-law situation is progressing, Ed is more than pleased to digress.

He tells Phil, who seems genuinely interested, how close Carly and Susan have become. How the children have taken to her. How all their lives have changed—and for the better—since she moved in. How full of admiration he is for this woman. What she's been through. How she's survived it.

'You know, Phil,' he says slowly, 'I thought things were good before. That what we, that what Susan and I had was enough, was all I needed.'

'But?' Phil's eyes are wide.

'But having Carly around has really changed things. She's made me ... made us,' Ed has to grope for the right words, '... see things in a new light. A new perspective.' He leaves it there, knowing that he has failed to explain his existential revelation clearly to Phil, that he can't even explain it to himself.

Phil snorts, pulls his chair in closer, hunches over the table towards him.

'Mate,' he says softly, conspiratorially, 'you know what I think?'

'What?'

'Ed, mate, don't think I'm judging you, and don't take this the wrong way, but I think you ought to cut through all this relationship enhancement bullshit and just face it.'

'Face what?'

'Ed, it's so bloody obvious, mate. You're dying to get into her pants. You want to fuck her.'

Ed is staggered. His indignation renders him momentarily speechless. Fuck her? Fuck his wife's sister? He'd swear the thought had never crossed his mind.

Susan

Aunty Di is not a real aunt, but an old friend of their mother. Her only friend, really. Her youngest daughter, Joanne, had been a classmate of Karen's, and Di stayed in contact over the years, sending Christmas and birthday cards, and was one of the few people to attend their mother's funeral. She has found out, somehow, about Karen's return and has called excitedly several times, made wistful comments about how much she'd like to meet her, how lovely it would be to see her again. Carly is initially indifferent, unmoved. 'I didn't like her when I was a kid,' she says, 'why would I want to see her now.' But finally, after a plaintive card arrives, welcoming her back into the fold, she reluctantly agrees to Susan's suggestion that they invite Di over for morning tea.

'Why,' Aunty Di says to Carly now, her massive bosom heaving from exertion and emotion. 'My dear, I'd have recognised you anywhere. Anywhere. You've hardly changed. Oh, dear.' She dabs at her eyes, sits down heavily. 'Oh dear!'

'And you, Aunty Di,' Carly sits beside her on the lounge, pats her arm. 'You're still exactly the same.' As Susan moves into the kitchen to make the tea, she can hear Di laugh weakly at this.

'What's ten stone in twenty years? Between friends? I'm still the same inside, anyway. And they say that's what counts.'

When Susan comes back with the tray the two women are chatting happily. What's strange,' Carly is saying, 'is that I hardly remember anything. And what I think I remember, Susan's forgotten.' She looks up at her sister for support. Susan nods her head, pours the tea.

Aunty Di purses her lips, nods. 'It's true,' she says. 'I find the same thing with my children. They seem to only ever remember the dreadful parts of their childhood. Not the lovely times. Not the parts I recall. The parts I treasure. And there were plenty of them. And now with you coming back, Karen, Carly, I have to admit I had a hard time remembering what exactly you looked like. I had some sort of a picture in my head of course, but when I tried to—get it into focus—I found that I just couldn't. That I really couldn't. I spent last night going through all my old snaps, looking, but Jo's taken all her old school photographs. So until I saw you today I really didn't have any idea of what you looked like. Now that I've seen you, of course, I remember perfectly well.' She beams at them both, reaches for her tea. 'You must be so pleased,' this to Susan, 'it must be wonderful to have her back. To have a sister again.'

'When I think of you, Aunty Di,' Carly murmurs between sips, 'I always think of a red dress you wore once. You were going out—you and Mum—a movie or something, I can't remember what, but I always think of that red dress.'

Aunty Di frowns, shakes her head. 'No. It's no good. I can't remember ever really going out with your poor Mum—I just remember being too busy with the kids to ever go anywhere, or do anything much. Anyway, we were always complaining about our hard lots—I do remember that. It seems to be the odd little details that you remember as you get older, but so many of the larger events disappear. It's sad, really, isn't it?' She beams, dunks her biscuit.

'I rang Jo when I heard that you were back,' Aunty Di says. 'She was just so excited. And she'd love to see you again. She teaches primary school, has just had her first kiddie, Jason. Six months to the day, now isn't that a marvellous thing? D'you remember what a time she had getting pregnant, Susan? You were a sensible girl, to have them so young. But poor Jo—she waited too long—ten years it took them, poor old Jo was having injections, she was so miserable—and it cost them an arm and a leg. And now when finally they've got their beloved baby, all of a sudden the whole thing's falling apart. Her hubby says he can't handle the responsibility, that he didn't really know what he was getting into. He's always seemed a nice enough fellow, he's something in computers, don't ask me what, it's all a bit beyond me; but you never know, do you—what people are really like—not when push comes to shove?' She wipes at her eyes again. 'Deary me. It's a hard life for you young things. Having to work so hard just to have a roof over your head—and then it's all just as likely to go up in smoke anyway. Never getting time to have any kiddies, let alone see them.'

Her round face is suddenly grim. 'It was a terrible thing, you know, Karen,' she goes on, her voice serious now, all the earlier lightness completely gone, 'a dreadful thing that you did. It didn't just affect your immediate family, you know. All the girls in your class were questioned by the police. Awful it was. They had my poor Joanne in tears, something about some man she'd seen you with. They made her go down to the station, sign a statement. I can't quite recall the details, but I'm sure it was something about some fellow in a red car. She had nightmares for weeks after, you know. It was a dreadful time. We all thought you'd been abducted. Murdered.' She shudders as if even the memory is too much. 'You know that, don't you?'

Carly murmurs something unintelligible, looks away.

'And what it did to your mother.' Aunty Di sighs, shakes her head. 'That poor, poor woman. Losing a child like that. And then her husband. Not that you could really blame him, I suppose. She just never recovered. How could you do it to her?' Di doesn't wait for an answer. 'It was a terrible, terrible thing that you did. The worst thing that could happen to a mother.'

They are silent. All three women look down, away. Di is the first to move. She clears her throat, then smiles as if to lessen the effect of her words, reaches for another biscuit, gestures to Susan to refill her cup.

'Anyway,' Di's voice is determinedly cheery, 'that's all in the past, isn't it? No point in going over it, is there? Crying over spilt milk. Can't change a damned thing. Now tell me, lovey,' this to Susan, 'how's that handsome husband of yours? Funny fellow isn't he?' she says to Carly, eyes twinkling. 'So serious. So intense. But nice looking. Reminds me a little of that English chappie, what's his name? It's not his looks exactly, but there's just something about him. His chin, perhaps.'

'Richard Burton?' Susan offers, mindful of Di's vintage, 'Laurence Olivier?'

'Oh, no, no, no,' she is giggling girlishly, her cheeks quivering, 'much younger than that. He was in all the papers and on the telly—in trouble for doing something unmentionable with a prostitute in a taxi.'

Carly and Susan look at one another. Laugh. Hugh Grant? Ed?

When her taxi comes they both offer to walk Aunty Di to the car. 'Dear me,' she says, 'I don't need you both to hold me up. I'm not *that* old.'

She turns to Carly, gives her a hug, pats her cheek. 'Now, I'm sure you've got better things to do, Karen. I'll see you soon, I hope, and I'll get Jo to give you a ring. It'd be lovely for you girls to catch up. You were such good friends.' Her dismissal is obvious, but kindly.

Susan and Di make their way slowly down the footpath, through the gate. Di struggles to lower herself into the taxi, huffs and puffs as she fumbles with her seatbelt, while Susan pushes the door shut, steps back onto the footpath.

The window winds down and Di leans out. 'I'm glad you've got your sister back,' she wheezes. 'It's good—to have family. Can't live with em, can't live without em, I always think. But Susy,' she reaches out and grasps Susan's wrist, her plump face anxious, 'don't trust her. She seems nice enough—and much livelier than I recall. Good fun. I remember your sister as a nice girl, a good girl, but she couldn't have been, could she? No good person could do what she did to your mother. Dreadful. Just dreadful. That poor woman. You should be careful. Don't get too—attached.'

'Aunty Di,' Susan starts, 'I'm sure Carly had ...'

'And that stuff about the red dress. Rot. Utter rot. Never wore red in my life, was always told it would clash with my hair.' She frowns, gives her stiff, grey curls an absent pat.

'But Aunty Di ...' She tries again.

'No, no, enough of that.' She's beaming again. 'You enjoy having your sister back, deary.' She lets go of Susan's wrist and taps the driver on the shoulder. 'But don't trust her. Not as far as you can throw her.'

Ed

It is remarkable to him, a thing of wonder and mystery, genetics.

Ed marvels at the way his daughter's tiny hand carries the shape of his own—larger, coarser, certainly, but still recognisable. Or his son's eyes which seem (somewhat dauntingly) to contain Ed's own mother's expression at certain moments. Lately, Ed has caught glimpses of his father (whose face is plumper, less defined than his own—or so he'd always thought) staring back at him from the bathroom mirror.

He likes to imagine the endless chains of DNA connecting him backwards and forwards in time and, on bad nights (when he wakes up, heart pounding and soaked from some black dream of death), this image of connection never fails to give him some comfort. Now Ed is certain that he can see similarities between the two sisters.

'There's a sort of family resemblance,' he says, looking from one to the other during dinner. 'Nothing specific—not eyes, or nose, or mouth, or hair or bodies. It's hard to say what exactly. But there's something. And I can see Carly in Stell, too,' he says.

'In Stella?' Susan looks dubious, and he knows that she's only thinking of the most obvious elements of their daughter's appearance. Stella is dark-haired, dark-skinned. Short but round, sturdy. A cherub. Her features are small and contained and solemn.

But Carly takes him seriously, the way she always does, pauses in her eating, looks over at Stella thoughtfully. Stella slurps her spaghetti, heedless of their regard. 'I guess,' Carly says, 'I was little and stocky like that as a kid, but that's the only thing I can see.'

Ed is disappointed that Carly doesn't recognise—and he was so sure she would—the body part that she shares with his daughter. With their hair pushed back it seems unmistakable. Both his daughter and his new sister-in-law have funny little close-set ears. He cannot point it out himself, it seems too intimate, suddenly, that whorled and curling part, that soft pale space above, tender skin behind. He shrugs, agrees.

'Yeah, that must be it.' Carly smiles, resumes eating, but Susan is gazing at him, frowning, and he blushes, though he doesn't know why.

'No, you weren't.' It takes Ed a moment to realise that Susan is addressing Carly, not him. 'You weren't at all stocky as a kid,' she says. 'Neither of us were. I've got photos of you, and you were like me. Skinny. Bony. The kids are both like Ed physically. Nothing like us.'

Carly shrugs. 'Memory's a strange thing,' she says casually. 'Especially mine.' She laughs suddenly (oh how he enjoys her sudden bursts of merriment). 'And people's ideas about resemblances can be vee-rrry strange. Like today, what Aunt Di said about Ed and Hugh Grant. Will you tell him or should I, Suse?'

Both women are chuckling now, look first at one another and then at him, laugh again. The children are smiling expectantly, only too willing to join in.

'What is it? What's so amusing?'

Now, with the full force of their combined humour directed at him, he can feel their similarity strongly, even if he can't see it. He enjoys the sensation, feels warmed by their affection for one another, for him, waits for them to share the joke, laughs along with them without knowing why.

Later, Ed studies a photograph of Hugh Grant taken from a magazine, inspects his own face in the bathroom mirror, searches for the resemblance. After all, Susan's Aunt Di has recognised it—has thought it worth commenting on. And, though both Susan and Carly clearly regard it as a hilarious comparison, completely undeserved, he cannot get it out of his head that there must be something significant in his appearance, something—a look, an attitude—that he shares with the infamous philanderer.

He looks at the magazine image again, and then at himself. Surely not. Ed imagines that he can actually see the weakness in Grant, that he can read it in his face—the way he has sometimes imagined a sign of approaching mortality in photographs of those who died tragically young. The actor's mouth is soft, loose, slightly petulant, his expression vaguely shifty, his chin lacking definition. Ed's jaw is square, his lips full and firm, his hair thick and springy, his eyes clear, set well apart. There is no resemblance, none at all. She's confused him with somebody else, surely.

III

Carly

You say you want to know about my life? About what I've done, where I've been, who I am? I say you don't. I say you don't need to know. I say you can't know.

Look at this—look at you—at your world. It's a world I know about. A world we all know about. Tree-lined streets, picket fences, happy children riding their bicycles up and down well-kept footpaths. Wall-to-wall carpets. Air-conditioned cars. Summer holidays. Happy marriages. Baked dinners. Stories before bed. Flowerbeds and cocker spaniels. Wholesome breakfasts. Burglar alarms. Nutritious packed lunches. Ensuites and built-ins. Please and thank you. The smell of jasmine. The buzz of lawnmowers on long weekends. Piano lessons. Remote-controlled garage doors. Fire insurance, car insurance, life insurance, insurance insurance. Chats over the back fence. Library books. A glass of red with dinner. The whites washed separately. Plastic bag-lined garbage bins.

That's the main thing, isn't it?—all the garbage is put in plastic bags here—that way you can't see it, can't smell it, don't have to think about it. All that mucky stuff. Just seal it up and someone else will take it away.

But you don't know, do you? You don't actually know where the garbage goes.

That's the difference, you see. The difference between us. I know. I know what happens to the garbage after you tidy it away.

Susan

The young real estate agent rings to let her know that he has an interested client. That a young couple have taken a contract and he's confident they'll be collecting the deposit in the next few days. Susan comments on the speed of the sale—the house has been on the market for less than a month.

'I reckon you could've asked for more, Mrs Middleton. For another, say, sixty-five grand, and you'd still have sold it, no worries. It was a bit of a bargain, y'know. And then if you'd sold it at auction ...' he adds regretfully.

He tells her he can organise the rest of the business with their solicitor. There'll probably be some documents to sign, the contracts and so on, but he's pretty sure that the lawyer has power of attorney anyway.

'That's right,' says Susan. 'I probably don't have to really be involved.'

'Yeah. I probably should have rung him first, but I just thought you'd like to know ...'

'I'm grateful. Thank you.'

There's a lengthy pause.

'Well, thanks.' She wonders what he's waiting for. 'You've done a great job. We're really pleased ...'

'Look,' he interrupts, 'it's probably none of my business, but you said that was your sister, right? That woman who was with you when you went through the house?'

'Ye-es ...'

'Well, you know how you said she's just moved here from Melbourne?'

'Yes.'

'Well, I'm certain that I saw her in Sydney, not so long ago. Maybe—oh—around three months ago.'

'Well, perhaps she was here ... She just hasn't mentioned it. I'll ask her if you like. Where did you see her?'

'No, no. I don't want you to tell her.' He sounds panicked.

'Look, this is kind of awkward.'

'What is?' Susan is nonplussed, has no idea where the conversation is heading.

'Well, it was at this bucks night. We'd organised this—um—this girl for my mate.' He clears his throat. 'A girl for the night. You know what I mean.' His extreme embarrassment is obvious, even over the phone.

'A girl?' Suddenly she understands. 'Oh. That sort of girl.'

'It was a high class kind of escort agency. Expensive.'

'What's that got to do with my sister?' Susan is in a hurry, is getting ready for work, and is really not in the mood for confidences from total strangers.

'That's the thing, you see. I don't know why I'm telling you this, it's probably not important. None of my business. But the girl ... we took a few photos, just so he would remember, you know, the experience. And I checked them after I met you both that day.'

'And?'

'Well, it's her. Your sister.'

'Who is? I don't understand what you're trying to tell me ...'

She can hear him take a breath. 'The girl we hired for the night. It was her. It was your sister.'

'My sister? I think you must be mistaken ... People can look so different in a photo, you know. My sister's never ...' she trails off, can't finish the sentence.

'No, look, I'm sorry. It wasn't just the photo. I recognised her, and I'm pretty sure she recognised me too. You see I'm certain of it—I couldn't really get it wrong if you know what I mean ...' he clears his throat again.

'Well, no, I don't know. I'm sure you could ... get it wrong. After all the—the girl was for your mate ... I don't suppose you really saw her for that long?' Susan's voice is tiny, the frightened squeak of a hunted mouse.

'The thing is ... I did. I mean my mate, the groom, he didn't want to, he wouldn't ... Anyway, we'd paid for her, couldn't get our money back.' He takes a deep breath. 'So, in the end we drew straws. And it was me. I won. Look, I don't want you to think badly of me—I don't have a girlfriend or a wife or anything. I wasn't cheating on anyone, and we'd paid our dough, it was only fair ...'

He pauses, obviously waiting for Susan to say something, to excuse him, perhaps, but there's nothing she can say.

'So I couldn't really mistake her, could I? It'd be hard to mistake someone you've been so—so intimate with.' His voice seems a little louder, more confident, slightly belligerent, she can imagine his chest swelling a little. 'In fact, you could say I know your sister pretty intimately.' He adds darkly, 'Better'n some, anyway.'

'Well, um. I guess I should thank you for that information.' She's polite as she can manage, 'So thanks very much.'

'Yeah, but that's not the only thing. There's more.'

'More?'

'The thing is—she took off with my wallet. I'd just had a big win on the pokies, and there was more than a thousand bucks cash in it ... and all my credit cards. I rang the agency when I realised, but she'd done a runner that night. She'd been using a false name anyway, so there was no way of catching up with her.' He sounds almost apologetic.

Susan can think of no way of answering this, ponders hanging up.

'Anyway,' he says briskly, 'the whole thing's pretty seedy, I guess, and I'm not going to rake things up, go to the police or anything, but I thought you probably ought to know, having kids and all that. Just thought I ought to warn you. You never know, with people like that, do you? Where they'll take you? What they'll do.'

Susan's not sure what to do with this information. One minute she thinks it could be true, the whole squalid scenario, the next that it's impossible, the most outrageous libel, that she should contact someone—the man's boss, the real estate commission or whatever organisation keeps these people under control; even the police. But then, what if it is true, what then? So she keeps it to herself, doesn't mention it to Ed, certainly doesn't mention it to Carly. But she tells them about the possible sale, later that evening. Watches Carly's face carefully when she passes on the young real estate agent's certainty that they could have got a little more.

'I wouldn't listen to that little sleaze,' she says dismissively, 'Doubt he knows what day of the week it is. He doesn't have a clue.'

'Oh,' Susan keeps her voice even, casual, her expression deadpan. 'I thought he seemed pretty smart. And cute. I don't know why you think he's a sleaze ...'

Her sister snorts. 'No. I guess you wouldn't, Susan. Why would you?'

Ed

Moira puts a call through to him. 'It's your sister-in-law,' she says.

He wonders why Cathy is ringing him, worries that something may have happened to Derek, or perhaps his parents, then wonders how she would know before him anyway.

'Ed.' It takes him a moment to realise that it's Carly—they've never spoken over the phone—but her voice is unmistakable, that husky burr. His own voice deepens in response.

'Carly. Hi. How're ...'

'Ed, look I'm really sorry, but Stella's broken her arm. She fell off a slippery slide at the park. We're at the hospital—Manly. In Casualty.' She's suddenly breathy, anxious.

'Oh, shit.'

'I think you'd better get down here now. They're talking about surgery. I've rung Anna, but she hasn't been able to get hold of Susan yet.'

'Oh, shit.' Ed has a meeting scheduled at four-fifteen and the

client is travelling all the way from Penrith. It's too late to put
him off.

'Ed?'

'Sorry, Carly. I'll be there. Fast as I can. Fifteen minutes, thirty maybe. Depends on the traffic.' Almost an afterthought: 'Is it
a bad break? Is Stella okay?'

He grabs his coat, his briefcase, tells Moira the news on his
way out.

'Go,' she says, shooing him out the door. 'Go. And don't worry,
this guy's got a mobile, it'll be fine. Hurry, she'll be needing you.'

He hurries out to his car, checks himself in the sun visor
mirror. Pats at his hair, straightens his tie. He tells himself that
it's his anxiety about his daughter's broken arm, that it's the
overwhelming fact of the thought of his daughter, his baby,
broken, in pain, in danger, that and nothing else, that is making
his heart pound, his breath come faster. She'll be needing him.

He reverses too fast out of the factory driveway, has to swerve
to avoid an oncoming truck.

The poor little thing—she'll be needing him.

Susan

It is after seven before they manage to contact Susan, and by the
time she arrives at the hospital Stella is already out of surgery,
in recovery. Stella's ulna had dislocated and her radius has frac-
tured badly enough to warrant a plate. It's hard to get any clear
idea as to what actually happened—Carly has taken Mitchell
to Ed's parents for the night—and Ed is vague, isn't quite sure.

'Carly said she fell off the slippery dip, I think. But Mitch
said it was the fireman's pole.' The surgeon has recommended
an overnight stay.

'I'll stay with her,' Susan tells Ed as they wait outside recovery
for Stella to regain consciousness. 'She'll only need one of us.'

'Perhaps it should be me,' he says half-heartedly. 'You stayed
over when Mitch had gastro. I guess it's my turn.'

'Ed. Go home. Honestly. What good would you be? I'm a nurse, remember.'

'Well, I should at least wait until she's out of recovery. What if ...?'

'Go now. She'll be fine.'

'Really?' He sounds doubtful, but is obviously relieved, eager to be gone.

'Really.'

'Should I bring you anything? Change of clothes, a book, toothpaste, pyjamas? Food?'

'Nothing. I've already eaten. And I can just sleep in what I'm wearing. Just go home and relax.'

He hugs her briefly, hurries away.

When Stella's wheeled back to the children's ward Susan hovers nervously over her daughter, listens to her drugged mutterings, watches closely as she drifts in and out of consciousness. Though she has downplayed her concerns to Ed, she is worried (how could she not be?), is particularly anxious about the effects of morphine on Stella's infant system. She checks her daughter's oxygen levels, her pulse, her pinprick pupils, every few minutes. She has never seen it happen, but knows that seriously adverse reactions are always a possibility with young children. Eventually the exasperated charge sister unplugs the monitor and takes it away.

'You have to let her sleep, Mrs Middleton. She's fine, everything's perfectly normal. We'll check on her every half-hour. That's really all that's required. Now, why don't you try and get some rest.'

'Mummy? *Muummmmeee?*'

Susan's by her bedside immediately. 'I'm here, darling. You're okay. Mummy's here.'

Stella clutches Susan's wrist with her. good hand. 'Mummy?'

'Here, sweetheart. I'm here.' Susan brushes a stray hair back from her face. Stella's skin is pale, clammy.

'Mummy. I wish I didn't.'

'Didn't what, darling? What did you do?'

'Why can't you change it, Mummy?' Her voice is light, dreamy. 'One minute everything's normal and then it's not and you can't change it. Why can't you go back to before? Before was better. If I could just go back to before I wouldn't have to be here.' She closes her eyes wearily, but tears squeeze beneath the lids, and slide down her cheeks.

Susan says nothing, wipes her daughter's face gently with a tissue.

Stella's breathing slows, deepens. 'It's not fair,' she whispers, 'not fair.'

It isn't fair, thinks Susan, Stella's right: there should be some way to get back to before.

Ed

Ed can't sleep. He is worried about Stella, is feeling slightly guilty about Susan having to stay overnight at the hospital. Guilty too, about leaving Mitchell with his mother, whose reluctance was evident even over the telephone.

'You'll have to pick him up early tomorrow, Edward. Before seven. I've got a busy day. I do have a life, you know.'

His awareness of Carly in the bedroom across the hall only increases his anxiety. They have never really been alone in the house together. Not without the children, and not all night. He's uncomfortable, tries moving from his side to his back. Turns over and pushes his face into the pillow. Looks at the clock. Three thirty-four. Moans. It's no good, he can't sleep.

She comes into his bedroom quietly. He is not even aware of her presence until she slips in beside him. Doesn't know she's there until it's too late.

No moment is wasted. They do it fully clothed, with the necessary coverings dragged down, rucked up. There is no flesh on flesh. And none of the familiar sensations and sounds that accompanies his marital lovemaking. Or if there are, he's completely unaware of them, utterly oblivious. And the anxiety, the what-ifs (Susan arrives back early, his mother calls in unexpectedly). Somehow, strangely, this anxiety only increases his pleasure, provides an unlikely turn-on.

The sex is feverish and furious, not loving. Carly is a demon. There is no slow discovery of one another's bodies, no gentling or fondling or tender caressing. It is urgent, desperate, and somehow, all through it, they remain quite separate. There are no words of love and no discussions afterwards. There is no future and no past. It is all physical sensation—wetness and heat, grinding and pounding. Sucking, biting, thrusting, pulling.

They do not make love, they fuck. It's fission, not fusion.

Carly

In the beginning the game plan was simple. Reappear. Satisfy the trustees. Make the claim. Disappear again. Exquisitely simple.

She isn't quite sure why she's complicated the whole game so radically when all the rules were hers to make—but it seems she is playing for a stake in something much larger now.

Still, one thing remains constant, there's one rule she never breaks: when she plays, whatever she plays, she plays hard. She only ever plays to win.

Susan

For the first two days after Stella's discharge from hospital Susan wonders whether she's been transported to some parallel universe. It's as if she's in some impossibly slowed down scene from a bad horror flick, Susan thinks, or has been taken back to those days of early motherhood, but without the euphoria. Poor Stella: the paediatric painkillers give her barely any relief and, despite the bottle's promise, don't make her sleepy. She's awake all night and all day, it seems, moaning and crying, her arm aching far beyond what the medical staff had led them to expect, her only comfort her mother's continual presence. So Susan's up all the night with her—has moved her into the marital bed, and Ed's sharing with Mitchell.

Ed, for some unfathomable reason, can't meet her eyes, appears to be avoiding her. He seems to be disproportionately upset about Stella's arm—wanders in and out of the room when he's at home, but won't stay more than a few minutes; it's as if he can't bear to see his daughter in such pain. Susan's surprised by this, had not thought he would be so fainthearted, thinks perhaps he's feeling guilty—though of course there's nothing he—nothing any of them could do. And anyway, she knows that really it's no big deal, that Stella's intact and will be pain free and ready to get back to school in a week or so—that in no time at all, the hardest thing will be getting her to be careful—not to run, not to play too roughly. She'd reassure Ed if she wasn't so damned tired, if she didn't have so many other things to do …

Carly

She likes to save the best till last. She eats all her vegetables first, chews them fast, then savours the steak. Stories are like that, too, she thinks. The climax needs to be held back, held tight, delayed until the optimum moment. She's good at sensing just when that moment comes. When she can do the most damage.

But it's a mistake to think that the climax is ever the end. After steak comes dessert. And anyway, she's always been a multiple orgasm kind of girl.

Susan

'You want the *real* truth? I'll give it to you. I know you don't believe, that you've never believed that I left for no particular reason. I guess it's hard to imagine. So I'll give you the truth. But I warn you—you won't like it. You'll wish I never told you.'

'No, I won't wish that, whatever it is, whatever it was. You don't understand, Carly. I really need to know ...'

'Okay.' Carly takes a deep breath, 'It was your father,' she says, looking straight at Susan, her gaze level, cool. 'I left because of your father.'

She doesn't have to say more—to give details. Just mentioning her father is sufficient. It's not as if Susan has never considered this possibility—but when Carly actually says the words, makes the accusation, she feels as if she has been hit hard in the stomach.

'Oh, no,' she whispers. 'Not Dad.'

'And Mum,' Carly continues. 'Mum was worse than useless. When I finally plucked up the courage and told her what was going on—despite the fact he said he'd kill me if I opened my mouth—she said I was lying. Said that I was just a jealous little bitch. Sometimes I think that she knew all along. That the frigid cow thought it was a good way to keep him away from her.' Carly's voice hasn't wavered through all this, her face is expressionless.

'So there you go, Susy. Now you know. Happy?'

Susan doesn't really want to probe any further, can hardly bear to speak, but there is something she needs to know— something she has to know. She blows her nose, sits up straight, takes a deep breath:

'How old were you, Carly, when he—when it—started?'

She frowns, thinks. 'Oh, I was seventeen I guess, almost eighteen. But it didn't go on for too long, y'know. I got out of there quick smart. I wasn't stupid.'

Seventeen. It's not exactly a reprieve, Susan thinks, but it's something. Some aspect of her father salvaged. At least (and she is amazed by her vague feeling of relief, by the desperate and endlessly elastic nature of love, the way it recovers, like one of those clowns that can't be knocked down), at least Carly was more or less an adult, and her father, however wrong, however depraved, was not—legally, at any rate—that worst of all modern monsters—a pedophile.

Small mercies.

She tells Ed later that night, when they're in bed. She waits until he has finished reading, has put out his bedside lamp, waits until they're lying in the dark. She can't bear to face him, to see his face.

'Ed,' she whispers, though she knows Carly, in the room across the hall, can't hear even if she speaks normally.

'Mmmm.' She can tell that he's already almost asleep. He goes to sleep so quickly sometimes, like a little child with nothing on his conscience.

'Ed, she told me. Carly told me why she left.'

'Uh huh. You've already said. She just got bored. Left. Weird.'

'No. She told me the real reason. Today. There was a reason.'

'Oh?' She has his attention now, he's rolled over towards her, she can hear his suddenly rapid breathing, senses his anxiety. She wonders whether it's been at the back of his mind all this time, too.

'It's awful, Ed. It's really awful.'

'It's okay,' he gropes for her hand, clutches it tight. 'Tell me, Suse.'

She takes a deep breath. 'It was Dad.'

'Your father? What? He hit her or something? I find that pretty hard to believe. I mean, I know he was a grumpy old shit, but ... he never even smacked you, did he?'

'Oh, Ed.' She almost laughs. 'It's much worse than that. Dad ... he ... he raped her.'

'No.' It's barely a negative, but a sigh of disbelief, of disillusion, echoing her own. 'No.'

Susan needs badly to tell someone else, someone who knew her father. Ed's reaction has been too much like her own, she can't bear his appalled solicitude, his comforting smiles, she can't discuss it with him at all, she needs another perspective, a more detached perspective, so she calls Anna. It's suddenly occurred to her that her father's predatory behaviour may have extended beyond Carly—that there may have been other victims. Anna had been a frequent visitor when they were teenagers—and though Susan herself has no memory of inappropriate conversations, oglings, gropings—as far as she was aware her father had ignored Anna's presence—as he had ignored all of her girlfriends—she needs to know what Anna remembers.

She doesn't tell her what Carly has told her, not straight out. Instead she asks if Anna had ever noticed anything funny, anything sexual, with her father when they were growing up.

Susan is half-expecting an embarrassed admission, or some shameful revelation, so is surprised by Anna's laughter. 'Your father? You're kidding, aren't you? There's no way. Your father never so much as looked at me.'

'That's what I always thought, but are you sure there wasn't anything? He didn't walk in on you in the bathroom ... he didn't touch you ...?'

'I'm absolutely certain. Don't you remember me at that age, Suse? I tried it on with every bloke. With any bloke. I even flirted with your dad, the poor old bugger. Wanted to see what effect I had, how far I could take it. God, I was dreadful.'

She sounds slightly wistful and Susan understands why, remembering the teenage Anna. Short skirts, long hair, bosoms bursting out of low-cut tops, pretty as well as sexy. She'd had every boy they knew panting over her. Susan had never noticed her flirting with her father, but it was entirely probable, completely in character.

'Really?'

'Truly. There's no way. I really don't think he'd have noticed if I'd walked into a room naked.'

'Oh.' Susan's not sure whether to be relieved or disappointed. It seems there's no way to confirm Carly's story. And no reason. She has her sister back, at last—and she's glad. She wants her here, after all.

'Don't tell me that's what she's telling you. Carly's not saying that your father abused her or something, is she?' Anna's voice is loud, indignant.

Susan says nothing.

'Oh, Suse. Come on. That's bullshit. That bitch. She's lying. She has to be lying.'

Susan hopes she is. But why would she lie? There's no reason for it, there's nothing to be gained by such a monstrous accusation, is there?

Ed

Carly laughs when Ed confides that, other than her, Susan is the only woman he's ever slept with. Oh, he'd come close a few times with an earlier girlfriend, he tells her, but had never quite made it.

'Christ, Ed. You two are like a couple of bloody Christians. I don't believe it!'

'It's true.' Ed doesn't mind her laughter—he knows his sexual inexperience must seem a little bizarre—that it is bizarre. It worried him once, especially in those long ago days when he was constantly regaled with Derek's outrageous—and, frankly, unlikely—tales of sexual conquest. These days he's resigned to it, has come to regard it as one fairly insignificant aspect of his personal history. 'And anyway, it wasn't planned—it just worked out that way. We got together fairly young.'

'Fairly young! You were nineteen. You could vote, drink, drive, go to war. You were hardly babies. You have to admit, Eddy, that you two have got the best excuse I've ever heard for having affairs. Nineteen! By the time I was nineteen ...' Carly lets the sentence trail, grins.

'Probably can't even remember your first time,' Ed realises his mistake even as he speaks, is stricken, horrified by his tactlessness.

She says nothing for a moment. 'Oh, I remember that occasion, Ed.' She stubs out her cigarette carefully, speaks quietly: 'I remember it only too well.'

Susan

The two women are waiting in the express check-out queue at
Coles. It is early afternoon, and the queue is a long one, though
the supermarket is not crowded. They have only a half-dozen
items to pay for, and Carly is impatient, paces, flips through magazines, sighs, rolls her eyes to the ceiling every now and then.
'Jesus Christ,' she mutters, 'Why is this girl so fucken slow?'

Susan murmurs something soothing, suggests her sister
waits outside.

'Oh no,' Carly says, 'I guess I should get used to this sort of
thing.'

Finally they are at the head of the queue and Susan greets the
cashier politely, offers a commiserating smile. The cashier—a
young woman, plump and pale—says nothing, scans the items
and bags them automatically, without looking up.

'Hey,' Carly says. 'Hey, we said hello.'

The girl remains silent, reaches for the next item and runs
it over the scanner. She keeps her head down, presses her lips
together firmly.

'Hellooo.' Carly's voice is getting louder. Susan glares at her.
'Sssh. Don't.' Her sister rolls her eyes, taps her fingers on the
counter, stares at the cashier.

'Forty-three dollars and forty-five cents.' The cashier is looking up now, not at the women, but somewhere to the left of Susan's shoulder, her face blank, a mask. Susan sorts out the notes
and holds them out to her, but the girl ignores her gesture,
keeps her hands clasped together at her chest, immobile. Only
when Susan places the notes on the counter does she respond,
pincering them carefully between two fingers. Susan holds out
her hand for the change but the cashier ignores this too. Drops
the coins one by one onto the counter and turns back to the
cash register. Susan scoops the money up and into her wallet,
grabs the bags. Heads for the exit without turning back or saying thank you. She has assumed Carly is following her, but then

hears her voice, turns back.

Carly is still at the counter, is leaning close to the girl. 'Why don't you wear gloves, you silly little bitch,' Susan hears her hiss, 'if you're that afraid of catching something.' Carly's face is contorted, hard, is suddenly unfamiliar. 'If you've got some kind of transmissible disease you shouldn't be working here. And if it's some kind of mental fucken problem there are places,' her voice is sharp, vicious, 'places you can go.'

The cashier's face remains stony, expressionless. The young woman standing next in line flinches, turns away. An elderly woman looks shocked, embarrassed, her cheeks glow. Carly glares at them all, stalks off without a backward glance.

'Carly,' Susan says, when they are safely in the car, 'there might have been something wrong with that poor girl,' she searches for a possible explanation. 'Perhaps she has some dreadful skin complaint. Some disease.'

Carly is unrepentant. 'Come on Sue, she was obviously a nutcase. She shouldn't be in the job if she can't even cope with exchanging money.'

'But you—you didn't have to react the way you did. It was awful, Carly, unkind.'

Carly turns to her, eyes wide. 'I've offended you, haven't I? Your suburban sensibilities. People don't ever behave like that here, do they? You lot are always so polite—never say what you think. Sorry, Suse,' she says not sounding it, 'I'll try to control myself in future.'

Susan makes no reply. She starts the car, pulls on her seat-belt, puts the car into reverse. Carly jabs at the radio dial, look-ing for a suitable station.

'But it's no different here, Sue,' she says quietly. 'However it looks, however you all behave, people are just as awful, bad things happen.' She turns the stereo up loud, leans back, closes her eyes. 'It's dangerous here, too, Susan.' Susan can only just hear her, 'You just can't see it.'

Susan says nothing. What can she say? She has no right to

admonish her sister; no right to judge her. Now, underlying their every exchange there is the knowledge that without the actions of her father, Susan's father, Carly's life would have been very different, would probably have resembled Susan's, in its neat and heedless middle-class progression. This life, that she takes so much for granted—husband, kids, career, home, car, trips to the coast, dinner out; what Anna laughingly refers to as their blessed double-garage life—has been denied Carly, and another one of unspeakable deprivation and degradation has been given in its place. Whatever Carly is, whoever she is, Susan has no right to say anything.

Susan knows she can't be held responsible, is hardly accountable for the actions, the crimes, of her dead father, but nevertheless she carries the burden of his wrongdoing. There is no one else to carry it, after all.

Ed

'There was a time,' she tells him, 'there was a time a long time ago when I could have been one of you ...'

'One of you? You who? What do you mean?' His voice is thick with sleep, his questions half-hearted.

She ignores him, doesn't need an audience anyway, continues: 'Sometimes I think I would enjoy it, you know, having a big house, a big car, a husband, children.' She runs long fingernails across his chest absent-mindedly. 'A garden with flowers in it.' Traces around one nipple. 'It'd be a nice life, wouldn't it?' Moves slowly, gently, slowly down his body.

'Would it?' his voice is still thick, but he's no longer sleepy.

'Oh I think so. Geraniums, petunias ...' Her fingers pause just below his belly button. 'Sex every second Saturday. No surprises.'

'Every second Saturday? That wouldn't suit you.' He gropes for her hand in the dark, but it's not anywhere. Switches on the bedside lamp. She's gone.

They have four hours, four certain hours, four safe hours. Two hours twice a week.

And for almost the entirety of those two scant hours between nine and eleven on Tuesday and then on Wednesday evenings (when the children are deeply asleep, unlikely to wake, and Susan still has another two hours of her shift to work), Ed is ashamed and terrified (Mitchell will wake, Susan will arrive home early), but still he cannot help himself. He obsesses about it all day. He frequently finds that he has been sitting daydreaming, fantasising; an hour, two hours will have disappeared. Caught out by Moira's abrupt entrance into his office, or Derek's impatient enquiries, interrupted by the insistent ring of the telephone. Imagines her fingers sliding and fluttering, every which way across his body; her tongue darting and flickering, insinuating itself in this tender part or that. He considers new ways to pleasure her—a solicitude he has long ceased to extend (did he ever, really, like this? he wonders) to Susan.

After the first few occasions it is only ever in Carly's bedroom (that this is actually his daughter's bed, his little Stella's bed, he tries hard not to think about). He does not take all his clothes off, and nor does she—and other than the odd, quickly suppressed moan, they conduct their lovemaking in silence, though Ed wants to shout, to weep with joy and terror. When he is with Carly he becomes someone he does not recognise. Their coupling is swift, animal, unconscious. With Susan he is often weirdly— though comfortably—aware of himself, of them both—of the absurdity of the sexual act—of the games they play over and over, all to the same inevitable end. But with Carly he has no such consciousness, he is lost, possessed, completely overtaken by desire. All Ed's planned and imagined caresses are forgotten, swept away in the heat and thrust of their animal rutting.

And afterwards, when he has scurried back to the marital bedroom, has washed every trace of his sister-in-law from his body, afterwards, as he lies feigning sleep, exhausted, his heart racing madly, waiting for Susan's return, he finds he has no real memory of the event itself. All he can recall is the shame that comes almost simultaneously with his climax. A shame that endures long after any orgasmic pleasure has been forgotten.

Susan

Before they sleep the children ask Susan to read them *The Emperor's New Clothes*. It is an old book, a favourite, read and read and read again. It is a fun version of the fairytale, with gaudy pictures of the fat old king in the briefest underwear. The stupidity of the admiring court and the king's absurd pomposity always makes them giggle. Tonight, though, they are both subdued as she reads, and when she closes the book and goes to say goodnight, they are unresponsive, cheerless. Stella in particular surveys her mother solemnly. Her plastered arm is propped awkwardly on a pillow beside her, her face pale and drawn.

'Mum,' she asks, 'what does that story mean? What's the—the moral?'

Susan is amazed, as she frequently is, by her daughter's fledgling resemblance to Ed, by her inability, her obvious disinclination, even at this tender age, to just let things be, to enjoy what's on the surface. Susan smiles down at the serious little face, strokes the soft brown curls.

'Mum?'

Susan thinks for a moment. She finds it difficult to reduce such a story, to assign it a single meaning, and dislikes having to do so—it's not the way she reads, and isn't really, she supposes, the way she approaches anything. 'I guess,' she offers eventually, 'the main point is that you should stick by your beliefs, when you know they're real and true, even when everyone else disagrees. Otherwise you'll be made a fool of like the emperor.'

Stella nods her head sagely. 'I thought that's what it meant. That's what I told Mitch. Didn't I, Mitch? Didn't I say it was like *The Emperor's New Clothes*? That whatever they said, we know what the truth was.'

'What do you mean?' Susan's stomach lurches, her heart pounds. Who are they? What are you talking about?' She has visions of pedophile rings, child pornography. 'Stella? Mitchell. What are you talking about?'

Stella looks over at her older brother.

'It's just that—well you know how I fell off the slippery-dip?'

'Yes?' Susan's terror dissipates as quickly as it came. This is, then, just another of Stella's crises of conscience. There have been many of these. As a very small child Stella came to them once in the middle of the night, crying piteously, wracked with guilt over a favourite teddy bear thrown from a bedroom window. ('It was a wicked thing to do, mummy. Wicked!')

Knowing what is likely to follow—an admission of some sort of mildly reckless behaviour—Susan takes a deep breath, has to work hard to maintain a suitably solemn expression. 'What is it, darling?'

'Well ... you know how we said that Aunty Carly was there, all the time, watching us? Well, she wasn't, ac-tu-ally. We were looking for her for ages before that, all over the park, we were bored and hungry and wanted to go home. She takes us to the park every single time you're at work, and we just get sick of it. We'd rather watch telly. Anyway we couldn't find her anywhere and then when I fell off the slippery-dip it was ages—it was hours, probably—before she got there. Some old man had to stay with me ...'

There is a slight quaver of indignation in Stella's voice.

'Oh, Stell, I'm sure she was there, she was probably just—behind a tree or something. Or maybe she was walking around the park trying to find you and you kept on missing one another.'

'That's just what her and that other lady said. That they were there all along, that they couldn't find us, that we were just being silly. Telling stories. But me and Mitch know that it isn't true, and we don't want to lie about it anymore. Anyway we can never find her, she always goes off with that other lady when she takes us to the park.'

It only takes Susan a moment to assimilate this information, to find the salient point, the question that needs answering.

'What other lady, Stella?'

'The one with the red car. We followed her one time and she got in a car with this lady and drove off.'

'You mean Carly takes ... Carly took you to the park and just left you?'

'Uh huh.'

'Maybe she just saw an old friend, just the once ... and, perhaps they went for a drive around the block ...?' The explanation sounds lame, even to Susan.

'No, Mum.' Mitchell's voice is firm. 'It's all the time.' Adds darkly: 'But she doesn't know that we know.'

'Once we saw her go off with a man.' Now their mother's response has been gauged, Stella is eager to tell all. 'He had sunglasses on when it was raining ...'

'Yeah. And his car was hot. One of those black BMWs ...'

'Are you telling me the truth?' Now it is Susan's voice that quavers.

Stella glares at her mother. 'Mum! But that's why we told you. We were lying before. Now, we wanted to tell you the truth.'

'Mummy,' Stella calls anxiously, as Susan dims the light, 'you do believe us, don't you?'

Believe?

'Of course I do, darling.'

'Good,' her daughter gives a little sigh, closes her eyes. 'See you in the morning.'

Right now it's Susan who'd like to know the meaning of the story. The moral. But who's there to tell her?

She'd question Carly if she could, but Carly's away on one of her weekend jaunts (with the woman in the red car, the unsuitably sunglassed man in the black BMW—and why does that particular vehicle ring a bell?). She wonders about Carly's weekends away: every couple of weeks, her sister packs an overnight bag, phones for a taxi. A friend, she'll tell Susan. She's visiting a friend, or she's spending time with some old mate just passing through. *You can always ask them over here*, Susan makes the offer casually, doesn't want to appear pushy, inquisitive. Carly always thanks her, declines. *Not really someone you'd want to know, Susy. Not your type at all.* There are never any names or destinations and she never mentions whether the friend is male or female. Susan never asks. That would be intrusive, an unnecessary infringement of Carly's space, Carly's freedom. *You can get me on my mobile*, she calls, blowing a kiss from the taxi, *if you need me for anything. But why would you?*

Susan has never called, and she can't call now. Why would she?

Susan doesn't know quite what to make of the information Stella and Mitchell have given her. She has no idea what it means. It's clear that Carly wasn't around when Stella broke her arm, but not at all clear where she was. In a red car with a lady? Why? Who? She can't begin to make it out and isn't sure that she really wants to.

There's a tale to be unravelled here. Oh, not just the story that Mitchell and Stella have just revealed, but something bigger, something deeper. Something fundamental to her, to Ed, to the way they live their lives. She knows that somewhere, *somewhere*, if she just knew where to look, she'd find, if not the answer, some sort of precedent—some way of understanding what's happening. The moral, if you like.

She vaguely remembers the tale of the prodigal son from childhood scripture classes, recalls that the story dealt with a good and loyal son; and another son who runs away, lives wantonly and destructively, but is welcomed by his father on his return home, much to the remaining son's disgust. She knows the story well enough, she thinks, but finds the reference in Ed's family Bible; Luke 15:11–13, reads the verses curiously:

There was a man who had two sons. The younger of them said to his father, 'Father give me the share of the property that will belong to me.' So he divided the property between them. A few days later the younger son gathered all he had and travelled to a distant country, and there he squandered his property in dissolute living.

When he had spent everything, a severe famine took place throughout that country, and he began to be in need. So he went and hired himself out to one of the citizens of that country, who sent him to his fields to feed the pigs. He would gladly have filled himself with the pods that the pigs were eating; and no one gave him anything. But when he came to himself he said, 'How many of my father's hired hands have bread enough and to spare, but here I am dying of hunger! I will get up and go to my father, and I will say to him, "Father, I have sinned against heaven and before you; I am no longer worthy to be called your son, treat me like one of your hired hands."' So he set off and went to his father.

But while he was still far off, his father saw him and was filled with compassion; he ran and put his arms around him and kissed him. Then the son said to him, 'Father, I have sinned against heaven and before you; I am no longer worthy to be called your son.' But the father said to his slaves, 'Quickly, bring out a robe—the best one— and put it on him; put a ring on his finger and sandals on his feet. And get the fatted calf and kill it, and let us eat and celebrate; for this son of mine was dead and is alive again; he was lost and is found.' And they began to celebrate.

Now his elder son was in the field; and when he came and approached the house, he heard music and dancing. He called one of the slaves and asked what was going on. He replied, 'Your brother has come, and your father has killed the fatted calf because he has got him back safe and sound.' Then he became angry and refused to go in. His father came out and began to plead with him. But he answered his father, 'Listen! For all these years I have been working like a slave for you, and I have never disobeyed your command; yet you have never given me even a young goat so that I might celebrate with my friends. But when this son of yours came back, who has devoured your property with prostitutes, you killed the fatted calf for him!'

Then the father said to him, 'Son, you are always with me, and all that is mine is yours. But we had to celebrate and rejoice, because this brother of yours was dead and has come to life; he was lost and has been found.'

The story's pretty much as she remembers it—and the similarities to her own situation are striking. But the differences are even more arresting. For one thing, she and Carly are sisters, not brothers. And the only father in their story is, according to Carly anyway, the villain—not the wise and loving parent of the parable. As for Carly's welcome, the robe, the ring, the sandals, the fatted calf, the eating and celebrating—well, it's been more symbolic than actual, she supposes, fairly low-key—with only Susan, and to a lesser extent, Ed, available to fall upon Carly's neck.

And Susan isn't at all like the angry, well-behaved brother—she hasn't experienced even the most remote pang of resentment. It's been quite the reverse: she'd been happy, more than happy, ecstatic about her sibling's return, more than willing to share the inheritance—and the future.

There are no clues in this parable—no answers to her own dilemma. Susan would like to know a little more about this biblical family, however. She'd like to know what happened next; wonders whether they all lived happily ever after.

She doubts it somehow.

Carly arrives home early on Sunday evening, full of energy, cheerful, light-hearted, she plays hide and seek with the kids, chaffs Ed about this and that, even offers to clean the kitchen after dinner. She's obviously had a good weekend, though she barely makes a reply when Ed, uncharacteristically, asks her what she's done, where she's been.

'Oh, you know,' she replies with a casual shrug, 'this and that; here and there. The usual.'

Susan hasn't mentioned it to Ed yet, he's been a bit off since Stella's accident—oddly distant, quiet. She had thought that she'd just casually mention Stella and Mitchell's account of the park visit, perhaps around the dinner table, introduce the subject breezily, as if it was of little importance, perhaps even let the kids do most of the talking. But she realises that that's not going to work, that in fact it's hard to be casual about such a thing. Stella's getting better, but she's still in some pain, she's pale, cries easily, hasn't yet recovered her starry twinkle. There's no way she can broach the subject of Carly's absence lightly— her daughter's been damaged, after all—and there's no way of avoiding the fact, no way of stepping over it, that if she really was elsewhere ... that Carly's responsible, Carly's to blame.

So she waits until the following morning—both children at school, Stella's first day back—and Ed at work. Carly's sitting in the lounge room with her coffee, she's lit up a cigarette, is ashing in a teacup, flicking impatiently through the television channels.

'Oh, this is hopeless.' She turns the television off, tosses the remote onto the lounge in disgust. 'Who do they think's watching at this hour?' she asks Susan, who's passing through with a basket of washing.

'People like me, probably. You know. Housewives. Or small children.'

'Housewives. What's a bloody housewife? How can you be married to a fucking house, Susan?'

Susan's wondered this herself, recently, but shrugs, not in the mood for this sort of conversation. She starts up the hallway with her basket, but Carly follows her.

'Come on, Suse, you've got to admit it's a bit of a bloody bore. That it's not really a life.'

'What are you talking about, Carly?'

'All this crap. Keeping the house clean. Cooking. Washing clothes. What's it all for? What's the point of it? Why aren't you out there, in the world, the real world—doing something useful. How do you settle for this?'

'That's not fair, Carly. It's not nothing. You just don't understand. I've got what I want. This is what most people want. To have people that they love around them. It's simple, Carly, really, it's simple.' Though Susan senses that she's hit on something, feels the truth lurking in her trite explanation, this obviously doesn't satisfy her sister.

'But it's so little.'

'What do you mean?'

'How can you bear the thought of just being one person? Living one life?'

'But that's all we get, Carly. We all only get to live one life.'

'You don't have to, Susan. That's just from your narrow perspective.'

'But you do—the only alternative is hurting people. Your life isn't just about you.'

'So what's it about, then, Susy? It can't just be about other people.'

'It's not. That's not what I'm saying. It's about—it has to be about—both. You have to find a ... a balance.'

'Why are you so sure that you've found it?'

'What do you mean?'

'From where I'm standing, Susan, you know, just observing from the sidelines, your life seems to be all about other people. Susan Middleton—who *is* she? Are you sure she even exists?'

Now Susan's beyond patience, she's been stung, has had enough.

'I'm pretty sure that I exist, Carly, everyone can see just how I exist, what I do to justify that existence. It might look boring, but it's real, Carly. I don't just sit around someone else's house, whingeing about the television programming. Eating their food. Leaving whenever I feel like it. Disappearing with strange women when you're meant to be looking after your sister's kids. Letting your niece—your own bloody niece—break her arm because you're too irresponsible to be where you've said— where you've promised you'll be.'

Susan's in the kids' bedroom, shoving their clothes into drawers, the wrong drawers, any drawer, slamming them shut. Carly's standing against the doorway, a forgotten cigarette burning away in her fingers, her mouth open, eyes wide.

'Wow, I didn't know you could get so angry, Suse. Very impressive, girl. Not the Mrs Middleton we've all come to know and love.' She laughs, but there's no merriment in the sound.

'I just want to know what happened, Carly. The kids have told me that you weren't there when Stella broke her arm. That in fact you were never actually there—that you'd dump them at the park the afternoons when you were meant to—and *you* offered—to look after them. That you'd disappear with some woman for an hour or so ... Carly, how could you? Mitch is only eight. Stella's virtually a baby. Anything could have happened.'

'So what are you accusing me of, Susan? Of breaking Stella's arm? Or of not telling you I have a friend? A girlfriend. What the fuck is your problem?'

'I'm not accusing you of anything, Carly. I just want to know ...' she takes a deep breath, 'Look, maybe you don't understand because you don't have kids; maybe Ed and I didn't make it clear—but you can't just leave them. They're too young ...'

'Jesus. Not accusing me? Not accusing me? Bullshit. I know an accusation when I hear one.' She purses her lips, speaks in a polite falsetto, 'Carly dear, don't you think it might be a nice thing to stick around when you take our little darlings to the park. Then you can push them on the swings and wipe their snotty little noses. What fun! And Carly dear, what's this I hear about you running off with some tart in a little red car. Perhaps you'd like to bring her home to dinner. Let Eddy and me check her over. Wouldn't that be just lover-ley.' Carly's face is contorted, thrust close to Susan's, her voice venomous. Susan steps away from her, tries to come up with a suitable, a soothing, response, through her own churning stomach, her breathlessness.

'Carly, you're taking it the wrong way. I really didn't mean to upset you. Why don't we ...'

'Fuck you. I've had enough of this. Had enough of the lot of you.'

'Carly ...'

'No. That's it. It's over. The whole thing makes me sick. Shelly was right—I should have just made the claim and pissed off.'

'Carly ...'

'And you can tell loverboy that it's like fucking a wet pillow.'

She slams the door on the way out. Susan finds a wall to lean against. *Loverboy*?

She's always suspected it was there, like a snake coiled in a corner, sleeping through winter, waiting patiently for the spring, for its moment of reawakening. Tragedy. Calamity. She's seen it raise its ugly head before, after all. She knows—don't we all?—that it's inevitable, unavoidable; it comes for everybody, eventually; in the end there's no possible way to escape. But she wonders whether this is it, whether this is her moment, their moment. Here. Now.

Carly

It's only confirmed what she's always suspected: that the complication quotient of domestic bliss is extremely high. Too high to risk.

She's had enough.

Story's told; game's over.

Susan

She tells Ed that Carly has decided on another night out, that she's not too sure when she'll be back. He seems surprised, but doesn't enquire too closely, retires to the lounge room with a newspaper while she gets on with the dinner. If he notices her blotchy face, her puffy eyes, he doesn't say anything, though maybe he doesn't notice—she can barely look at him.

She has left dinner till late—it is already past seven; the children are starving and tired. They are supposed to be in the bath ('Before dinner, Mum? That's stupid'), but are fighting in the hallway just beyond the kitchen.

'Dad says brothers should spect their sisters,' Susan can hear Stella shriek over the noise of the bathtub filling.

And Mitch's reply: 'Not when they're as stupid as you, dickhead.' There's the sound of flesh on flesh, a muffled scream, a thud. Silence—and then a howl.

'Mum, she's hit me with her plaster. *Muuum.*' Susan ignores all this, leaves it to Ed to intervene. She cuts through a sausage, but it's still pinkly raw inside. She drains the potatoes and mashes them. This requires a certain amount of effort—they're not quite cooked and won't pulp easily so she tips them straight out onto the bench top and hits them viciously with the meat tenderiser.

Eventually Stella's screams are shrill enough to disturb Ed and he rushes in from the lounge room, does a double take when he sees the mess Susan has made. 'Jesus, Susan. Jesus. What's going on?'

'Dinner's made, darling,' she says brightly. 'Just add some butter and salt to the potatoes and they'll be delicious. I'm going out.'

'What do you mean you're going out? You can't just go out. Get off your sister, Mitchell. Now!'

She finds a couple of addresses in the phone book; scribbles them down. She grabs her handbag, car keys.

'Going out where, Susan? Susan?'

She backs the car out of the garage, wondering vaguely if Ed will think to turn off the water before the bath overflows and if he'll split the sausages to make sure they're cooked right through. She turns left at the end of the street and heads towards the city.

She knows that she should have noticed there was something happening between them. There have been signs—small, but significant—and so clear, now, that she can't imagine how she ever managed to disregard them. (The way Ed watches Carly constantly, the way he smiles so widely, laughs so enthusiastically at her jokes, seeks out her glance when they're watching television, the way he includes her in their every conversation.) So stupid—she'd been so pleased that they genuinely seemed to like one another, that her husband and her sister—both so dear to her—were establishing such a strong, such a solid, relationship. Now, too, she's suddenly aware of how little time the three of them actually spent together. It seems remarkable—or perhaps it isn't—that in almost every memory, each encounter, there is nearly always a neat pairing—Carly and Susan, Ed and Carly. Almost as if it has been arranged that way. She wonders whether it's at all significant, whether these twosomes were somehow deliberate manoeuvrings, cunningly manipulated, in order to keep all their stories separate. To keep them all contained.

She parks illegally in a loading zone, in a small back street. According to her street directory, Darlinghurst Road should be only a short walk away, and the hotel itself several blocks along, but she's taken a wrong turn somewhere, can't quite work out where she is. Although Susan has lived in Sydney all of her life, she is unsure of herself in this part of the city. The buildings are high and crowded together, everything's grimy, even the air seems greasy. The street lighting is sparse, the narrow streets dim and curiously empty. Her footsteps seem officiously loud. She's walking fast, but even so her steps can't keep pace with her heartbeat, her rapid breathing. She's feeling strangely exhilarated—almost as if she's drunk—but simultaneously afraid, although she isn't quite sure what it is that she's afraid of: Carly, the night, some hidden danger lurking in the unfamiliar streets, her own rather vague intentions?

She wipes her forehead with her hand, and it comes away wet, though the night is not hot. A man shuffles towards her out of the dark and she automatically, instinctively, moves from the centre of the footpath towards the gutter. The man is weeping loudly, one hand covering his face. He is enormously, grotesquely fat and his other hand clutches at his unbuttoned pants, holding them up, holding them together. Susan looks the other way and hurries past. A shit smell wafts towards her. She walks faster.

At the next corner she pauses for a moment to check the street name against her directions. Brougham Street. She thinks if she turns back, and then takes the next left, she should be heading in the direction of her parked car—she can reorient herself there, start again. But then again she's not quite sure; perhaps she should turn right, head east. Brougham Street. The street name rings a bell, several bells. She checks the hastily scribbled addresses under a streetlight: 134 Brougham Street. Just in case, she'd thought at the time, but in case of what? Perhaps her disorientation is deliberate; perhaps Brougham Street has always been her objective.

His house is one in a row of almost identical Victorian terraces—all in various stages of disrepair. She pushes through a rusty wrought-iron gate at the front of number 134 and feels her way up a flight of sandstone steps. There's no doorbell and she has to rap hard on the heavy wooden door. There's a light, visible through a front window, but no movement from within. Just as she's about to bang on the door again, harder this time, using a closed fist, the door opens. A firm hand interrupts the downward trajectory of her own.

'Susan!' Howard says, the surprise evident in his expression, his voice. 'What on earth are you doing here?'

'I'm lost.' Susan smiles weakly. 'I thought you might be able to tell me where I am.'

Howard's terrace is obviously in the process of being renovated. All the downstairs walls have been knocked down, and the staircase to the upper level appears to have been partially dismantled—terminating abruptly at the first landing. There's a sink and an old upright stove in one corner, a futon in another, but no evidence of any bathroom facilities. Little mountains of rubble adorn every corner and an inch-thick layer of grey dust covers everything; what little furniture there is is draped in sheets for protection.

Howard offers her a seat on the futon, pours her a whisky and pulls up a dusty packing case for himself. He politely refrains from asking, but Susan tells him that she'd come here intending to look for Carly, thinking she may have gone back to the hotel she'd originally stayed at, the Capital. She tells him about the children's revised account of Stella's accident—though it seems so trivial now, so lame in the telling, in the aftermath—about the fight, about Carly's departure. Susan plays the whole thing down, it was just a misunderstanding, a minor spat, she says. A sister thing. She feels she should offer some sort of explanation, after all, she doesn't want him to imagine that she's purposely driven here to see him, that her story about Carly is some sort of a pretext, though she thinks perhaps he does, anyway.

'Anyway, I'm hopeless—I'm nowhere near the Capital, am I? I was going to head back and start again, but I got a bit muddled—and I can't quite remember where I left my car. And when I saw Brougham Street I thought of you. I thought you might help me get my bearings. Anyway, I don't really know what I thought I could do—the whole thing was silly, really. Impulsive. But I guess I wanted to see if we could sort things out. Patch things up.'

There's no possible way to patch things up, she knows that. But Howard doesn't—she hasn't told him about Carly's terrible rage, her parting revelation.

'But what made you think she'd be at the Capital, Susan? She could be anywhere.'

He shakes his head disbelievingly from side to side, his lips pursed in such a very lawyerly way that Susan can't help laughing.

'What? What's funny?'

'It's nothing.'

Suddenly everything looks slightly surreal, upside down. 'It's Carly. Everything. Nothing fits. Being here, now ... Your house ...'

Even Howard is not who he ought to be. Nor she. They are both being so circumspect, so polite, like children playing at being grown-up, desperately pretending that their professional relationship is intact. 'It's all crazy.' Susan giggles, sips her whisky.

'I'm not sure I get you.' Howard's smiling now, but warily.

'No, it's okay. There's nothing to get.' She stands up, still giggling. 'Well, I'd better get home, Ed'll be wondering where I've got to.'

'You're sure you're alright?' Howard stands too, takes the empty glass Susan proffers.

'I'm fine,' she says, not feeling fine at all. 'Thank you,' brightly. 'You've been terribly ... terribly solicitous.'

She isn't giggling anymore, but crying, and Hamilton offers her a handkerchief, another drink, the slight comforting pressure of his warm hand on her shoulder.

And then, she doesn't know how, can't recall the precise sequence of events (then or later), Susan finds herself lying prone on the futon, being kissed. Or perhaps it's Susan that's doing the kissing. She can't be sure.

Ed

Tonight, though Ed is tired, he sits on the edge of their bed, waiting for Susan's return. He has managed to feed and bed the children—though both were quite distressed by their mother's inexplicable absence, and—although he couldn't quite face the potato encrusted benchtop—he has even stacked the dishwasher, scrubbed the pots. He has done the crossword on his own (but needs Susan's help with seven down), has showered and cleaned his teeth. He is ready for sleep, but sleep won't come.

Over the years Ed has watched various friends' marriages break down, has counselled, lent a willing ear, given advice. It has always seemed to him, watching objectively (though not, he hopes, judgementally) from the sidelines, that many of these relationships have foundered not through any great rancorous disagreement, or unforgivable betrayal, nor because of any discernible personality change in either of the partners (these being the most common explanations, and excuses), but through a simple lack of trying. A lack of will. A successful marriage, Ed maintains (has always maintained) is based not upon romance or similar interests or whatever drew a couple together in the first instance, but on a conscious decision to settle for what it is you've got, to not yearn after other people, other lives, other things. To admit the impossibility of having everything and to be content, happy (insofar as happiness actually exists other than as a memory or an ideal—which he's not so sure about) with your lot.

Now, as a not-so-objective participant in what he can't avoid recognising as his own impending relationship breakdown, his own test of will, Ed can see that it's far more complicated than that. That it's not so much to do with trying (and he is trying), that trying achieves very little. Now all his theorising seems laughable, inadequate, incredibly naive. The smug pronouncements of the complacent. This isn't about will, he realises now, will counts for nothing here. He's willed none of this. It's inescapable, and he's without volition.

The only thing he can liken the experience to—and he knows it's a laughably cliched analogy, tired and trite—is being picked up and swept along by a current. Ed feels he's done his level best to swim across the flow, but that's just not working—any attempt to escape is wearying beyond belief and, anyway, impossible. He thinks perhaps the only way to survive is to stop resisting, to let the tide pull him out. And if he can somehow survive the journey, the voyage (and he knows he might be taken miles and miles offshore, he might end up somewhere unrecognisable, another continent, a desert island; he might even be eaten by sharks en route), if he can just stay afloat, he might preserve some small bit of his strength.

And that way he just might make the long swim back.

Susan

Susan wakes with difficulty, her head thick, eyes sticky. The room is full of sunshine, the space beside her—well, there is no space beside her, she's not in her own bed. She's in Carly's room, Stella's old room—is lying, fully clothed, but uncovered, on top of Carly's single bed. She doesn't know, can't remember, why it is that she's there, why she hasn't slept in her own bed, why she's still in bed at this hour. What hour? A glance at the bedside clock tells her that it's late, past ten, and she panics—Stella, Mitchell, school!—goes to get up, but can't—her stomach lurches, head spins.

She lies back gingerly and closes her eyes again. She tries to remember what day it is, but can't; hopes that it's Saturday, but doubts it somehow. Her stomach's churning, but her mind is churning even more violently. She can't remember why she's here, what she's done—and isn't at all sure that she wants to.

By the time the phone call comes, she's just begun to feel human. She's showered, dressed, drunk copious cups of black coffee (and vomited them back up again), has ascertained (from a scrawled note on the kitchen table) that Ed has taken the children to school. She's even managed to dredge up her memories of the night before—most of them, anyway. Susan's certain that she left Howard's terrace with her marriage vows—if not her dignity—intact. Certain that she drove home without mishap, despite having drunk somewhat more than the legally prescribed quantity of liquor.

She can distinctly recall opening a bottle of champagne on her return, less distinct are her memories of the drink itself. She has a dim recollection of rummaging through the photograph box, of weeping over this and that family snap, of reading through the articles relating to her missing sister, again, of opening an envelope, trying to focus on some dull documents, of giving up, of pouring more champagne ... After that—a blank. She's satisfied, though, that she, at least, has done nothing that requires forgiveness, nothing she need ever apologise for, nothing that will endanger the future happiness of their little family. She's beginning to fill with a righteous anger—feels swollen with the weight, the magnitude—leaving no room for the inevitable sorrow; the despair that she knows will follow hard and fast. She's ready, primed for action, for confrontation, and when the telephone rings, she hopes that it's Ed.

But it's Howard's secretary calling to tell her that the settlement has gone through as planned—it was a two week settlement rather than the usual six—and that the funds have been deposited into a trust account. 'Less agents' fees and the solicitor's—your share is four hundred and fourteen thousand dollars, Mrs Middleton.'

The woman gives her the figure with an uncharacteristic enthusiasm, obviously impressed and, despite her pounding head, Susan manages to make the appropriate noises. 'The money's ready for disbursement, and we don't seem to have instructions for transferring your share of the funds. Do you want a cheque, or do you want your portion of the money deposited directly into an account?'

Susan rattles off her account details, realises she has made a mistake, then, picturing the secretary's bored disdain, can't remember, has to make several attempts before she gets it right.

'What about my sister's funds—what about her details?' She tries hard to make the question seem spontaneous, the sort of question anybody might ask—idle, inconsequential—but Susan is flustered, she's breathless, she knows she sounds nervous, even guilty. And the secretary's reply is icy:

'Miss Brown has made her arrangements with us, Mrs Middleton. I'm sorry, but I can't give you any information. You'll have to ask her yourself.'

Susan phones Ed.

'Susan. You're awake. Is everything alright?'

Susan has lost the urge to discuss their situation, to confront him with her knowledge. She's too tired, her head's begun to pound again—the whole thing's too hard.

'Everything's fine, Ed.' She tells him about the secretary's call.

'Wow.' He sounds vague, distracted. 'We're rich.'

She tells him that she has to take Stella to the orthopaedic surgeon at lunchtime and then she has some shopping to do, errands to run, they'll be home too late home to cook, could he organise takeaway, buy champagne? 'Good champagne,' she adds, 'we can afford it.'

'I guess we can. Do you need me to get Mitch from school? Will you be back in time?'

'Mitch is going to after-school care. I've booked him in for the afternoon. He wants to go. I'll pick him up on the way home.'

'Oh. Sure.' A long pause, then: 'Is she back? Is Carly back?'

'No.'

'Have you heard from her?'

'No, Ed, I haven't.' Then casually, without emphasis: 'Have you?'

Susan

She is flicking impatiently through an old newspaper in the surgeon's waiting room when she comes across the story. *Missing Teenagers*, the headline announces, *Murder Victims or Runaways? The Anguish of Uncertainty.*

Every year, she reads, *hundreds of Australian teenagers disappear, most of whom leave of their own free will and return or are returned to their families within days or weeks. Others never come home and police files remain open indefinitely. Unless evidence of foul play can be proven or a body is found, these young people remain in an official and personal no-man's-land. For their families the uncertainty is agonising—and for some it will never end. Recently a taskforce investigating a number of disappearances of young women from Sydney's inner west between March 1975 and May 1976—a series of disappearances investigators initially feared was serially linked—has come to the conclusion that at least two of the missing girls left of their own accord and that these cases can now be officially closed.*

The families of Jane Harkness, who disappeared from Leichhardt in April 1975, soon after her 17th birthday, and Carleen Potter, aged 18, who disappeared from Marrickville, in March 1976—were recently informed that NSW police had good reason to believe that their daughters are both alive and well. For these families, the knowledge of their daughters' safety has given some relief. Mrs Enid Harkness, mother of Jane, stated today that she had always feared the worst and that just knowing that Jane was alive somewhere was enough. Gerald Potter, father of Carleen, and her only remaining parent, now terminally ill with lung cancer, expressed his great relief, but added, 'If you're reading this, Carl, how 'bout you get in contact with your Dad. I'm not going to last long. Let me die knowing you're safe and happy. Let's put the past to rest, love.'

Inspector Dal Whitehouse, who heads the taskforce, emphasises Mr Potter's sentiment: 'Let me make it clear that it's not a crime to disappear—there are often legitimate reasons for leaving—but there's no harm in dropping a line or making a quick phone call, just to say you're safe. It would save a great deal of heartache and worry. Not to mention paperwork.'

Susan looks closely at the two grainy photographs. They are similar in appearance, in type, these two girls: both fair, with Farrah Fawcett flicks, plucked eyebrows, cheeky grins. There's little enough to distinguish between the two, but the picture of Carleen Potter is somehow familiar. There's a certain something in this girl's smile that Susan knows well, but can't quite place, and in the way she has her head tilted. It shouldn't be surprising, no doubt this woman's life is going on somewhere— just as Carly's did for all those years. She could be anyone—a schoolteacher, shopkeeper, bus driver, even a neighbour. And it could just be Susan's imagination ...

It *could* just be her imagination, but even so she nudges Stella, who is sitting patiently beside her, and points to the photograph, raises her eyebrows. Often the kids see things she can't—lost needles for instance, or the sunglasses that have been left in the fruit bowl—and this is no exception. Stella doesn't hesitate.

'That's Carly, Mum,' she says, excited. 'She looks really different, though, doesn't she? With long hair. Must of been in the olden days. Look,' she puts her finger on the girl's mouth. 'Her broken tooth's just the same.' Then: 'Why's Aunty Carly in a newspaper? Mum? Is she famous?'

Susan tears out the article, ignoring the receptionist's glare, and shoves it into her handbag. 'I'll tell you later, sweetheart.' She grabs Stella's good hand, pulls her up. 'I've just remembered that I've left the stove on, Stell. We'll have to see the doctor another day. We have to go right now.'

She takes the bemused Stella back to school ('But *Muuum*, what about the stove?'), arranges for her to join Mitchell at after-school care—a family emergency, she explains—and rushes home. The photos and clippings she'd gone through the night before are still out, strewn untidily across the lounge room coffee table. She finds the old *Sun* clipping, then smoothes out the new article, lays them side by side, looks closely at the featured portraits. There's an undeniable resemblance between these three lost girls: they're all fair, all roughly the same age, seventeen or eighteen. Karen: missing, presumed dead—by her at least—for over twenty years; the face in that photograph is almost as familiar as her own. Jane Harkness, evidently alive somewhere, but completely unknown, quite unfamiliar.

The third photograph—head tilted slightly, the smile: wise, knowing—is of Carleen Potter. Like Karen's, this face is familiar, but more urgently, more recently, so. Her eyebrows are thinner, hair longer, face slightly rounder, more open. But the chipped tooth, as Stella has pointed out, is unmistakable.

Susan sorts through the other papers strewn across the coffee table—what a mess she'd made last night—the entire contents of her photo box seem to be out, and all the family documents—the articles detailing her sister's disappearance, her children's birth certificates, her own, their marriage certificate, deeds to their house. Right at the bottom of the pile she finds a large manila envelope—the one Gillian sent. It had arrived a couple of weeks ago, and she'd put it in a drawer, unopened, and then forgotten all about it. She must have opened it last night, half-remembers an abandoned attempt to decipher the contents, must have shoved them back in willy-nilly. She slides the papers out now and sorts them carefully, puts them in chronological order, then reads through them, quickly, compulsively.

She looks back at the cuttings. Even without the chipped tooth there'd be no doubt.

No doubt at all.

Howard's secretary puts her straight through. She gives him a rushed and garbled account of events—of Carly's continued absence, the pictures in the newspaper article, the reports from Gillian.

'Oh, dear. Dear, dear. This is ... I think perhaps you'd better come over now. We'll see what can be done to ... er ... sort things out.'

Sort things out. The sorting's been done, though, hasn't it? They've all been thoroughly sorted.

Ed

Ed takes a long lunch break. He usually takes none, gulps down a quick sandwich in his office, so feels he is justified. He isn't working, anyway. He can't. He tells Moira that he will be gone for an hour or so, maybe more.

He wanders along the busy industrial streets, tramps south, then east, heads back into the beachside suburbs, not seeing anything, or anyone; thinking of his life, what he wants, where he's heading. It seems he's forgotten. Lost his certainty, his focus, his direction.

Looking back, he's amazed by how effortlessly the framework of their family life expanded to accommodate Carly, how the structure of their existence seemed initially unchanged: as if the new addition really dovetailed effortlessly with the original. He supposes that for a while it, she, did: and even when it didn't quite, the differences were exhilarating, striking—like rosewood marquetry in a maple door.

But now, when the new construction has revealed itself fully, he can see that the apparent durability was deceptive—it's like a cupboard that's missing a screw, lacking some glue: it's been put together well enough, can withstand the usual wear and tear, but put under additional pressure—bearing the weight of a solid granite benchtop, say—the doors won't align, drawers won't close, and eventually the cupboard will buckle under the strain, maybe even collapse. You'll be left with nothing but worthless bits of board—warped and battered out of all recognition.

And way beyond repair.

He finds himself at the end of his own street—he's walked for more than two hours, headed for home, almost unwittingly. He speeds up, thinks that he will call Moira, get a taxi back, he has things to do, an appointment at three, quotes to phone in. He's a few houses away when he notices the little red car parked in his driveway, a woman sits waiting in the driver's seat. The woman—blonde, slender, dressed all in black—climbs out and opens the boot, and then Carly comes into view, bulging green garbage bags slung over each shoulder. Ed goes to call out, but thinks again. He steps back a little, conceals himself behind a large jacaranda in a neighbour's yard, watches as Carly hoists the bags carelessly into the boot, slams it shut.

The women stay behind the car for a moment, talking; they turn to look back up the driveway, Carly points something out, and they laugh. Then Carly slings her arm around the unknown woman's waist, pulls her towards her, pulls her close, closer. They stay like that for a moment, one woman gathered into the other, shoulder to shoulder, chest to chest, and then their separate profiles merge. The two women kiss. And even from this distance, even though he has to squint to focus properly, Ed knows that this is not a kiss between friends. It is a slow kiss, a hungry kiss.

A kiss between lovers. Between Carly and her lover. It's a kiss he recognises. It's a kiss he knows.

Carly

Pussy Cat Pussy Cat
Where have you been?
Poor little mousies,
The cat's got the cream ...

Susan

She passes Howard the two newspaper articles. When he puts his glasses on, little half-moon reading spectacles, he seems years older, reminds her suddenly of her father, becomes a fussy dry little man. Whatever it was between them, whatever crazy spark or magnetism flared briefly between them, has dissolved, evaporated as quickly as it appeared.

He smoothes the papers on his desk, looks from one article to the next, then back again. Shakes his head. Sighs. He looks at Susan anxiously. 'I see what you mean,' he says slowly. 'There's a definite resemblance. It's unmistakable. Oh dear.'

'There's more. Gillian—my stepmother—sent me these a few weeks ago. I'd put them away, forgotten about them, hadn't even thought to look at them until now. They're reports from an agency that my mother hired years ago. Dad ended up with the reports because he paid the accounts. By that time Mum was barely lucid. And of course nobody ever bothered to tell me about them. She'd hired a private detective.'

The story sounds absurd to Susan, melodramatic; the entire situation is looking increasingly like something from a bad film. Howard holds out his hand for the files, but she hesitates, finds she cannot hand them over so easily. They're something to hold onto after all. Something solid. 'Perhaps I could read them to you?'

'It would be quicker if I go through them myself ...' He must sense her determination, her desperation. Shrugs, 'Whatever you like, Susan.'

She has put the reports in order, pinned them together at the top. 'The agency was called Marlowe and Co Investigative Agents.'

Susan winces, but Howard nods, 'They're quite a reputable firm—and still in business. I've had dealings with them myself occasionally. It's all quite regular.'

'This first letter is dated 21st June, 1984.' She's surprised by the clarity and strength of her voice. 'That's almost ten years after Karen ... left. She'd have been twenty-seven.'

Howard gives an encouraging nod.

'*Dear Mrs Carter*,' Susan reads slowly.

'*Just a brief letter to inform you that as yet no information regarding your daughter Karen has come to light. Our agents have made extensive enquiries in the Kings Cross district as per your request, but have not yet had any positive identification. As discussed, the time element is against us, as is the transient nature of the neighbourhood.*

Please find account attached.

Yours sincerely

J.D. Nicholson, Marlowe and Co.'

She prises the letter from its clip and passes it across the desk. Hamilton reads through quickly, then looks up at Susan, raises his eyebrows. 'Go on.'

She goes on.

'*Dear Mrs Carter,*

We have had at last some slight success. A Mr Joseph Giannopoulos, proprietor of Gianni's Cafe, Darlinghurst, has identified your daughter as being one of two female tenants who lived in the flat above the cafe from 1980–1981. Though he claims that he knew very little about her (he cannot remember her name, isn't certain that she did go by the name Karen), he does recall her telling him that she was moving to St. Kilda, Melbourne. She left sometime around April 1981.

Please let us know if you wish us to continue our investigation in Melbourne. Our interstate costs will comprise the daily rate, plus travel—return by air—and accommodation.

Yours sincerely,

J.D. Nicholson, Marlowe and Co.'

She hands this letter over, begins reading the next.

'*Dear Mrs Carter,*

We have had a positive identification here in Melbourne. The local constabulary are certain that a young woman who strongly resembles your daughter goes by the name Michelle or Shelly Brown and has lived in the St. Kilda area for several years. Unfortunately, according to several acquaintances, she has recently moved—allegedly to Western Australia—in company with another young woman, one Carleen Taylor. They have left no forwarding address. We have requested that we be informed if anyone receives information as to their present whereabouts.

We enclose our account.'

It's all there, but she reads him the last letter anyway. It provides an ending, of sorts.

'*Dear Mrs Carter,*

As discussed over the phone we feel that it is very unlikely that any further information regarding your daughter will come to light. We have received no further information as to her current whereabouts from any of our numerous contacts, and as it has now been over six months, we very much doubt that we will.

We hereby tender our final account.'

They sit in silence for a long moment. Susan places the last letter carefully on the desk, smoothes it out gently, almost caressingly. She looks around the bland office, some part of her vaguely amazed that such a place could provide the backdrop to such drama, such melodrama. She's amazed, too, by an inexplicable feeling of calm, of lightness; a creeping sense of relief.

The hangover wearing off, perhaps.

Howard Hamilton has taken his glasses off, rubs his eyes tiredly. 'What makes you so certain?' he asks. 'The investigators could have made a mistake. The name—Carleen, Carly—it could just be a coincidence.'

'It's not just that. My sister's middle name was Michelle,' she points out. 'Michelle. Shelly.'

He clears his throat. 'I think at this stage, Susan,' he says almost apologetically, 'we really need to call in the police.'

Ed

Ed walks on and on and on. North, east, south, west. North again. He loses track. When his feet can't take it any longer—he's wearing work brogues, not joggers—he stops at a garage and phones for a taxi. He has to ask the mechanic where he is exactly, he hasn't got a clue.

And when the driver asks him where he's going, he answers without thinking: 'home'.

'Yeah, man,' he can see the driver's expression in the rear vision mirror, the exaggerated eye roll. 'But where's that? Where's home?'

He'd like to tell the man that he's not sure, that he's not certain that it even exists any more. That it's possible that his home only exists somewhere in the past. And that's a destination no taxi can ever take him—a place of no return.

'Head to the coast,' he says, eventually. It's the best he can do, for now.

Susan

This time the police are brisk, businesslike. After all, this is not a disappearance, not a time for compassion, for counselling. This time it is quite straightforward. There may be warrants to issue, accounts to trace, people to interview. This time it is not a sister she has lost, but money. It is all very fast, very efficient.

When Susan arrives home with the kids in the early evening there is a message on the answerphone. Howard's voice, cool, remote: 'There's news. But it's not good I'm afraid. Call me.'

She calls him.

He's matter-of-fact, formal, lawyerly. He doesn't call her Mrs Middleton—he doesn't call her anything. 'The upshot of it is, that it's all above board. There's nothing the police can do. Nothing anyone can do. We deposited the money straight into the account Carly gave us—the account was in the name of Karen Michelle Brown ... The police contacted the bank about an hour ago and evidently the account had been opened several weeks ago at the ANZ George Street. Everything was done properly—a hundred point check to verify identity and so forth.'

'And she had documents in that name?'

'Evidently she had more than enough ID—the teller sighted a passport and a licence as well as a birth certificate. The teller was questioned, she remembered her quite well. She insists that the photo ID tallied, that they were recent shots.'

'Recent photographs ... but how? Carly was, she is, Karen, then?'

'Well, no, not exactly.'

'What do you mean, not exactly? I don't understand.'

Howard gives a big breathy sigh: 'I'm sorry to have to tell you this, Susan, but Carly wasn't the one who opened the account, there were two women. The teller was quite certain about this. She was able to identify Carly from the photograph the police showed her, but the woman said that she, that Carly, had only accompanied the woman who called herself Karen Brown. She was introduced to her as the woman's ... partner.'

Susan is stunned, can't think of what to say next, how to respond. Eventually says in a very small voice: 'What did she call herself?'

'Who?'

'Carly? Did she say her surname was Potter ... or Taylor?'

There's a long silence.

'I don't know, Susan. I don't think anybody thought to ask. And quite frankly, I can't see that it's important in this circumstance.'

'So what happens next? Can we trace the money, find out where she's gone?'

'The police can't enquire any further—there's absolutely no reason to suppose that the woman's identity was anything but authentic. No evidence of fraud, whatsoever. The money belonged to Karen Michelle Brown, and as far as anyone can ascertain, Karen Michelle Brown has taken receipt of the money.'

Howard has given her, reluctantly, the name of the detective in charge of the case. The officer sounds harried, slightly bored, as if he's got far more interesting, more urgent cases to investigate.

'Look, I'm sorry, Ma'am,' he says, 'but there's really nothing we can do.' He speaks patiently, as if explaining to a child. 'You see, it isn't actually fraud. It's not regular, of course, and quite possibly it has been done with some illegal practice in mind, but there's no law against having that much cash,' he sounds slightly regretful. 'Not when it's your own money.'

'But you don't understand,' Susan says, 'it's not the money.'

'Then what is it, Mrs Middleton?'

'She can't just go, can she? Surely she can't just leave?'

'Well, yes she can. She's an adult.'

'But she could be anywhere. With anyone. She could be in some sort of danger.' Susan isn't sure who she's referring to now—who it is that might be in danger. Does she mean her sister, her real sister, or the impostor, Carly? And what sort of danger?

'Well, Ma'am, if you have any concerns for your sister's well-being, I'd strongly advise you to contact our missing persons unit.' Eagerly: 'I can put you through to them now if you like.'

'Your missing persons unit? But you don't understand. I don't even know if she's actually my sister. My sister went missing over twenty years ago. Oh God, surely she just can't disappear again?'

'Oh, yes she can. People disappear all the time,' the detective says. 'There are a lot of people out there, you know, people who just don't want to be found. For whatever reason,' he says darkly. 'And then sometimes for no real reason. You'd be surprised.'

Surprised? She's way beyond surprise.

Susan collects the kids from after-school care and goes down to Freshie. She knows that's where he'll be; she's found his work clothes neatly folded in the garage, his board is missing, and his wetsuit. She stands for a while, squinting into the setting sun. There are four or five black shapes out there, surfers waiting patiently for the next decent wave, and from this distance, really, they all look pretty much alike. But somehow, Susan fancies she can distinguish Ed from the rest, is certain that she recognises his particular stance, a certain straight-backed upright attitude that could only be his. The way he faces the waves with such certainty—faces that risk, that fear, those unknown depths, without any evident lessening of that uprightness. She notices that this particular figure hangs back till the last, starts paddling maybe a full second later than the others, but still manages to catch the wave, and somehow, somehow, is always the one who's left standing the longest, way after the others have given up, are paddling back out into the depths, he'll be determinedly trying to stay, riding some petering-out swell, or else, being ignominiously dumped ...

But it might just be imagined. When she asks the children, digging tunnels nearby, they can't tell which particular shape is their father—even closer to the shore there's no way to be certain. Sitting herself on the sand, she loses sight of that particular surfer eventually, loses that certainty, and by the time Ed runs out of the surf she's completely uncertain—about everything.

She watches him as he jogs up the beach, shaking the water out of his hair, rubbing his eyes. He doesn't look at all surprised to see them there. 'Daddy!' Stella runs up to give him a hug, and squeals at his rubbery wetness, pulls on his arm, entreats: 'Look at what me and Mitch have made, Dad. Come and look. We've digged this hugest tunnel!' But she gives up when her father shakes her off gently.

'Hold on, Stell. Give me a minute. You go and do some more digging, I'll be there shortly.' When she goes back to her trench, he squats down beside Susan. He wipes his eyes again—and it's not just the salt water, they're red-rimmed, puffy.

'I guess she told you?'

'She did.'

'I don't suppose sorry ...'

'No.'

He looks down, makes patterns in the sand. 'So what are we going to do?'

'I don't know, Ed,' she keeps her voice gentle. 'I really don't know. What can we do?'

He reaches for her hand, she doesn't resist, takes it tentatively. 'I guess we just have to play it by ear; take it day by day ...'

Susan laughs. It sounds so trite, so banal. So Ed.

He clears his throat. 'We've worked too hard ...'

For once, it seems, Ed is struggling to say what he means. She thinks perhaps he's struggling to even know what he means, what he thinks.

'We have to think of the children. We can't ...' He turns his head to watch their busy excavations. 'It was madness, Susan, you know that ... You know that I love you—that whatever it was with Carly, that it wasn't real ... It was like an illness. A madness. It didn't really exist. And in a way,' he squeezes her hand, still looking away, 'Carly didn't really exist either ... did she?'

Susan doesn't answer. What can she say? She doesn't want to go into details about Carly's non-existence now, here. There'll be time for all that later. For some reason she recalls the detective's words: People disappear all the time, he'd said. People disappear all the time for no particular reason.

But there are different ways of disappearing, she thinks, not all of them obvious. Sometimes nobody even notices. Sometimes there are no missing person reports, no police enquiries, no headlines, no grieving families. And sometimes, Susan thinks, returning Ed's squeeze, nobody even notices that they've come back.

Susan is eight years old. She is sitting on a bed watching her big sister get ready for her high school formal. It is 1975 and her sister Karen is eighteen and has just finished her final exams. Karen has blonde hair, long and usually straight, but tonight fat curls tumble about her shoulders, wispy tendrils coil around her ears. The dress she wears is glorious, long and elegant: the fabric a swirling combination of purple colours—lilac, violet, mauve, indigo—with a delicate tracery of silver that glints and shimmers in the light. It is not the dress that Karen wanted—it's too long, she says, hopelessly old-fashioned. She has pointed out a dress at a local boutique—short, black, halter-necked. It's not appropriate, said their mother. You're too young.

But Susan likes this dress far better anyway. The dress that their mother has made is a dress fit for a princess. She has been given some scraps of the fabric for her craft box, but it is too soft, too precious, and she can think of no proper way to use it.

Karen is sitting in front of her dressing table, putting on make-up. Susan sits very still on the bed, and watches the reflection in the mirror. She could sit for hours, watching. Karen is more beautiful than any television star. Prettier than Jeannie, prettier even than Samantha in *Bewitched*. Susan thinks she would be happy to sit here forever, just watching.

Karen draws a heavy blue line around her eyes, and her mouth opens just a little, the tip of her tongue flickering occasionally at one side of her mouth. Susan follows the path of the pencil around her sister's eyes. Feels her jaw slacken. Suddenly her big sister is grinning at her reflection in the mirror. 'You'll catch flies, Sukey,' she says, 'if you don't watch out.' Susan snaps shut her mouth, smiles back at Karen without showing her teeth.

Karen turns back to the mirror, but somehow she has moved a little, has tilted her head, twisted her torso. And suddenly, from her position curled up against the pillows of the bed, Susan can't see her sister anymore.

Can see only herself.

ACKNOWLEDGEMENTS

A heartfelt thank you—

To the friends who, despite initial setbacks, made me feel it was worthwhile persevering: Winifred Belmont, Rebecca James, Sophie Masson and Felicity Plunkett.

To the amazing team at UWA Publishing: Terri-ann White, Kate McLeod, Jade Knight, Sylvia Defendi; and the incomparable Linda Martin, whose brilliant editing *really* made all the difference.

To Benython Oldfield of Zeitgeist Media: in advance, because I know what he can do.

To Kim Witherspoon and Alexis Hurley of Inkwell Management: for believing, and expecting that little bit more.

To Ashil Davawala and Paul McLeman: for invaluable—and idiot-proof—information on DNA testing.

To Penni Russon: for introducing me to the wonderful *Mousewife.*

To Darren, Sam, Abi, Nell & Will Shepherd: for obvious reasons.

www.ingramcontent.com/pod-product-compliance
Lightning Source LLC
Chambersburg PA
CBHW061433210726
48287CB00007B/2192